To Audrey,

With best wishes.

Peggy Savage.

AMY

AMY

Peggy Savage

ROBERT HALE · LONDON

ISBN 978-0-7090-8816-5

Robert Hale Limited
Clerkenwell House
Clerkenwell Green
London EC1R 0HT

www.halebooks.com

2 4 6 8 10 9 7 5 3 1

Typeset in 10/13½pt Palatino
by Derek Doyle & Associates, Shaw Heath
Printed in Great Britain by
the MPG Books Group, Bodmin and King's Lynn

CHAPTER ONE

August 1914

A MY sat alone in front of the long table, watching the men who were sitting behind it. Not one of them smiled or relaxed their grim faces. They were eminent men – certainly. Were they men who believed in justice, or simply too prejudiced even to listen to her? Prejudice, she thought, was almost universal. She had no way of knowing, but, just or not, they held her future in their hands. Was this the end, then? Was this the end of all the effort, all the years, all the struggle?

She tried to catch their eyes, tried to look calm and confident, but only one of them actually looked at her. She thought he had a sympathetic face, but he put his finger inside his stiff winged collar and stretched his neck. Then he looked away.

She wanted to scream out, 'For goodness sake get on with it,' but they shuffled their papers, inclined their heads and nodded to each other. No women, of course, Amy thought. Women on the General Medical Council? What a joke! How many years would it take – how long before they were really accepted, and not just tolerated? She sat still, rigid on the hard chair.

I can't bear this, she thought. I really can't bear it. There was so much at stake, not just for herself but for all the other women doctors in the profession – women she didn't even know. How would they take it? It would be such a knock to all of them. It already was. The very fact that she was here at all must be a blow to their collective esteem, and to their hopes and expectations. They would – they must – all think that she had let them down. Very badly. She wouldn't even have a chance to vindicate herself.

The whole scene began to take on a nightmarish, dream-like quality. The panelled walls seemed to close in and the faces of the men behind the table faded and blurred. She looked down at her hands in their neat black gloves. She pressed them together to stop their shaking. She had taken care to dress for this – occasion – a sober black coat and skirt, a high-necked white blouse, her hair in a severe chignon, and a respectable hat. She raised her head and looked across the room. Sir William Bulford was sitting with his arms crossed, a half smile on his face. He met her eye quite deliberately and the smile changed to a look of private triumph. Amy glared back at him, making no effort to conceal her contempt and bitter anger. How dare he even look at her? He obviously thought that he had won. Perhaps he knew that he had. Perhaps he had been slipped a bit of private information at his club or at a dinner party. Most of them stuck together, had been at public school or medical school together.

The chairman cleared his throat. 'Perhaps you would stand, Dr Richmond.'

Amy stood up. She tried to look calm and untroubled but she was trembling so much that she had to hold the back of her chair. She heard the words, but at first they didn't make sense – so awful that her mind would not accept them.

'The decision of the General Medical Council is that you should be removed from the Register of Medical Practitioners for a period of at least five years, and then not reinstated until you have proved to the council that you are retrained and fit to practise in a reliable and professional manner.'

She put out her hand as if to ward off an aggressor. 'No,' she whispered, 'Please, no.'

They did not appear to hear her. The chairman murmured a few more words, but she didn't hear them. Then the one man who seemed to have some sympathy looked up at her.

'You are still young, Miss Richmond,' he said. He looked down at his papers. 'Twenty-seven, isn't it? There is time for you to put it right.'

'You realize of course,' the chairman said, 'that if you make any attempt to practise during this time you will never be reinstated.'

She didn't reply. There was nothing to say.

They gathered up their papers and filed out, leaving her standing, clutching the chair. She turned slowly, feeling the blood draining from her face, her mouth dry. Sir William Bulford was almost at the door but he turned and looked at her, his florid face smug and satisfied, his thumb in the watch chain that strained over his stomach. Then he, too, left the room.

She was struck with a feeling of utter helplessness, and rage and frustration that almost choked her. So Bulford had won. Of course he had won. He was an eminent surgeon – a knight. Of course they would believe him. She was only a woman. Because of that simple fact she could no longer do the only thing that she had ever wanted to do. She couldn't practise medicine. She might as well be dead. And it was all because of Bulford's lies, lies and deliberate misleading and a deliber- ate twisting of the truth. She had fallen victim to that man, with his outrageous prejudices and lofty superiority. She had not been able even to mention his sick, sexual advances. No one would have believed her, and it would have gone against her – of course it would. It would have been regarded as a vicious woman's weapon – sly and under- hand.

'Would you come this way, madam?' One of the council's servants was holding the door open for her, ushering her out. She crossed the room and left the building, stepping out into the street, into a sunny London afternoon.

For a while she walked blindly, not looking where she was going, stumbling into people on the street. A motor car blared its horn when she stepped unseeing into the road, causing a cab horse to shy and whinny. I don't care, she thought. I don't care if I die. I've nothing to live for.

Eventually, exhausted, she came across a little tearoom; she sat down inside and ordered tea. 'No,' she said to the waitress, 'thank you. Nothing to eat – just tea.' She took off her gloves, peeling them away from her fingers. The action reminded her sickeningly of everything that she had lost, of taking off her surgical gloves at the end of an oper- ation, of the feeling of exhilaration at a job well done, of a patient who would heal and live. Never again? Would she never do that again?

The tea was hot and strong. It calmed her body a little, but not her mind. What will I do now? she thought. How will I live? She was not thinking about a roof over her head or her daily bread. She could go home to her father. He would welcome her as ever. He would be waiting there now, waiting for the results of the council hearing. He would be outraged on her behalf, but he couldn't change anything. She could keep house for him, eat and walk and read and go to bed, and all the time she would be dead; it would be a living death.

She began to cry silently, dabbing the tears away with her handkerchief and hiding her face in her teacup until she could steady herself. She couldn't think about the events that had led to this. Her mind shied away, skirted around them. She had known all along that Bulford had opposed her appointment, that he had tried to get rid of her. He had belittled and opposed her at every turn. But she hadn't imagined that even he would go this far. She ordered more tea. She didn't want to leave the safety and normality of the little tearoom. She couldn't face the world yet. Eventually the waitress began to look at her strangely.

'Are you all right, madam?' she said. 'Are you not well?'

Amy forced a smile and paid for her tea and went out into the bleak world again. How could this have happened to her when her services would be needed so much, when the news was already so bad? Would she be in the papers? WOMAN DOCTOR STRUCK OFF IN MEDICAL SCANDAL. When she came to the newspaper stand by the tube station she realized that no one now would have the slightest interest in her problem. It would probably never even be reported. There were other, more dreadful things to worry about. The paperboy was frantically handing out papers, the crowd jostling, throwing coppers into his cap on the pavement. Amy eased her way through the crowd. One woman was openly crying. The headline on the billboard leapt out: WAR, it said, WAR WITH THE KAISER'S GERMANY.

'We've got to do something about it. That man Bulford can't be allowed to get away with it. I can't believe that any gentleman could behave like that.'

Her father had said more or less the same thing for several days now, over and over. Her own distress was so overwhelming that she had taken several days to truly realize his devastation.

She had moments of resolution. She would fight the General Medical Council's decision. She would fight Bulford, expose him for what he was, and then her helplessness would destroy her again. Now, as she looked at her father, he seemed to shrink, to stoop. He seemed to be becoming obsessed. She did not seem to be able to get him to talk about anything else, not even the war.

'All those years,' he said. 'All those years wiped out.'

She knew that her academic successes had given him deep joy; that she had tried to make up for the loss of his son, dying at birth, with her mother. He had lost them both in one terrible disaster. That she should have matched his interests so completely had made an even deeper connection than that of just father and daughter. He had taught her all the science that he had taught the boys at school. Medicine was their mutual goal, jointly achieved, and now, horribly, jointly lost. All those years, he said. All those years of his patient teaching and her eager learning. He had even persuaded his headmaster to let her join in some of the practical work in the laboratories at his school. The boys had been baffled, and then much amused that Mr Richmond's daughter was going to join them for science lessons. 'Why do you want to know about Boyle's Law?' one of them said. 'You should be learning to boil an egg,' and then laughed hugely at his own joke. Typical she had thought. Typical male attitude.

'Bulford isn't a gentleman, Father. He's drunk with his own power and he loathes women doctors. I think he just hates women. I met his wife once when she came to the hospital. She was a grey little thing, too frightened to speak.'

She sat beside her father on the sofa in the drawing-room. She was close to tears. His face was lined with distress, his grey hair ruffled and on end, so unlike his usual careful neatness.

'We must do something, Amy. Quite apart from your reputation, it's your career, your livelihood. You know you can't expect much from me when I'm gone, only the house. All my savings went on your training.'

'I don't know what we can do, Father. They won't believe me. They'd much rather believe Bulford. He's a man, and a knight – one of them.' She took his hand. 'You do believe me, don't you? You know I wouldn't be negligent and just carelessly harm a patient?'

He squeezed her hand. 'Of course I believe you, Amy. I've known you all your life. You couldn't have qualified at all if you'd been careless and negligent. And I assume that if you'd made a mistake you would say so and ask for help.'

'No one is perfect Father, but I didn't make a mistake on that occasion, and certainly not the parade of negligent mistakes that old Bulford said I did.' Utter helplessness filled her again. She felt trapped, hounded. Her eyes filled with tears, more of rage than of weakness.

'What's to become of you?' he said. 'I won't live for ever.' Then he looked suddenly a little more hopeful. 'Perhaps you'll get married. You'd have someone to look after you then.'

'Have you got anyone in mind?' she said drily, 'because I certainly haven't.'

He put an arm around her shoulders and held her against him.

'My dear,' he said, his voice breaking, 'don't worry. We'll fight it. We'll get the best lawyer in London.'

She raised her head and looked at him in alarm. 'You know we can't. We haven't got the money. It would cost hundreds, if not thousands. I had a lawyer anyway.'

'Much good he turned out to be. We'll get someone else. I'll get the money. I'll take out another mortgage on the house.'

She leapt to her feet. 'No! No you won't! I'm not going to let you put the house in danger. You might – we both might find ourselves out on the street. I won't let you do it.'

He put his face in his hands. 'I can't bear to see you hurt like this.'

She knelt beside him, looking painfully at his bent head. His anxiety added to her own and that seemed to rise and expand, half choking her. For days now she had not been able to sleep, lying in bed, exhausted with rage and frustration. Night after night the memory returned, and she would make herself wretched wondering what more she could have done or said to defend herself. When she did take an hour or so of black unconsciousness she would wake feeling normal, and then the fear and helpless pain would be upon her again. In some dreadful synchronicity her own despair was combined with and heightened by the coming of the war. That her dismissal had happened at all was bad enough, but for it to happen now, when she would be so much needed, made it all the more unbearable. What would this war be like? Things had changed, science leapt on. There were so many more ways now to kill.

A few days crept by. She got up each morning with nothing to do, nowhere to go. Her father went to his school every day, so she spent the days alone. She scoured the papers every morning, her heart in her mouth, but there was nothing about her. They were filled almost exclusively with news about the war. The only other detailed reports were about cricket, as if to maintain a tiny breath of normality.

She did the shopping for the house and it became more difficult every day. 'We have no sugar left, madam,' the grocer said. 'People are stocking up on everything.' The shelves emptied of sugar, rice, flour, tinned stuff. Women hurried from shop to shop, carrying their baskets; groups of men stood on street corners talking in low, urgent voices. She passed a crowd of men, perhaps fifty of them, waiting to get into the recruitment centre. Overnight more uniforms appeared.

I have to find something to do, she thought, over and over again. Anything to be useful. Troops were already moving in huge numbers, ready for battle, and here she was, idle, useless, unemployed.

The advertisement was in THE TIMES, *Wanted urgently, orderlies, cooks, cleaners, to join a group of women doctors who are forming a surgical unit in France. Write or telephone. . . .* She felt as if some kind of salvation had been handed to her. She couldn't offer herself as a nurse; she had no nursing qualifications, but she could be an orderly, a humble ward orderly. At least she would be there, in France. She hurried out to the post office to telephone. She was given an appointment for the next day in London at a hotel in Russell Square. 'My name,' she said, 'Is Amy Osborne.'

Next day she took the train from Bromley Station, paying her one and ninepence at the ticket office. She stared out of the window as they passed through the fields, and then the suburbs, into London. They must take me, she thought desperately. I must get in.

There were several women waiting. There were two older women, wearing the careful clothes of those who had to work hard for their living. They looked calm and capable – cooks and cleaners, she supposed. There were a few girls chatting and giggling as if they thought the whole thing was a bit of a lark. They are far too young, Amy thought. They wouldn't last a week. There was one girl who looked different, older than the others, more mature. She had flaming red hair under her hat and was wearing the purple, white and green badge of the suffragists. She'd be good value, Amy thought, brave anyway, not easily intimidated.

She fought down the fear that the doctor interviewing might know who she was, but it seemed unlikely. She had given a different name, and there were more than 500 women doctors in Britain now.

The women went in one by one and came out again, some of the girls looking petulant and disappointed. The girl with the red hair caught her eye and smiled and then went in herself, her hair shining like a beacon. She came out again, looking pleased.

Amy was the last. There were two women behind the desk. One of them was slender, with a thin, capable face, her grey hair in a tight bun. 'I am Dr Hanfield,' she said. 'I will be heading the surgical department, and this is our matron.'

They both questioned her. No, she was not married and had no dependents. No, she had no experience as an orderly, which was true. At least, it wasn't a lie. Yes, she had experience in running a house and caring for her father. She knew how to organize, to take responsibility.

Dr Hanfield smiled at her. 'We would be glad to take you, Miss Osborne but we are leaving very soon. Can you be ready in two weeks?'

Amy nodded. 'Yes, I'm sure I could.'

'We're nearly ready to go,' Dr Hanfield said. 'It was obvious to me that there was going to be a war. We will be working for the French Red Cross, seeing that the British Army won't take women doctors.' She smiled. 'I'm sorry it's such short notice. Unfortunately a few applicants cancelled at the last moment.'

'I can be ready,' Amy said.

'Go to Gamages for your uniform and ward dresses,' Matron said. 'I'll send you the arrangements and your tickets.'

Amy thanked them and left the room. The redheaded girl was still there.

'Did you get in?' she asked, her eyes bright.

'Yes, I did.' Amy smiled with relief.

The girl held out her hand. 'I'm Helen,' she said. 'I got in too.'

'Amy.' They shook hands.

Helen fingered her badge. 'Something real to do at last,' she said. 'Deeds, not words. That's our motto. See you soon then, Amy.' She almost danced out of the door.

Amy smiled. Deeds, not words, at last.

She waited for her father that evening, dreading telling him, knowing what his reaction would be.

He came in, looking tired and drawn. 'Any news?' he said.

'Not from the General Medical Council, Father,' she said. 'If that's what you mean.'

She sat down on her mother's old chair and watched her father as he raised his head and looked around the room, stopping here and there to look at little things that were precious to him – things that her mother had left behind. He paused at a china cherub that her mother had bought on their honeymoon, at a tapestry fire screen that her mother had worked herself, and then at her mother's photograph placed carefully and alone on a side table. The room still had a Victorian air, too cluttered for Amy's taste, but the taste had been her mother's, and her father would never change it. It kept her alive for him. He had said so often, 'She would have been so proud of you Amy. I wish so much that she could have seen you qualify.'

It seemed to be the right moment to tell him of her decision, if any moment was right. 'Father,' she said, 'there's one thing that we haven't talked about – this terrible war. My problems hardly seem important, except that I could have helped so much more.'

His face became even more agonized. 'I know,' he said bitterly. 'Half the boys in the sixth form have left and enlisted. Young Frensham says he's going to join the Flying Corps. I can't bear to think of them. . . .'

She sat beside him again. 'There's something I want to tell you, Father.' He raised his eyes to hers. 'You must go on teaching, and you must keep this house safe because it's our home and I shall want to come back to it whenever I can.'

He was quickly alert. He looked almost frightened, 'What do you mean – to come back to? Where are you going?'

'I'm going to France.'

He opened his mouth to protest, but she went on, 'I've found out that there are a few British women surgeons going out to form surgical units. I'm going as a medical orderly.'

'No,' he said, 'No, you can't. It will be too dangerous. You are too young to. . . . You are too young. Why can't you do it here in England?'

She got up and stood beside the window, looking out into the street. A young man walked by, wearing khaki. He was walking proudly, very straight. As he got closer and passed the house she saw how young he looked – just a boy.

'Because,' she said, 'because the War Office in its wisdom has turned down the services of women surgeons. Can you believe that? They can't have their soldiers' lives saved by mere women, can they? Or perhaps they think we'd all have hysterics and run away. So the women are going to France to work for the French Red Cross.' The young man walked out of sight. 'And there are boys out there much younger than I am who are suffering and dying.'

She came back to sit beside him. He said nothing for a while, his face white and stricken.

'How can you?' he said eventually. 'Won't they know who you are?'

'They won't know my face. They'll know my name, that's all. So I'll change it. I'll use another name. The war is the only thing that anyone is thinking about. They won't think about me.'

He was still now, resigned. She's made up her mind, he thought. Nothing will change her when she's made up her mind.

'I don't suppose that I can say anything that will stop you?'

'No, Father. I'm sorry.'

'What will I tell people? What shall I say?'

'There's no need to say anything. No need to tell anyone what's happened. Just say that I've gone to France.'

'And what name will you use?'

She smiled. 'My mother's maiden name, of course: I'll be Amy Osborne.'

His eyes filled with tears. She's going out to die, he thought. She's going to go into danger, deliberately. He looked around the room again. He could see a young girl at the table by the window, sitting upright, her elbows on the table, her chin in her hand. Her quick eyes were on her book, studying, always studying the science that he taught her. And now it had come to this. His tears began to fall. Perhaps he had been wrong to so encourage her – such a quick, such a purposeful mind. But she was all he had. They spent so much of their time together. How could he not transfer to her his own passion for the growing, expanding, thrilling science that filled his own mind? I blame myself, he thought. I blame myself. He took out his handkerchief to wipe his face.

'Father, don't. I'll be all right, really I will. I'll be careful. You know me.'

'Yes,' he said, 'I do know you.' His look was clear: hopelessness and fear.

She knew what he was thinking. 'You're so wrong,' she said. 'I have every intention of coming through it, hale and hearty. I'll be back, you'll see. And Father' – he seemed to be waiting for the next blow – 'I'm going to get it back. I'm going to clear my name and get myself back on the Register without any marks against me. I don't know how, but I'm going to do it.'

How was she going to do it? That night she lay in bed, restless and unsleeping. Was there anything that she could have done, anything that she could have said? She relived that last time over and over again.

She and the theatre sister spread the sterile sheets over the patient on the operating table. There was always some apprehension – taking out an inflamed appendix was not a procedure to be taken lightly. Opening the abdomen at all was a risk, but she had done the operation twice now, and both her patients had survived. She had been able to remove the appendix before it burst, spreading infection into the abdomen, causing peritonitis and almost inevitable death.

The theatre nurse switched on the big overhead light, the anaesthetist adjusted the cylinders on his machine, the young student who was to assist her took up his position across the table.

She knew when Sir William Bulford entered the theatre. She could tell by the change in the atmosphere, the straightening of backs, the slight intake of breaths. She could tell by the way her hair rose on the back of her neck, under her cap. He had every right to be there. As senior surgeon he could do what he wished, watch what he wished. It was his right, his privilege, his duty. The knowledge made a little bile rise in her throat. Out of the corner of her eye she saw him put on his gown and gloves. He came to stand beside her.

'Good morning, Dr Richmond,' he said.

She made no reply. She thrust out her elbow to spread the last sterile sheet and he moved away a little.

'He's asleep,' the anaesthetist said. 'You can start now.'

On the right side of the abdomen she located McBurney's Point, the junction of the lower and middle third of a line from the anterior superior iliac spine to the umbilicus, under which she might expect to find the appendix. She held out her hand for sister to give her a scalpel, and it rested familiarly in her palm.

She took a breath, then she cut through the skin, clipping off and tying the bleeding points. Then through the muscles – the external oblique, the internal oblique, the transverse. She placed a retractor for the student to hold open the incision.

Beneath the muscles the peritoneum glistened whitely – the protective covering of the abdominal organs. Once through this the die was cast. She must find the appendix and remove it – remove it without damage, without allowing any of the killing pus to escape into the abdomen to cause peritonitis, septicaemia and death. It was infection that killed – infection about which they could do very little, once it had taken hold. These were the invisible murderers – the staphylococci and the streptococci and all the others. It all depended on the strength of the patient – and the skill of the surgeon.

She raised a small pinch of the peritoneum, careful not to pick up the bowel beneath, and then she cut through, opening the abdomen. She gave a small sigh of relief. There was no stench of corruption, just a faint smell not unlike fresh meat. The bowel lay exposed, and by good chance the appendix lay in full view, the swollen red infected tip clearly visible.

Now that she was inside the abdomen she must be quick and accurate. She could not move away. With a sick feeling of expectation fulfilled she felt Sir William Bulford move beside her so that his thigh was against hers. She clipped off the base of the appendix.

'That appears to be a fairly easy one,' he said. He turned slightly, so that the front of his body was against her now, rubbing against her thigh.

She had to ignore him, to concentrate. She removed the appendix, dropping it into the dish that sister offered. She tied off the stump and buried it with a purse-string suture. She checked the rest of the abdomen and all seemed well. She made to take the threaded needle from Sister's hand, but Bulford put out his hand and stopped her.

'I'll close up,' he said.

She looked round at him. He was looking down at her, a look of bland innocence.

'That's not necessary,' she began, but he took the suture from Sister.

'You look tired,' he said. 'Perhaps you didn't sleep well last night.'

She didn't move.

'There is no need to stay, Miss Richmond,' he said. 'I can manage without you. I should go and get some rest if I were you.'

It was an order – there was no doubt about that. She left the theatre, helplessly fuming, and went into the female changing-room. She took off her theatre clothes, putting on her skirt and blouse and lacing up her boots. Anger made her breathless. The man was appalling, brutish. His red, florid face and thick fingers filled her with the utmost repulsion.

She sat on a stool and leant against the wall. Perhaps he was a good surgeon, but she was no longer sure even about that. He was too set in his ways – too resistant to change. He made no secret of his violent opposition to women doctors, especially to women surgeons, but when she was appointed he had been narrowly over-ridden by the Board of Governors. He was clever, though, and ruthless. But even then she hadn't imagined what he would do.

The next day her patient had a slight but worrying temperature. She arrived to find that Bulford had asked for the dressing to be taken down.

'Miss Richmond,' he said. 'I see that you forgot to put in a drain yesterday. Surely you know how important that is. How else is any fluid or pus to escape?'

She opened her mouth in shock, but he forestalled her.

'I cannot tolerate this,' he said. 'It isn't the first time. If you are too busy gadding about at night to get your proper rest you shouldn't be doing surgery.'

'What on earth do you mean?' she said. 'You closed up this patient yourself. You made me leave the theatre.'

He frowned. 'You really cannot try to make me responsible for your mistakes,' he said. 'I have had to put them right too often.' He walked away from her and into Sister's office, and she followed him.

She remembered her helpless fury. 'That is a complete lie,' she said. 'How dare you say that in front of the patient and the nursing staff. You know it isn't true. All my patients have recovered well – and without your help. As for gadding about! I usually spend my evenings studying – the latest methods, in case you haven't heard of that.' She shouldn't have said that, she knew it now. It could only have made things worse. He was white with anger.

'That's all, Miss Richmond,' he said. 'That is quite enough.'

As she left the ward she passed Sister. She thought she saw a look of sympathy in Sister's eyes, before she lowered them hurriedly and looked away.

She worked through the morning outpatient clinic and then she walked across the hospital grounds to the nurses' home. She had been given a room there where she could stay when she was on duty at night. It was raining, and she pulled up the collar of her coat and bent her head, the rain dripping off her hat.

The nurses' home was bleak – long corridors with the wall below the dado painted a dark yellowy green. It was nearly lunchtime and the smell of boiled cabbage hung about everywhere.

Her room was in the section reserved for the senior sisters. It was hardly comfortable. It was sparsely furnished – linoleum on the floor, a bed, a chest of drawers, a small wardrobe and a washbasin in the corner.

She took off her hat and coat and hung up her coat to dry. She sat down on the bed, staring at the opposite wall. What was she to do? She could leave the hospital and try to get a post somewhere else. That would mean asking Bulford for a reference, and what would he say? With a feeling of sick despair she knew what he would say, or she could guess. His approaches to her were becoming bolder, more frequent. At first she thought it was accidental, an unavoidable aspect of their work – the standing close to her, the innocent seeming touches that no one else would notice. Now his behaviour was unmistakable. On the occasions when they were alone, perhaps in Sister's office or the theatre office, he would stare at her, looking her up and down, his eyes bulging and lustful, like an animal. Once he had put his hand on her shoulder, his thumb straying to the top of her breast, and she had shrugged him off and backed away. Oh yes, she knew what he would say.

She got up and took a glass of water and stared out of the window. She could see the nurses walking across the quadrangle, their cloaks huddled round them. Carriages and occasional motor cars arrived at the hospital doors. Ambulances brought patients on stretchers, the porters hurrying out to meet them. This was her life.

She rested her forehead against the window. She could leave the hospital without a reference, but where would that get her? She could go to some other town, put up her plate outside the door and hope for the best. The thought filled her with despair. That wasn't what she wanted, what she had trained for.

She drew back a little, and saw her reflection in the glass, her drawn, slender face, hair in the severe chignon. That was it, wasn't it? In the eyes of some men, that was her original sin. She was a woman. And that made her incapable of rational thought, fit only to run a house and bear children. Even some women were against women doctors. Even female voices were raised against them. So much for the sisterhood.

Shockingly, horribly, she did not have to decide what to do. Bulford had arranged her life for her. Someone had knocked on her door and told her that Sir William wished to see her in his office. He began at once.

'I can no longer tolerate your behaviour, Miss Richmond.'

She tried to speak calmly. 'What do you mean? I have done nothing wrong. It is your behaviour that is intolerable.'

'Really?' He smiled at her – a frightening smile. 'And how many people do you think would support you in that? The students? The nursing staff? I think not.'

She stared at him, wordless, knowing that he had the better of her.

'I am putting you on suspension,' he said. 'And I am going to make a report to the General Medical Council. I shall make it clear that I do not think that you are fit to practise medicine.'

'You can't do that,' she said, appalled. 'You can't do that to me.'

He smiled again. 'Oh, yes, I can.'

The rest was a blur. Days and weeks of waiting, of fear, of almost unbearable rage, of tears, of her father's distress. And now this – this nothingness, these endless days and sleepless nights.

She lay in her bed and stared into the dark. Her own problems were nothing now. Out there, outside her horrors and troubles there was a war, so savage that the world was already reeling in shock and horror. 'I'm coming,' she said to herself, aloud, in the dark. 'I'm coming. I'll do what I can – whatever it is.' Knowing that she could have done so much more was a pain that was hardly bearable.

CHAPTER TWO

1914

TWO weeks later she and her father were standing on a platform at Victoria Station. The platform was crowded and the noise frightful – shouting voices, pounding feet, slamming doors. Even the pigeons had retreated up into the roof. She could see them flying, agitated, up above.

Streams of men in khaki, kitbags on their shoulders, struggled up and down the platform. Corporals with lists shouted orders and the men threw their kitbags into the carriages and followed them, leaning out of the doors and windows, cigarettes hanging out of the corners of their mouths. Many of them stared at the group of women in uniform and one rosy-cheeked boy gave Amy a cheeky wink. A packed troop train left the station in a clanking of wheels and a cloud of steam, the men shouting and cheering. The station smelt of burning coal and oil and the sharp, acrid smell of new uniforms and new boots.

Amy's father stood straight and calm, but his face was as white as the newspaper under his arm. He gave a strained smile.

'You all look splendid, Amy. Very smart and efficient.'

Amy smiled back, trying to hide her own apprehension and keep up the sense of excitement and purpose. The news was too dreadful for words, so many casualties already, so many dead. The men on the trains didn't seem to be worried, laughing and larking about, but here and there she saw a strained white face and anxious, haunted eyes. Many of them looked little more than schoolboys.

The group of women stood loosely together, friends and relations gathered about them. They were all wearing the uniform of the group that the doctors had called The Women's Surgical Group. The station master had made a special concession for them and allowed their friends on to the platform to see them off.

'I'm so glad you're here, Father.' Amy squeezed his arm. Quite apart from the comfort of his being there, it meant that she didn't have to circulate or talk much to anyone else. And thank God for the uniform, she thought. It was a sensible colour, mid-grey. The skirt was short, just above the ankle, not like the fashionable hobble skirts that she thought were so ridiculous. The jacket buttoned up over a blue shirt and tie and the small hat had a little veil at the back to cover the hair.

She glanced across at the group of doctors. They wore the same uniform; they had designed it themselves. The same dress, but that was where it ended. They would be doing the surgery, while she? She felt bereft, as if the whole purpose of her life had been taken away from her, and sick that she had to hide her identity, pretending that she knew nothing. She didn't know what she would be doing; washing the wounded, probably, feeding, changing beds. If she was lucky she might be promoted to changing dressings.

She looked away. She felt reasonably safe in the uniform, especially as an orderly. She could become totally anonymous – disappear.

She had one or two nasty moments. One of the well-wishers with the group of doctors had a face that she knew – a woman doctor who had been a year or two ahead of her at the Royal Free where she trained. She felt a moment's shock and turned hurriedly away, but she hadn't been recognized. She was safe, invisible among the orderlies. Then a photographer pointed his camera in her direction. She turned her face to her father, hiding it against his coat and he understood and put his arm around her and waved the man away.

Beyond the platform barrier she could see a mass of colour, the fluttering shapes of women's hats and dresses, moving and jostling as the wives and mothers, sisters and daughters, said goodbye to the men who surged through. This side of the barrier there was no colour at all, just khaki and grey. It was, she thought, as if someone had drawn a line across the world. On that side, England and home; on this side, the unknown horror of what was to come. She felt as if all the colour and joy of life were back there on the shore, and that she was drifting out into an unknown sea on a mud-coloured tide.

'Are you all right, Amy?' Beside her Helen put her hand on her arm.

Amy shook her head briefly, clearing her thoughts away. 'Yes, it's nothing.' She turned to her father. 'This is Helen, Father. We met when we joined up. Helen, I would like you to meet my father.'

Helen's freckled face smiled up into his. 'How do you do, Mr Osborne.'

He gave a slight start at the name, and then smiled and shook her hand. She looks sensible, he thought. He noticed the purple, white and green badge on her lapel. A suffragist, though. Impetuous, perhaps.

'I hope you two young women will look after each other,' he said.

Helen gave a broad grin. 'Oh we will.' A porter came down the platform with a loaded barrow. 'Oh look,' she said, 'there's my luggage. I'd better go and look after it.' She bounded away, her bright red hair glowing under her veil.

'She's a nice girl,' Amy said, 'and fun, I should think. And she's very sensible.'

'And a suffragist,' her father said. He smiled. 'I don't suppose she'll be chaining herself to anything in Paris.'

'We're all suffragists, aren't we?' she said. 'Even if we don't wear the badge.'

'Of course,' he said. He was frightened again. These girls seemed so strong these days, so confident. Too confident perhaps.

There was a sudden movement among the women. The rest of the luggage was piled into their reserved carriages and the women began to climb aboard.

'I've got to go, Father.'

'Oh, Amy.'

'It's all right, dear, don't look so tragic. I won't be in any danger. We're only going to Paris.'

'Promise me, Amy,' he said, 'promise me that if the Germans get anywhere near Paris you'll leave. They are not far away now.'

'I'll have to do what the unit does,' she said. 'I'll have to do my duty.'

He sighed. 'Write to me. Regularly.'

'Of course.'

She kissed his cheek and climbed aboard. The train gave a great gout of steam. There were shouts and a clattering of doors. The guard blew his whistle and waved his flag and the train gave a lurch and began to move. From the window she watched his tall, thin figure retreat from her view, and behind him the colour and movement of the world she once knew.

They arrived in France in the late afternoon. The boat steamed into the harbour at Dieppe, Amy and Helen standing by the rail on deck with the others. The long quay was lined with people, strangely still and silent, watching the boat come in.

Amy looked along the line of silent figures. It was unnerving, this stillness. It was, Amy thought, as if these people themselves were the strangers, cast up in an unknown foreign place, not knowing where to go or what to do. She shivered a little, though the day was still warm.

'Strange, isn't it?' Helen said beside her. 'What are they waiting for, do you think?'

'I don't know.' Amy's throat was dry. Perhaps these stunned, overwhelmed people were waiting for someone to give them an explanation – why is this happening to us? Why France? They were standing on the very edge of their country, as if they wanted to leave, to flee. They looked, she thought, like the rows of birds in autumn, waiting on wires and trees for the signal to go, to get away. And these were the French, so proud of their nation and their heritage. The sight chilled her.

An agent met them on the boat, to help them with their luggage through Customs. They walked in a line off the boat and into the Douane, watched by groups of sailors and porters. In their own grey uniforms they were, Amy thought, as colourless as the watchers. Was this the first effect of war, the draining of all colour, the first bloodletting?

'Why are they staring at us?' Helen said. 'They look as if they think we're some strange undiscovered tribe.'

'I expect it's the uniform,' Amy said. 'I suppose we are an undiscovered tribe, in a way. They're not used to women in uniform. Nobody is. Not yet.'

They went into the Customs building.

'Good Lord,' Helen said. 'They look like a flock of crows.'

The Douane was manned by women, old women, in thick black dresses decently down to their black boots. The few porters were old men – too old to fight.

'Get ready for some arguments,' Helen whispered. The French

Customs were notorious for their thorough inspections. But the women merely stared at them and chalked on their hand luggage and waved them through.

They walked in a group to the station and boarded the train. Amy watched as the doctors and senior nurses got into a carriage of their own and then climbed aboard with the other orderlies. They waited for half an hour while their heavy luggage and boxes of equipment were loaded, with much noise and the raising of French voices. Then they slowly chugged away.

After Pontoise the train stopped at every little halt and station, and often in between for no apparent reason. The stations were mostly deserted, apart from women selling water and wine and fruit, and who gazed at them in puzzled surprise. No one, it seemed, was eager to go to Paris. The French countryside, lush and green, drifted by. It slowly grew dark.

'I've never been to France before,' one of the girls said. 'Isn't it exciting?'

They ate sandwiches and cake that they had brought from England. The simple food seemed to Amy to be oddly exotic, a piece of an England that now seemed so far away, so different, so safe. France was a different world now, a world that had become strange, fierce and dangerous. But it was an England that she wanted to leave. Whatever she had to do in France, it was better than sitting at home doing nothing, or doing something meaningless to her – rolling bandages or knitting socks. Those activities were useful, of course, and the women at home would feel that they were contributing in any way that they could. She would have gone mad.

At every small station a group of young men was waiting, surrounded by haggard, tearful women. At every station the young men kissed their goodbyes to mothers and sisters and wives and climbed aboard.

'They've all been conscripted,' one of the young orderlies said. 'Our men have all volunteered. I think that's much braver.'

Young men, Amy thought; many of them just boys. It must take courage, conscripted or not.

'They'll all be fighting the same battles,' Helen said sharply, 'however they got there. They'll all be taking the same risks.'

The girl blushed and looked shamefaced and Amy smiled at her, trying to comfort her, and the girl smiled back. She was young, nine-teen or twenty, Amy guessed. She wondered if the girl would survive here and stay, or hurry back to England, frightened and appalled. She would certainly never have seen real injury or suffering.

'I wonder what it'll be like,' Helen said, 'the hotel that's going to be our hospital. Some little building tucked away somewhere in a back street I expect. God knows how we'll manage.'

'We'll manage.' Amy said. 'Dr Louisa Garrett Anderson is forming a group as well, and she won't put up with any nonsense.'

'Who is she?' one of the young girls asked.

Amy looked at her in amazement. 'Her mother, Elizabeth, was the first woman doctor in England.'

'My grandmother doesn't approve of women doctors,' the girl said. 'She's very old-fashioned. She says it's indecent.'

Amy looked out of the window. What do we have to do? she thought. What on earth do we have to do to make our way, to be even heard? British women surgeons rejected by the army! How crass, how stupid, how wasteful of their expertise. The French countryside slipped by.

It was nearly midnight when they arrived in Paris. They climbed stiffly out of the train into the dimly lit Gare du Nord. Amy breathed in the atmosphere, a mixture of garlic and anise and Turkish tobacco. So this was Paris, the smart, ultra-fashionable, self-confident and self-satisfied Paris. Surely such a wonderful city couldn't have lost its beauty and its charm. Why was this happening? There seemed to be no logical reason for this dreadful war. There seemed to be no logical reason for half the things that human beings did to each other.

'I'm dying for a cup of tea,' Helen said. 'And then bed. Bed for days and days.'

Amy laughed. 'You might just get the tea, but I have a feeling that we're going to be rather busy tomorrow.'

There was more delay while carriages were found to take them to the hotel. They were put down, at last, on the pavement outside the hotel, cold with tiredness. They all stood for a moment in a group, looking at the big, impressive glass doors.

'Goodness,' Helen said. 'It's not what I imagined. It's certainly not in any back street, is it?'

'Come along then.' Dr Hanfield opened the door and they trooped inside. Waiting for them was a small plump man with glistening moustaches, an elegant black suit, black boots gleaming. Beside him stood a woman, taller than himself, wearing a well-cut brown dress and coat and a large, impressive hat. Despite their elegant clothes there was a very un-English air of rather too much fashion about them. They couldn't be anything but French. Helen dug Amy gently in the ribs and glanced at her impishly out of the corner of her eye.

He stepped forward, smiling. 'I am M. Le Blanc,' he said in heavily accented English. 'And this is my wife. I come to welcome you on behalf of the French Red Cross. Welcome to Paris.'

Dr Hanfield stepped forward and shook his hand. 'We are very pleased to be here.'

'We are very pleased that you are here,' he said. 'We urgently need more hospitals, more surgeons, more nurses. We never expected—' He stopped suddenly and cleared his throat.

Dr Hanfield looked grim. 'We will do our best, M. Le Blanc,' she said. 'You can be sure of that.'

They stood in a group inside the door, silenced by the sight of this magnificent hotel. The floor of the foyer was tiled in white marble, covered here and there with Persian rugs in rich colours, blue and red. There were soft settees in tan leather and glass-topped tables. From the ceiling hung opulent crystal chandeliers, glittering in the modern electric light. A wide staircase swept up to the first floor – white marble treads with a deep red carpet in the centre, held in place with shining brass rods. The public rooms opening out of the foyer were in darkness.

'Good Lord,' Helen said. She was looking about her with her eyes wide and her mouth half open. 'I didn't think I'd ever be staying in a place like this.'

The carts arrived with their numerous chests and boxes and the porters piled them on the marble floor. M. Le Blanc's eyes widened.

'You have brought much equipment, I see. We have done what we can before you arrived. We have cleared the lounges and the dining-room and the beds will arrive tomorrow.'

'Good.' Dr Hanfield smiled. 'In that case we should be able to open the day after tomorrow.'

'So soon!' he said, surprised. 'You English ladies work very hard. We already have many patients waiting for you.'

'We'll be ready.'

'Is there anything that we can do for you tonight?'

Dr Hanfield shook her head. 'I think we all need to go to bed,' she said. 'We can do nothing more until the morning.'

'The bedrooms on the first floor are ready,' Mme Le Blanc said in careful English, 'but some of you will have to share, I think. There are sheets and blankets to make your beds, and there is hot water in the bedrooms and the bathrooms.'

Matron shepherded them towards the staircase. 'Come along, young ladies. Let's sort ourselves out and get to bed. I've no idea where anything is. We can't unpack anything tonight, I'm afraid. We have a lot to do in the morning.'

'Share with me, Amy?' Helen whispered, and Amy nodded.

'No tea,' Helen said.

Amy smiled. 'It must be lost in one of these packing cases. I think I'd be too tired to drink it.'

They trailed up the marble staircase to the bedrooms. The floors of the corridors were laid with red and blue tiles, and the walls hung with cream silk wallpaper and huge gilt mirrors. Matron opened each door in turn. She reserved the rooms nearest the staircase for the doctors and senior nurses, and then quickly settled the rest of the staff into the other rooms.

Amy and Helen dumped their bags on the carpet, looking round them at the luxury, the deep windows with their rich blue curtains, the thick carpets, a cheval mirror and linen-covered dressing table. There were two neat single beds with the bedding neatly folded at the foot. A water carafe stood on each bedside table.

'I hope it's been boiled,' Helen said. 'That would be a good start, wouldn't it, if we all went down with food poisoning.' She opened a cupboard door. 'Oh look. There's a wash basin with hot and cold taps.'

'I'm sure they would have boiled it,' Amy said. 'They seem to be very efficient. I'll start making the beds. You go and locate the lavatories and the bathroom, Helen.' Helen left the room and Amy took off her hat and coat and put them in the wardrobe. She was weary to her bones, partly with the fatigues of the day, but mostly, she knew, with apprehension. She began to spread out the bottom sheets and put on the pillowcases. At least everything seemed to be dry and aired.

Helen came back. 'Just down the corridor,' she said. 'On the left.' She gave an enormous yawn. 'I'm too tired to do more than wash my face tonight. Baths in the morning.'

They finished making the beds and then they undressed and put on their cotton nightdresses and got in. Amy turned off the bedside light.

'I didn't think I'd ever be sleeping in a place like this,' Helen said. 'Utter luxury.'

'For the moment, yes.'

'We've never had a chance to talk, have we?' Helen said cheerfully. 'Where do you come from? Where is your home?'

Amy didn't want to have this kind of conversation. She would just have to be careful. 'Bromley,' she said.

'Do your parents live there?'

'My father does,' Amy said. 'My mother died when I was a young child. I hardly remember her.'

'I'm sorry about that. Do you have any brothers or sisters?'

Amy shook her head in the dark. 'No. Just me.'

'Any passionate swain waiting for you?'

Amy laughed, a short humourless laugh. A horrible image of Sir William Bulford rose in her mind. 'No. Nothing like that. Just as well really, the way things are now. It must be dreadful to have someone to worry about. It must be appalling.'

'I just have two sisters,' Helen said. 'Younger than me, and my parents, of course. No brothers, fortunately. My father's too old to be a soldier but I know he'd like to go. I don't have a swain either. My mother was always trying to marry me off.' She giggled. 'I think she was trying to get rid of me.'

Amy laughed. 'So you didn't find anyone who took your fancy?'

'Goodness no. Everyone my mother found was far too immature, or boring. Anyway, I wasn't ready to settle down and have children. I wanted to do something first – have an adventure. My father always said I was the boy of the family.' She was silent for a moment. 'I suppose this is an adventure, isn't it?'

'I don't know if I'd call it that exactly. It's going to be very hard work.'

'Have you done anything like this before, Amy?'

Amy hesitated. This was another question she wanted to avoid. She would have to be prepared and phrase her answers accordingly. 'No,' she said at last. 'I have never been an orderly before.'

'Neither have I. I just stayed at home and helped my mother. Deadly boring. That was until I joined the suffragists. I don't think my mother is very pleased about that. She was always frightened that I'd end up in prison. Now she's frightened that I'll end up as a prisoner of war.' She yawned loudly. 'I don't think I can stay awake any longer. Good night, Amy.'

Amy heard her turn over, and she seemed to be instantly asleep.

Amy lay awake. Outside the windows Paris seemed to be strangely quiet and very dark. The street lights were apparently out, or the gas turned down very low. Utter luxury, Helen had said. Amy could imagine what might have been here, the carriages and motor cars coming and going, the flowers, the music, voices and laughter. She could see the guests arriving, the women beautifully dressed, Worth and Fortuny and Patou, greeted by porters and pageboys and an obsequious receptionist. They would be shown to their rooms, champagne and fruit waiting, all the trappings of luxurious living. This beautiful hotel should be filled with elegant tourists and travellers, with silks and furs and the haunting scents of French perfumes. It was not meant for what she knew was to come. Death was coming. Death and suffering and sorrow. She shivered, though the night was warm.

The news from the Front was already so bad, the casualties so high. There was a memory, an image that she couldn't get out of her head. A year ago, a lifetime ago, she and her father had been to a slide lecture in London. The speaker was an old man who had actually fought in the American Civil War, on the Southern side. That lecture came back to her, almost a premonition, a preparation. The old man spoke haltingly, and now and again, even after all those years, struggled to hold back his tears. His descriptions of the carnage had been utterly horrifying. He told how he had watched his best friend die beside him, shot through the head; how he had watched a man die holding his own bowel: how he had nearly died in a prison camp of pneumonia and malnutrition. This was not a battle, he said, this was a new kind of war, a war that lasted for years, that drained the country of its finest young men. Could it really be true that civilized men did this to each other? Could it be true that thousands and thousands had died in agony, had limbs removed without anaesthetic when they ran out of chloroform and morphine, had died of dysentery and pneumonia because there was no way to treat them? He told of barns discovered, half filled with rotting, stinking amputated limbs, of mass graves, of farms and home-steads devastated, women and children starving. She and her father had been shocked and horrified, but it seemed like fiction then, too far away to be real, too horrible to have happened. Yes, the suffering human body had been exposed to her, but in the best conditions, in an English hospital; not the kind of suffering that was happening now, here, in France. The rumours had been appalling, thousands already dead and injured, shocking injuries, tetanus, gas gangrene, dysentery. She lay awake until sheer exhaustion put her to sleep.

The next morning they woke early.

'Come on,' Helen said. 'Let's get to the bathrooms first. There's going to be a rush.'

They bathed and dressed and put on their uniforms over their bodices and bloomers.

'At least we don't have to wear corsets.' Helen said. 'They're an invention of the devil anyway.' She picked up her suffragist's badge. 'I don't suppose they'll let me wear this,' she said, 'but I've still got it in my head. I won't be giving up.'

'After the war,' Amy said grimly. 'After the war, perhaps. They wouldn't be bothered with it now.'

'Breakfast,' Helen said. 'And lots of cups of tea.'

They walked along the silk-lined corridor and down the marble staircase. Matron and Dr Hanfield were standing in the hall.

'In here, girls,' Matron said. 'Get your breakfast quickly and get to work. We have to be ready tomorrow.'

They went into a small room with bare tables and chairs and the comforting smell of bacon.

'The cooks must have got up at the crack of dawn,' Amy said.

'I don't know why we brought our own cooks,' Helen said. 'I was looking forward to a bit of French cooking.' She grinned. 'Though I don't suppose the Tommies would fancy snails and frogs' legs.'

Amy took porridge and a boiled egg. They reminded her achingly of home.

Matron was waiting for them in the hall. 'Aprons and long cuffs, girls,' she said. 'You can start making the beds as soon as the cleaners have finished the floors.'

'It's chaos, isn't it?' Helen whispered.

The crates and boxes were open and strewn about. Amy watched the doctors unpacking the surgical instruments, enamel basins and kidney dishes, scalpels, saws, retractors, hypodermic syringes, packs of needles. She found herself gazing at them, almost unable to bear it.

Dr Hanfield looked up and saw her. 'It's Amy, isn't it? Help me with these, dear. We're setting up the operating theatre in the ladies powder room. There are sinks and water in there already. M. Le Blanc has worked wonders – he's found us an operating table and an electrician to put up the light.'

Amy carried in the bundles of familiar instruments. Sister Cox, the theatre sister, was already sorting them and putting them away in boxes and drawers.

'Where shall I put these retractors?' Amy said. She knew she had made a mistake as soon as the words were out of her mouth.

Sister gave her an odd look. 'What do you know about retractors?' she said.

'Oh – nothing,' Amy stammered. 'Dr Hanfield said that's what they were.' I'll have to be careful, she thought. That was a close one, but Sister appeared to be satisfied.

'Thank you, Amy,' she said. 'That's all you can do in here.'

The words were like a blow. No it isn't, she thought. I could do everything in here. Men were dying and she could do nothing.

She turned abruptly and hurried out. 'Help in the wards, Amy,' Matron said. 'The beds have come. They all need making up.'

The big luxurious lounges and the dining-room had been stripped and emptied and scrubbed and the beds arranged in rows, a strict four feet apart. Amy wrinkled her nose. The wards smelt strongly of carbolic, astringent and sharp. An efficient smell. So much for French perfume. Helen was already there, spreading sheets and tucking in neat corners.

'You have to do the corners right,' she said, 'or the nurses will shout at you.'

The nurses moved about, crisp in apron and headdress, and crisp in manner. One bed was piled with dressings and bandages, thermometers and pairs of scissors. There was a crate of hydrogen peroxide and a box ominously marked in red letters – Morphine.

The morning wore on. They scrubbed and dusted and made beds and put away supplies. A brief lunch of roast beef and potatoes and cabbage, and then they began again. Slowly the piles of boxes disappeared. Slowly the equipment was put away.

Amy stood in the doorway of the biggest ward, looking back. The rows of beds stood silently in the late afternoon light, waiting in terrible expectancy. The empty beds had a soul-chilling air of impersonal indifference, as if all feeling, all emotion, had left the world. Who knew who would lie there? Does it matter, they seemed to say? Does anyone care? They will lie here and die, and more will come and lie here and die and this is just the way it is. Men have always killed each other. They always will. It will never end. Does anyone care? Not the heads of state, she thought, who cause it all, not the generals in their fine uniforms, safe behind the lines.

We care, she thought. We care. The beds waited. She was too horrified to cry.

The next day they arrived. One after another the ambulances unloaded their dreadful cargo. The whole staff watched them arrive, standing in the foyer. Amy was overcome with pity and dismay.

'My God,' Helen whispered bedside her. 'Oh my God.'

The orderlies and nurses got the men to bed and stripped them of their lice-ridden clothes and washed them. The doctors hurried round the wards; the chest of morphine was opened. Dr Hanfield and the other surgeons operated all the day and far into the night. In the hospital, the war had begun.

CHAPTER THREE

1914

THE work was relentless. Amy had not really known what to expect, but certainly not this endless flow of wounded men, many of them already dying of their wounds, of infection, gas gangrene, septicaemia, blood loss. They arrived filthy, in tattered uniforms, most of them covered in lice. They brought every wound imaginable; limbs shot away, abdominal wounds, head injuries, eyes missing and facial injuries almost too dreadful to look at. The operating theatre was working all day and half the night. She and Helen fell into bed every night, utterly exhausted. Helen cried herself to sleep for the first few nights. 'Oh, those men,' she sobbed. 'Those boys. How can they be so quiet, so patient? They should be raging. I don't understand what this war is about. It's about nothing, just men wanting power – more and more power.' Amy could only agree, horrified and sickened.

Every day those men whose wounds had been treated and were fit to travel were taken to the railway station and loaded on to hospital boat trains *en route* for the many hospitals that had been set up in England, set up in schools, church halls and country houses, and largely staffed with women volunteer VADs and orderlies. And every day the orderlies and ambulance drivers collected more shattered men from the trains that carried them from the trenches and brought them back to fill the waiting beds in Paris. On too many nights a heart-rending cargo of plain coffins was moved hurriedly through the corridors and loaded on to carts and lorries at the back of the hotel to be transported home, invisibly, in the night. Often the dead were not taken back to England but were buried in France. Sometimes there was no way of even knowing who they were. Their funerals took place in the early morning. Usually the coffins were placed on an open hearse, and the people in the streets would cover them with flowers. They were taken to cemeteries outside Paris where the local mayor would say a few words of sorrow and gratitude. The rows of graves and simple crosses grew every day.

Suffering and pain, courage and death were laid before them every day. Two of the young orderlies who had come out with them left almost immediately, their faces stiff and stretched with horror.

'What's that smell,' Helen said one day, her nose wrinkled. 'It's horrible. Smells fusty, like mice or something.'

'It's gas gangrene in the wounds,' Amy said. Another batch of men had just arrived and the dressings that had been applied hurriedly in the aid posts at the trenches or at the clearing stations were soaked and stinking. 'The wounds will have to be excised and irrigated.'

'What's gas gangrene?'

'An infection, a germ in the wound. The germ is one of those that doesn't need oxygen, and it goes very deep.' She paused, dismayed, knowing what might happen next to these men.' If it gets bad enough, they will have to amputate the limb. Otherwise it just spreads.'

'Oh my God.' Helen looked as if she were about to burst into tears. Then she looked puzzled. 'How do you know all that?'

I've done it again, Amy thought. I really must be more careful. 'I heard the doctors talking,' she said hurriedly. 'It's not something you see very often in England – apparently. They're trying some new method of irrigating the wounds. I don't know whether that will work, but it's worth trying, if it saves a limb.'

Some of the wounds were alive with maggots. To her surprise, Amy thought that the maggoty wounds looked cleaner than the others. She mentioned it to one of the nurses. 'It must be just a coincidence,' the nurse said stiffly. 'Maggots are horrible things.' Still, Amy wondered.

They wrote letters home for the men who could not use their hands or could not see. The letters were simple and brave and were all much the same:

Dear Mother
I am all right but wounded in the leg. The hospital here is very good and
all the doctors is ladies. They are very good. We are having good food.
Do not worry.

Then there were the letters to wives and sweethearts, sometimes very intimate, sometimes very descriptive. The younger orderlies often had flaming cheeks.

The dreadful letters, those to tell the appalling news to the bereaved families, were written by the doctors. It was one task that Amy was glad that she didn't have to do. What could you possibly say?

Occasionally they got an English newspaper. There were lists and lists of the dead, or the 'missing, believed dead, believed wounded, taken prisoner', appalling, endless lists. Sometimes Amy could hardly bear to look. Often, in the same regiment, there were several dead men of the same name – William Weaver, Henry Weaver, John Weaver. She knew that men from the same area, the same towns and villages, often joined the same regiment. Were they related? Were they perhaps even brothers? Did some distraught mother see that dreaded boy with the telegram visit her home again and again, with the same ghastly news? She could hardly bear to think about it.

Some of the news from home seemed so trivial. 'Look,' Helen said one day. 'It says the Duchess of Devonshire has asked people not to wear mourning in the streets for fear of lowering morale and Selfridges is going to put up an honour board of all their men.' She gave a wry, bitter smile. 'That should help a lot.'

'I suppose they have to find ways,' Amy said, 'to bear it.'

The news from the front at the beginning of September was dire. The British Expeditionary Force had retreated at Mons, and the Germans were even closer to Paris. Very close, apparently. M. Le Blanc kept them informed, as much as he could. He came to the hospital every few days to see the doctors, to ask if they needed anything that he could possible get for them. His face became more clouded every day, his fear more obvious. The news was as bad as it could be. Paris was in great danger. At any time the people who had bravely stayed in the capital expected to hear the screech of shells bombarding the city, or even worse, the apocalyptic clatter of hoofs as the German cavalry rode through the city streets.

'Do you think they will get here, Amy?' Helen was obviously nervous, though she tried to sound jaunty and calm.

'No,' Amy said firmly. 'Of course they won't.' We must believe that, she thought. We can't let fear overcome us. Unfounded fear is more destructive than anything. We must believe that.

They were given a few hours off one afternoon. 'Let's go out,' Helen said. 'I've never seen Paris and I must get out, just for a little while. I'm getting claustrophobic. We need to look at something different.'

Matron was dubious. 'Don't go far,' she said. 'We don't know what is happening.'

'I don't think the Germans are going to come today,' Helen said. 'Surely we would have heard something. There would have been some news, some shelling, or something.'

Matron still looked worried. 'Well, keep together,' she said. 'and if there's the slightest sign of trouble, come back at once.'

Paris was surprisingly quiet; there was no sign of panic or confusion. In the side streets the shops and apartments were nearly all closed and shuttered and the streets almost empty of people. They passed a little church, with the doors open, and it was packed with women and children and old men, praying on their knees, rosaries in their hands. Their prayers spilled out into the street, in desperate chanting. '*Je vous salue, Marie, pleine de grâce.*' The many candles flickered and wavered in the gloom; the plaster saints stood inscrutable in their niches.

Here and there in the streets they saw small groups of people clustered about a young man, and they would hold him and kiss him until he turned and walked away, leaving behind their shocked, white, tearful faces. Very soon they realized that these were families, saying goodbye to their sons and husbands and brothers. Helen clutched Amy's hand. 'Oh, Amy!' By now they knew what was waiting for these men. In every street there were more and more women, bent with grief, wearing their widows' veils.

The people who were left seemed to be steadfastly going about their usual business, an old cobbler in his shop still mending shoes, a little milliner's shop, open, but bereft of customers, a dressmaker, sitting alone in her little shop, staring out of her window. There were signs of jobs half done – a strong smell of horse dung in some of the streets where there was no one to clear it away.

There was none of the usual cheerful tables and chairs outside the cafés, no one sitting in the sunshine with their coffee or wine. M. Le Blanc had told them that they were no longer allowed, that the French had to drink inside now like Englishmen in their pubs. The cafés had to close at eight o'clock, and the restaurants at half past nine and there was to be no music after ten. The Louvre was closed, but the most frightening news of all was that the government had decamped to Bordeaux.

'They must think the Germans are coming,' Helen said, 'or they wouldn't have gone. Why didn't they warn everybody? And I suppose everybody has to stay inside in case they start shelling. And why do they have to close at eight o'clock?'

'M. Le Blanc says there is a curfew,' Amy said. 'No one goes out at night. Apparently they have policemen patrolling the streets in case anyone is up to no good.' There were constant rumours of spies. Shops with German sounding names had been hurriedly abandoned, and their owners fled. Some of them had been wrecked by angry Parisians, the broken windows boarded up.

They walked on. Many of the monuments and statues were completely surrounded by sandbags, the history and beauty of Paris covered and obscured.

'Look, Amy. There's the Eiffel Tower.' They looked up at the great structure that was now the signature of Paris, known all over the world. 'I wish we could go up to the top, but M. Le Blanc says we can't. They have searchlights up there at night, and there is a machine-gun post on the top. In case of Zeppelins or aeroplanes, I suppose.'

Aeroplanes, Amy thought; such a wonderful invention, such a leap forward in man's ingenuity. Her father had been so delighted when he heard of the first powered flight. 'I knew it would happen,' he said. 'I knew someone would do it one day.' And now aeroplanes were just another weapon of war, just another way to kill. Could such a thought ever have entered the Wright brothers' minds when they flew for the first time? Could they ever have imagined this? Did every wonderful thing have to be used for destruction?

They walked on. 'It feels peculiar, doesn't it?' Helen said. 'Creepy.' Amy nodded. There was an atmosphere of deep apprehension that showed clearly in the strained, white faces, the hurried steps. The words hung in the air – are the Germans coming? Will they be here, in Paris, tomorrow? What will they do to us? The memory of the siege of

Paris in 1870 had returned, with all its terror.

They walked into the wide boulevards. There was a scattering of bright uniforms; the red of the Zoave – the North African soldiers; the Turkos – the Algerian riflemen in their blue jackets, and the splendour of the French Hussars in their light blue tunics. Amy wondered at the bright colours. Surely they would be easier for the German riflemen to see. They would surely stand out against the greens and browns of the land. The British Army had long used khaki – ever since the Boer War.

They reached the great boulevards and stopped in shock at the most dismaying sight of all, the steady streams of people moving south. The streets were filled with slowly moving lines of traffic, refugees from the north in their carts pulled by farm horses or donkeys, taking whatever they could from their abandoned houses and farms, pots and pans, bottles of wine, a flitch of ham, a fat yellow cheese – and children; so many children, gazing about them at the sights of the city. Here and there were carriages or motor cars carrying the more prosperous French from their fine homes in the 16th Arrondissement or Neuilly-sur-Seine, all going south or west, away from Paris.

'Look, Amy.' Helen plucked at her sleeve and they watched, astonished, as a farmer drove his flock of sheep down the Bois de Boulogne. 'I didn't realize,' Helen said, her voice shaking. 'Shut up in the hospital all the time, I didn't know this was going on. They must really believe that Paris is going to be invaded. They must think it is lost.'

Amy put her hands in her pockets to hide their trembling. The rumours were rife, and worse than rumours. They had all heard about the German atrocities in Belgium. They had burned Louvain and its precious medieval library. There was a dreadful report in the papers that they had shot hundreds of civilian men and women and children at Dinant. Did the country that had given the world Goethe and Beethoven really do such things? There were worse rumours for women. There had been a horrible cartoon in one of the French newspapers of a fat German soldier with a woman at his feet, a woman, half stripped, bound and gagged. The caption read 'The Seduction'. Its meaning was obvious: the fear of rape was yet another horror for women. It brought into her mind another hideous memory, hurriedly suppressed, of Sir William Bulford.

'No, not Paris,' she said firmly. 'The Germans will never get Paris.'

Helen looked doubtful. 'I hope you're right.'

'Lots of people are staying,' Amy said. 'We're staying.'

'Let's go back to the hotel,' Helen said, 'I think I've seen enough. We don't know how lucky we are in England half the time, do we? Never been invaded since 1066. Thank God we're an island and we have the sea and the Royal Navy.'

'This Sceptred Isle.' Amy said. 'Thank God indeed.'

They made their way back to the hotel. 'I wish we hadn't gone out at all,' Helen said. 'I'm more worried now.'

Later in the day Dr Hanfield called a meeting of all the staff. 'We must make plans,' she said, 'for a possible evacuation. I think the American hospital would help us with an ambulance or two and I would have to find whatever transport I could. I want you all to be ready – a small suitcase only. Just essentials.'

'It's getting bad, Amy,' Helen whispered.

'Meanwhile,' Dr Hanfield went on, 'you are to continue your duties. And under no circumstances upset the men. No nasty rumours, no panicking. Remember who you are. British women. And these men are in your care.'

A letter arrived for Amy from her father.

My dearest Amy

It isn't any use you telling me not to worry. I worry about you all the time. The news is so bad. I fear every day that you will be trapped in Paris at the mercy of the Germans, and it seems that they have no mercy.

Several of our boys from school are already dead. Young Frensham is dead. He was either in an accident or shot down with rifle fire, I don't know which. He had only been in the Flying Corps for three weeks. Other boys from the school have died in the trenches. They were so young, so full of life. I can hardly bear to think about it. I know that you will want to stay and do your duty, but is it really necessary for you to be there, in Paris? Couldn't you do your work at home in England? The hospitals here are overwhelmed. You know that you are all I have in the world. Of course, you must decide, and I must accept that. But I worry about you all the time.

Write to me soon

Your loving Father.

Amy sighed and put the letter in her pocket, to be answered as soon as she could. She couldn't go back. Perhaps she could work as an orderly in an English hospital but it wouldn't be the same. At least here she felt that she was at the heart of things, that she was doing her utmost, the utmost that she was allowed. She couldn't go back.

There were times, though, when she had to use all her self-control to repel fear. It was not, she thought, exactly fear that she felt now. The situation had to be accepted, overcome. It was more a heightening of awareness, a slight but constant tensing of the muscles, a sharpening of the senses. She was aware that her body seemed to be holding itself alert in readiness for whatever was going to happen. She must control her mind to control her body. Were the Germans as bad as everyone said, or was this just propaganda to fire the British populace into anger and fighting spirit? She tried to imagine what it must be like to be a man, to face something more real, something that was actually happening now, to go over the top of the trenches into an inevitable and expected hail of shells and machine-gun fire. What must it be like to face death or mutilation on such a scale? Her own fears seemed minor in comparison.

She felt also the responsibility of her profession. Giving way to fear was something that doctors must not do. She remembered how, newly qualified and in her first house job, she had lain awake at night, listening as the ambulances drew into the hospital yard, knowing that she would have to go down to the ward, make life or death decisions for other people, to take decisive action. That responsibility was so great that for a time she had found it terrifying. That fear went away with time and experience. There was, of course, no comparison with the present source of fear, but it had to be conquered just the same. She would not leave. Doctors did not, should not, run away, leaving their patients to face whatever was coming.

The world was full of fear even without the war. She thought of the women in the slums at home, living in damp, vermin-ridden rooms, struggling and fighting to feed their children, watching them day after wretched hungry day, willing them to survive. That was something that must be dealt with after the war – those barefoot, half starved children, children with scurvy, rickets, conditions that were not due to infection or disease, but to poverty and simple neglect and lack of nourishment. How many children to a family? Five? Six? Even more? Women who had a child year after year, who spent most of their lives pregnant, who went without food themselves to feed their ever growing families. There was a woman in America who had written articles about contraception and the need for impoverished women to have access to it. She had been pilloried by state and church groups, denounced as immoral and flying in the face of God. Had these people ever seen how these women lived? How they struggled and starved? It was that situation that was immoral. Her determination rose in her again, to do her job here, to get her licence back, to help these people when the war was over.

The wounded poured in. They continued their endless work, washing and delousing men, making beds, feeding, trying to ignore the threat that hung over them. Every day they expected the dreadful news that Paris had fallen. The strain of the work was enough, but none of them could sleep properly at night, except when they were too exhausted to think. Even then, often, Amy would wake in the early hours, her heart pounding, wondering what it was that had wakened her, listening for any noise that was unusual, that could signal disaster. Rain rattling at the windows would sound like machine-gun fire; a shout in the night would sound like a battle cry.

Then one day Helen rushed into the ward, laughing, beaming, doing a little dance. 'Amy, Amy, M. Le Blanc is here with such news! There's been a battle at the Marne and the Germans have been beaten back. They're retreating. They've gone back miles. They won't be coming to Paris.' The men in the beds were cheering, those who were on their feet slapping each other on the back.

The relief was overwhelming. Amy found that her first reaction was one of enormous fatigue, as if all her muscles had released their tension and left her limp and helpless. She slept that night in a deep, dreamless sleep. As long as it lasts, was her last thought. As long as it lasts.

The atmosphere in the hospital lightened. Hope was in the air.

'Perhaps this is the beginning of the end,' Helen said. 'Perhaps it will all be over soon.'

Amy could not begin to believe it, not while the men continued to pour into the hospital. The two armies seemed like two wild beasts, head to head, jaws locked in a kind of stationary combat, neither giving ground, blood pouring from their wounds.

CHAPTER FOUR

1914

A MY dressed in her uniform, putting on the shirt over her bodice. For a moment her fingers shook so badly that she couldn't do up the buttons. She stopped and made a little sound, puffing out her breath in exasperation. They had been here for nearly a month now, surely she should be used to it. As if anyone ever got used to it.

Helen looked up. She was sitting on the edge of her bed, buttoning up her shoes. 'Are you all right, Amy? Is anything wrong?'

Amy shook her head. There was no point in saying what she was thinking. What could she say? I'm going to see some terrible things today? How could such things happen? The words would give body to the thought. There was no point in saying this to Helen anyway. Helen knew. There were times when they had both stumbled into this room and clung to each other and burst into tears; times when the carnage and the suffering they had to witness was too much for anyone to bear. They had to stay strong; otherwise they would be useless to anyone. Helen was the only person who had ever seen her cry.

She shook her head again. 'Just these dratted little buttons.' She could see from Helen's strained face that she understood, that she understood not to say anything, not to pursue it. Helen gave a tight little smile. The skirt was loose, Amy noticed. She had lost weight since she came to France. She picked up her boots and turned them upside down and shook them.

Helen grinned. 'Find any spiders?'

Amy sat down on her bed and pulled on her boots. 'No. Horrible things. They're even bigger here than they are in England.'

'Autumn coming,' Helen said. 'They get everywhere.'

Amy got up. 'Worse things than spiders.' she said. 'Got to go.'

'You look very nice,' Helen said. 'Very crisp and efficient.'

Amy forced a smile. 'Not for long. It'll look very different by the time I get back.'

'I know,' Helen said. 'I'll see you tonight. Be careful, Amy.'

Amy left the room and walked down the corridor to the staircase. She stood at the top of the stairs, looking down. The big crystal chandeliers still hung from the ceiling. They caught the gleams of sunlight from the tall windows and cast all the colours of the rainbow on to the marble floor. She couldn't see into the other rooms, but she knew what was there; she saw it every day, the constant fight against infection, pain and death. She paused for a moment, gathering herself into a calm, controllable whole. She felt, not exactly fear, but a mounting tension that froze her muscles. She was aware of her shoulders rising up and her jaw clenching. She forced herself to relax, taking a few deep breaths. She felt slightly sick, as she always did when she had to go out with the ambulance; a nausea of apprehension.

The hall below was filled with uniforms. The crisp white aprons of the nurses and orderlies moved among the khaki and the plain blue uniforms of the wounded men, a strange contrast to the luxurious surroundings. It hardly seemed real. Only a few weeks ago she had been at home. Nothing much would have changed there. Her father would be getting ready to go to his school and Mrs Jones, the daily woman, would be starting on the housework. Normality. Did it really still exist, anywhere? A faint smell, a mixture of ether and carbolic and suppressed nastier things, reached up the stairs.

Dr Hanfield walked into the hall below, talking to a British officer in khaki – not a patient then. He looked quite young, Amy thought. Young enough to fight. She felt calmer now, and ready. She walked down the stairs into the hall. She stopped to let three wheelchairs go by. One of the men had no legs below the knee. She hurried towards the street door.

'Oh, Amy,' Dr Hanfield called. She was smiling and beckoning. 'Could I speak to you for a moment?'

Amy walked over to her, across one of the glowing Persian carpets, criss-crossed now with the wheel marks of the chairs.

'I'm on the ambulance today, Doctor,' she said. 'I think it's waiting.'

'I won't be a moment, Amy. 'Dr Hanfield turned to the officer. 'This is Miss Osborne, one of our orderlies. She has been with us from the beginning.'

Amy looked up at him. He was tall, in his thirties perhaps, broad-shouldered. He looked down at her, brown eyes under brown hair that curled a little. His eyes smiled, but they held the look that she had come to recognize. They were darkened with that particular horror-filled experience that all the men seemed to have – all the men who had been to the trenches.

'This is Captain Fielding, Amy,' Dr Hanfield said. 'He is a surgeon with the Royal Army Medical Corps. He's come to see what we do. The British Army apparently wants to know.' Her voice held an ironical note. Amy smiled but said nothing.

Dr Hanfield turned back to the Captain. 'We were all rather disap-pointed,' she said. 'We had hoped that the British Army might have been more open-minded. We hoped they might be glad of the services of women surgeons and physicians during the war, but it seems not. However, the French Red Cross seems to be quite pleased with our work here in Paris.'

He nodded. 'So I understand.'

'And not only the surgeons.' She turned to Amy. 'Miss Osborne is on her way out with the ambulance today.'

He raised his eyebrows. 'Out? Where?'

'One of the villages,' Amy said. 'To pick up the wounded.'

'Which village?' he said, frowning.

He looked surprised, she thought. Perhaps he didn't expect that women would be doing such things. Perhaps he thought that she should be at home knitting socks. She was prepared to be irritated.

She looked him in the eye. 'I'm not quite sure. The driver knows. One of the villages. They get word to us somehow about where the men are – the wounded.'

'Will you be near the Front?'

'Possibly,' she said shortly. 'That's where the wounded usually are, isn't it? Usually we don't know. They get the men back any way and anywhere they can.'

He looked at her in silence for a moment. She wondered if she had been too sharp, too outspoken. Maybe he didn't have the usual prejudices. Who knew? After all, it wasn't his fault that the British Army took the attitude that they did to women doctors. Most of the male population was the same, and many of the women too.

'May I ask what you will be doing, exactly?'

Amy looked at him and opened her mouth to reply, but the words wouldn't come. Her mind seemed to contract, trying to shut out the frightful images of what she would be doing. She couldn't hold them back, the severed limbs, exposed intestines, the moans and cries – 'Water; God; Mother; help me'. She stared at him for a moment, unable to speak. Dr Hanfield put her hand on her arm and gripped her. The firm pressure shook her, brought her back to the present. She took a deep breath. 'We will be bringing in the men,' she said. 'Bringing them back here to the hospital.'

He said nothing, but he smiled at her, a grim, complicit sort of smile. He seemed to understand. She could see compassion, even admiration, in his face, in the sudden warmth in his eyes.

'You are very brave,' he said at last.

'It's not only me,' Amy said. 'We all do it.'

'Then you are all very brave.' He smiled. 'Until the war, I didn't think ladies did that kind of thing.'

Amy looked at him calmly. 'We were underestimated.'

Dr Hanfield laughed softly and he looked a little sheepish. 'So I see.'

'Thank you, Amy.' Dr Hanfield put her hand briefly on Amy's shoulder. 'Take care.'

Amy nodded and walked on. At the door she turned and looked back. Captain Fielding was looking at her intently. Then he raised his hand and gave her a slow salute.

The ambulance was waiting outside the door. Bill, the driver, opened the door for her.

'Morning, Miss Amy. Nice day.'

'I hope so, Bill.'

She climbed aboard. Bill went to the front of the ambulance and put in the starting handle. He swung it several times before the engine caught. Then he climbed in beside her. They set off through the streets of Paris, going north.

The streets were busy, a few carriages and motor cars, but mostly carts and barrows going south. The carts were laden with whatever the people could rescue from their houses – trunks and boxes and pots and pans, bedding and small bits of furniture. Children or old men and women perched and clutched and swayed on the loads, the children with puzzled, frightened faces and the old people with faces that seemed already dead, frozen in fear and pain. Babies cried, or quietly suckled in their mother's arms as the carts went past. Often the traffic slowed and pulled to one side to let the ambulance through, and then closed in again in an endless stream.

The broad Parisian streets narrowed and diminished and then they were driving through the suburbs, and then through scattered groups of houses. The houses were shuttered and silent as if they had been abandoned, but here and there smoke rose from a chimney, thin poor-looking wisps rising up into the still air. Then they were out in the countryside.

She began to feel the tension rising again. She drew in her breath, and clasped her hands together. Bill turned to her briefly.

'Are you all right?'

'Yes,' she said. 'It's nothing, I'm fine.'

'It'll be all right,' he said, but she noticed that his jaw was clenched and his lips were curled in and pressed tight. He took a battered cigarette out of his top pocket and put it in the corner of his mouth. After a few seconds he lit it with a Lucifer, bending over the wheel, his eyes still carefully on the road.

It was late September and still warm and dry. The countryside looked peaceful enough as they drove along the long straight roads of northern France. The lines of tall, straight poplars filtered the bright sunlight and it flickered on their faces as they drove by. It seemed almost normal, a normal day in a normal country, until they came across the trenches dug by the roadside. They passed a lorry that had been burned out and abandoned, and a dead horse that had been pulled into a ditch, one leg sticking up in a grotesque salute. The sweet, nauseating smell of death thickened the air and she tried not to breathe as they went by. They passed through villages that seemed lost and deserted but once or twice, as they approached, they saw a woman clutch her child and run into the nearest house. How dreadful it must be, Amy thought, to have such fear for your children.

She watched the countryside going by, trying not to feel anything. Beside her Bill was silent, but she could see beads of sweat standing on his brow. He drove steadily, but his eyes constantly swept each side of the road, constantly watchful. Amy thought that they were well away from the enemy lines, but you could never be quite sure. Sometimes even the troops they met didn't know. Sometimes they saw an aircraft above them, a swooping biplane, never knowing whether it was friend or foe.

Amy looked about her. The fields and pastures looked so lush, so beautiful, but further on, she knew, the land itself was as shattered and wounded as the men. She had often wondered what France would be like, in those days that were so far away now. Holidays with her father had always been in England. She remembered how excited she had been as a child, taking the overnight train from Paddington to Cornwall, or the train up from Euston to the Lakes. Then when she was older, she had so wanted to travel, especially to France, but they never really had enough money, and she could never spare the time; her studies were all consuming. She had thought then to see a beautiful country, contented farms, prosperous towns and a Paris that led the world in fashion, sophistication and chic. She had never expected to see France like this, battered, exhausted, running with blood.

'Barricade,' Bill said. Amy jerked back to the present.

Every few miles they were stopped at a barricade and the ambulance searched by French or English soldiers, and they were able to ask directions. Some of the English soldiers they met were cheerful enough; they were wearing fresh, clean uniforms, joking and laughing. They've just come, Amy thought. They haven't been to the trenches yet. They were very grateful for the Woodbines and the books she brought with her.

One of them, a cheery, rosy-cheeked boy, came up to the ambulance window. 'Thanks a lot, miss,' he said. 'Thanks for the fags.'

Amy leant out. 'Where are you from?'

'Cheshire. Worked on a farm.' He glanced about him. 'Nice land here. I never knew France was so like England. I'd like to come back after the war – have a look round.'

Come back? Amy looked at his open, innocent face, her heart contracting. What were his chances of coming back? 'Good idea,' she said. 'Best of luck.'

'Won't be long,' he grinned. 'We'll soon get rid of them Huns. They can't beat us Tommies.'

He saluted and went back to his friends. They gave her the thumbs up sign, broad grins, and letters to be posted to England when she got back to Paris.

Amy watched them as they drove on, battling with her feelings of horror and despair. She knew, perhaps better than they did, what was in store for them. She had seen the results, the remnants. How did they do it? How did they make themselves do it? They must know the facts about what was happening. They had to shut their minds to it; they had no choice. They had to shut their minds to the likelihood of being killed or maimed among the trenches, the barbed wire, the shells, the machine-guns. She turned to Bill to say as much but the words stuck in her throat. Bill had been there and had lost half his left hand. He wouldn't want to hear her thoughts.

How do I do it, she thought, and Helen and all the others? There wasn't a single thing in her life that had prepared her for this. Her contacts with suffering humanity had taken place in the best conditions. She had no experience of raw, bestial, pain and death. She felt a wave of homesickness for the solid, comfortable house in Bromley, the sweet smell of her father's pipe tobacco. It had been so peaceful, so serene. They had thought it would go on for ever.

They passed more men marching in single file along the road. She looked at their faces as they drove by. Some of them looked so young. How long before they were wounded or dead, or went mad? Some of them did go mad, as she well knew. She cared for men with broken minds as well as broken bodies. Sometimes her personal rage was almost insupportable. She watched the doctors at the unit struggling to cope with endless waves of shattered men, knowing that she could have helped so much more. Sometimes the effort was almost too great, the effort not to step forward, to reveal herself.

'Here we are then, Miss Amy.' Bill stopped the ambulance in the village street. He took out his revolver and laid it across his knee, ready to hand.

Amy looked about her through the dusty windows. The village lay in a hollow with low hills all round, hills that could conceal anything. It looked dilapidated, shaken. This village couldn't be anywhere but in France, she thought. The whitewashed houses, close together, ran in a single file along each side of the roughly paved road. A covered wash-house stood at the end of the village, fed, Amy assumed, by a stream that must run behind the houses. Often they found the wounded in the washhouse, close to the source of water.

The houses were shrouded and empty looking, although it was the middle of the morning. A sign – Café Bar – hung in the still air, but the café was deserted. A thin black cat crept around a corner and fled when it saw them.

The silence stretched. Amy couldn't judge whether it was menacing or merely defensive.

'Where is everybody?' she said softly.

Bill shrugged. 'Must be somebody here somewhere.' One or two curtains twitched in the few windows that were unshuttered.

'There's someone in the houses,' Amy said. 'I'll get out first. Even if they think we're Germans I don't suppose they'd do anything to a woman.'

Bill picked up his revolver. 'I wouldn't be too sure about that.'

She opened the door and got out into the dusty street and stood beside the big red cross on the ambulance. She supposed that no one here would recognize her uniform. It was not one of the regular service uniforms. It seemed to be well known in Paris now, but here it might arouse some suspicion.

She waited. The silence stretched and the heat seemed to grow more intense. The light was clear and brilliant and cast deep sharp shadows beneath the eaves and in the doorways. In the field behind the houses a horse stood as still as a statue. She began to feel as if it were all unreal, as if they had driven into a static moment of time that would never change. Then one of the shutters moved a little and somewhere she heard the cry of a child that was suddenly silenced. She had no doubt that several hidden pairs of eyes were inspecting her. She broke out in a sweat and could feel it running down between her shoulder blades. She closed her eyes against the sun, and against whatever horror might erupt from these silent houses.

What am I doing here, she thought? Is this all there is for me? Perhaps I'll be shot. Perhaps I'll die here beside this ambulance before I have achieved anything, before my life is worth anything. The silence was more and more intimidating. Maybe this village had been occupied. Maybe these were German eyes watching her.

'You're a woman,' her father had said, trying, for the last time, to dissuade her. 'There are worse things for a woman than dying.' For a few moments she couldn't think what he meant and then she blushed and turned away. She must not ever think of horrors that might happen. The evil she could see was enough.

'There's someone coming,' Bill said. Amy opened her eyes and saw his hand appear at the window, holding his revolver.

'It's all right,' she said hurriedly. 'It's a priest.'

'I hope he speaks English.' Bill withdrew the revolver.

'It doesn't matter,' she said. 'We'll find the men.'

The priest stopped beside her and held out his hand. *'Bonjour,'* he said.

Amy shook his hand. 'Do you speak English? *Parlez-vous anglais?'*

'Yes, *mam'selle,'* he said. 'We are very glad that you have come. The men are very sick.'

He looks dreadful, she thought. He was gaunt, tense with strain, grubby and unshaven. His cassock was stained and dirty. Some of the stains were dark and stiff. Blood, she thought, always blood.

Slowly, some of the doors of the houses opened and the people came out hesitantly, looking at each other and at the priest for reassurance. Amy noticed, as she always did, that the few men were old, wearing the rough trousers and shirts of farm labourers. The women were almost all in black, some with a white scarf at the neck, and the children clung to their mothers' skirts, silent and unsmiling, their little faces wiped blank with sights that no child should ever see. The priest gestured to them to come out, that it was safe, and spoke to them in French that was too rapid for Amy to understand. They came out, smiling a shy, troubled welcome. Some of them brought gifts, a half bottle of wine, a small piece of cheese resting in a spotless linen handkerchief. An old woman, grey and bent and leaning on a stick, took Amy's hand and kissed it. 'Thank you,' she said in careful English. 'Thank you.' Amy's eyes filled with tears.

'The Germans have been through here twice,' the priest said. 'They took everything.'

Amy glanced up at the surrounding hills. God knew what was concealed, waiting, up there.

'We'd better get going then,' she said. 'Where are the men?'

The priest turned to lead the way. They walked down a little lane with high hedges on each side where blackberries were growing, gleaming like dark jewels, nearly ready for the villagers to pick. It looked so much like England that Amy was swept again with homesickness, longing to be in a quiet English country lane, her basket on her arm.

She needn't have asked where the men were. As they walked towards the church the foul smell of infected wounds rolled out and enveloped them. She gagged and swallowed. She could never get used to the smell and never seemed to be able to get rid of it. It seemed to cling in her hair and clothes and stay in her nostrils for days, sour and rotting.

The priest led her through a little cemetery beside the church. There were a few ancient gravestones, but most of the graves had simple wooden crosses. One of the graves was decorated with a wreath made entirely of beads that shone and glittered in the sun. Who had made that, she wondered? It was a work of art, a reminder of days of peace and leisure. Between the graves the grass was mown and here and there a late, lost poppy was still in bloom. At first sight the little grave-yard seemed filled with peace, with loving memories of villagers of the past, villagers who had died in the love and care of their families. But there were two fresh graves, each with a bunch of wild flowers in a jar. Amy stopped beside the graves. Often she was able to take the name and rank of the dead. At least their suffering families would know where they were.

'Two British soldiers,' the priest said. 'We don't know who they are. They only had half their clothes, and nothing to say who they are.'

Amy felt an immense sadness. These two young men had died here, far from home, with only strangers to bury them. They had mothers at home, back in England, who didn't know what had happened to them, who would probably never know.

They came to a tall, rusty cross, with a figure of Christ that had lost its head.

The priest stopped. 'A bullet,' he said. 'It was a bullet.'

The head with its crown of thorns looked up at her from the grass. She shivered, for a few moments unable to move on.

She steadied herself against the cross. The little churchyard reminded her of home. She saw herself going to church with her father every Sunday as a matter of course, but she had had doubts before. Her work at the hospital and the occasional suffragist meeting had opened her eyes to the dreadful privations of the poor in England. One Sunday, an idea, almost a blasphemy, had come into her head and shocked her.

Did God only live in comfortable places? Was He really in the slums and workhouses? Was He here on the battlefields? What kind of God would make a world like this? The face, looking up from the grass, had no answer to give her.

Over the hills there came a sound, a tearing, crashing boom, a shriek, a rumbling; the sound of great guns. The priest winced and shuddered. 'This way,' he said.

The door of the church was open and a cloud of fat, bloated flies buzzed around it. As she approached the foul smell hit her again like a blow, a solid wall of pestilence and putrefaction. She hesitated and slowed. For a few moments she was overcome. She began to tremble and leant against the church wall. She wanted to run away, run to the ambulance and drive away, away anywhere, as long as it was away from here. Slowly she gathered her strength and walked inside.

A dozen men, French and English, were lying in the straw on the floor. They lay close together, their uniforms tattered and filthy. Some of them were moaning in pain, some muttering and calling out in delirium. One man was laughing, a continuous high-pitched manic laugh behind empty, staring eyes. His left arm was in a crude sling and he held up his right hand as if he were holding a gun. He pointed it at Amy. 'Bang,' he said, and then the manic laugh again. An orderly from the RAMC and some of the village women were handing out tin mugs of water. Every head turned towards her. Some of the men gave a faint, ragged cheer. One man, an older man by the look of him, in a sergeant's uniform, called out, 'Thank God. God bless you.'

The orderly came towards her. 'You're a sight for sore eyes,' he said. He was small and thickset, with a strong Northern accent, Lancashire, perhaps, or Cumberland. He had a bloodstained bandage around his head.

'You're hit yourself,' Amy said.

'Just a scratch. Nothing to worry about.' His voice was light and cheerful, but behind that his face was deathly pale and his hands were shaking. He put them hurriedly in his pockets. His eyes seemed to have sunk, set back in their sockets, as if they didn't want to see the sights before them.

He's probably a Quaker, Amy thought. She had met several Quakers now; they often came from the North, from the Lakes. They wouldn't kill, but they were in the thick of it, caring for the wounded.

Her voice shook. 'How long have they been here?'

'Since yesterday morning.'

Bill gasped, 'My God,' and ran outside the door and Amy could hear him retching.

With a familiar effort, she faced what she had to do now. For a moment she closed her eyes. She tried to force down every feeling, every emotion. Pity and compassion had to be put by, stored away for another time, another need. What was needed now was efficiency, common sense. She steeled herself not to listen to the voices begging for help. She must take the men who could stand the journey; the men who had a chance of survival.

'Can any of you walk, or sit up?' she said. One or two hands were raised, one or two voices called out. Bill came in behind her with the stretchers and a few of the men from the village. She selected as many as the ambulance could take, some on stretchers, some sitting, a few able to walk with help. She gave morphine to those in severe pain and a measure of brandy in their dirty tin cups.

She came to a young man who was lying silently, his bottom lip bruised and bleeding from his biting, his muscles tense as he struggled not to move with every breath that he took. He was covered in filth and his left thigh was covered roughly with a blood-soaked bandage.

'We'll take this man, Bill,' she said.

'No you won't.' His voice, wrenched out from between set teeth, was cultured, confident and firm – used to command. Amy saw that his tattered rags were the remains of an officer's uniform – a lieutenant. 'Take the men,' he said. 'I'll wait.' His fair hair was thick with mud and his face stretched with pain but the blue eyes were clear and hard.

She knelt down beside him. 'I have to take whoever can stand the journey,' she said softly. 'I have to decide.'

'Take the men,' he said. 'That is an order.'

She met his eyes, hostile and angry. 'I'm going to give you some morphine,' she said. 'At least I can ease the pain.' She took out the syringe and morphine. Dr Hanfield had carefully taught the orderlies how to give injections, and she had allowed herself to be taught, carefully silent.

His eyes remained fixed on her as she filled the syringe, staring at her, glittering. She slipped the needle into his arm. She watched, as she had so often, as the lines of pain began to slide from his face. For the hundredth time she thanked God, or man, or both, for the drugs that eased pain. He continued to stare at her but soon his hard gaze changed to a look of puzzlement, as if trying to place her. Then, as the pain that was his overwhelming stimulus eased away, his eyes filmed and closed and he lost consciousness. His head fell forward.

'He's unconscious, Bill,' she said. 'We can take him now. He's probably got a fractured femur. We'll need a splint and we must be very careful. We don't want to damage his femoral artery.' Bill gave her a look that was half enquiring, half surprised, but he went off to get the splint without comment. I don't care, she thought, if he thinks I know more than I should. She and the army orderly fitted the splint and they lifted the young officer carefully on to a stretcher.

They loaded the ambulance, cramming in as many as they could. Amy said goodbye to the priest. She turned to the orderly.

'I'll send someone for the others,' she said. 'as soon as I can.' He looked grim, but said nothing. He didn't have to. 'Tomorrow,' she added hurriedly. His eyes glistened. They both knew the reality. Some of these men would not last the night. There would be more graves in the little cemetery.

Bill turned the ambulance carefully in the narrow street and they set off again, back the way they had come. He drove more slowly now and with care, but Amy winced at every jolt, thinking of the men behind her.

After an hour they stopped in a quiet country road that was lined and hidden by trees. 'They'll need some water,' Amy said. 'It's warm. They must be thirsty.'

She got out and opened the ambulance door. The foul smell swept out again. She turned her head away and took a few deep breaths of clean air. She had a sudden memory of a day when she was a little girl at home. Somehow a piece of raw meat had fallen behind a cupboard in the pantry. By the time they tracked it down it was crawling with maggots and the smell of rotting flesh had pervaded most of the house. This smell was the same. Rotting flesh.

She closed her mouth firmly and climbed inside. She gave out water, helping the men to drink. She came at last to the lieutenant. She realized that she had left him to the last, almost deliberately. She didn't want any more time-wasting arguments about who came first. He was conscious now, lying rigidly still, staring at the ambulance roof. As she came to him with the water he turned his cold, clear eyes towards her.

'You disobeyed me,' he said. 'You deliberately disobeyed my order.'

In spite of what had happened to him, Amy was suddenly annoyed. She was tired and dirty, and wouldn't feel that the men were safe until they were back in Paris. They were never absolutely sure that they were in friendly territory. Was that all that he could say? You disobeyed my order.

'I'm not one of your soldiers, Lieutenant,' she said sharply.

He hesitated; looked puzzled. 'What are you then? What is that uniform?'

'I'm a nursing orderly. With the Women's Surgical Group.'

'Never heard of it.'

Amy held out the mug. 'Drink the water. We must be getting on.'

He drank and lay back again, staring at the roof again. 'Where are we going?'

'To Paris, to our hospital. The Group hospital.'

'I don't need women,' he said, 'I need a surgeon. We all need a surgeon.'

Amy forced down her annoyance. 'We have surgeons,' she said. 'Excellent surgeons.'

His eyes shot round to her again. 'Women surgeons?'

'Yes,' Amy said firmly, and with pride. 'Women surgeons.'

'Oh my God,' he said, and closed his eyes.

Amy got out of the ambulance and closed the door. She climbed in beside Bill and they set off again.

'It makes me so mad,' she said.

'What?' Bill glanced at her briefly.

'The way everyone reacts to women doctors.'

'What?' he said again.

'They all seem to think that women aren't capable of doing anything apart from staying at home and doing the cooking and running a house. We can't even vote. Any drunken half-witted man can vote, but not a woman. Oh no.'

'They'll change their minds when we get there,' he said, 'when they see it's a bit of all right.'

'It's not the men,' she said. 'It's that lieutenant. You'd think he would be grateful.'

'Officers!' Bill said.

They drove on in silence. Amy gazed out of the window, not seeing the countryside going by. Why, she thought? Why is it like this? Why can't we vote? Why can't women be doctors, or anything they pleased? Even many women were against it. The row of men at the General Medical Council was seldom far from her mind. Perhaps this war would change their minds, the starch-collared, starched-brained establishment.

They drove over a bump in the road and she heard a muffled cry from the ambulance behind her.

'How long now, Bill?'

'We're getting on,' he said. 'There's that dead horse.'

CHAPTER FIVE

1914

THEY arrived in Paris and drove down the broad street to the hospital. The late afternoon sun lit up the trees that lined the pavements and glittered, orange and red, in the windows as they passed. Amy was weary to her bones. Her uniform was stained and soiled, blood and earth clinging to her skirt and jacket. The men behind her were moaning now, the effects of the morphine wearing off.

'We're there, Bill,' she said. 'We can get them inside, thank God. They've had enough.' She could not allow herself to think of the men they had left behind.

'Usual reception committee,' Bill said.

Every time they came home, they were there – a group of Parisians, a dozen or so, waiting by the hotel door. The individuals were not always the same, but the group seemed to have an individuality of its own. There were elderly men in black frock coats and top hats; their best clothes. There were women, dressed in black up to the neck, some of them with widow's veils. Their stricken faces seemed to Amy to be disembodied, pale, haunted ovals floating in a sea of black. The scene had etched itself into her mind like an Impressionist painting, but devoid of beauty or colour. As the ambulance approached, the faces would turn towards them, and the old men, in a gesture that brought a lump to her throat, took off their hats.

'It's a shame, isn't it?' Bill said. 'They can't really do anything.'

'I know.' Amy said, 'but it shows they care.'

'Oh they care all right.' Bill slowed down. The moans from behind them increased.

'They just want to be part of it,' Amy said. 'They just want to feel they are helping.' They are helping, she thought. They help the men and they help me. Sometimes, like today, she felt utterly drained, unable to feel anything, a fatigue of the spirit. These people helped to bring her back, to restore her spirit with a gentle word or touch.

There was usually someone in the crowd who spoke English, usually a man. She knew now what he would say, 'What can we do? Is there any news, *mam'selle*? What is happening?' She wished she knew. She wished she had something to tell them, something of hope. They filled her with sadness. They should have their families around them, their grandchildren on their knees; not like this, desperate for any news, frightened and alone. They should be able to see life renewing and growing. Instead it was bleeding away, their sons and all the children they would never have, dying on some battlefield.

Bill drew up outside the hotel and they got out. They opened the ambulance doors and helped out those who could walk. The hotel doors flew open and the orderlies and porters came out with stretchers and wheelchairs. The men came out of the ambulance, blinking in the light, many of them crying with relief.

The people crowded round them. As ever, an elderly man turned to her, his old hands shaking, his eyes rheumy and glistening. 'What can we do, *mam'selle*? Can we carry in their bags, their weapons? Can we help them?'

'Thank you,' she said gently, 'But I don't think they have anything.' Most of the men had lost all their kit and had nothing but the filthy clothes they lay in.

Then came the women, weeping and touching, stroking a forehead, taking a hand, '*Oh, les pauvres, les pauvres garçons.*' They showered the soldiers with gifts, cigarettes, sweets and flowers. It seemed that these women could do so little, but Amy knew what this meant to the men, to come back from that hell to a kindly face and a motherly touch. Many of them were just boys, crying for their mothers.

Sometimes a woman would hold up a photograph, 'Have you seen my son?' Once, on a day that Amy would never forget, one of the women in the crowd had actually found her own son being carried out of the ambulance. He was wounded and sick, but he was alive. She had screamed with joy and covered him, and then Amy, with kisses – her cheeks and her hands. Amy, and most of the other women in the crowd, cried too and Amy found that she couldn't stop. The tears had gone on and on until she could lie down on her bed and fall into an exhausted sleep.

Once again, the last out of the ambulance was the lieutenant. As his stretcher was lowered from the ambulance she could see that the lines of pain had come back to his face. He closed his eyes and groaned through his teeth as they moved him. Amy stood beside the stretcher looking down at him, and suddenly he opened his eyes. For a moment he seemed confused, his eyes empty and expressionless, and then he smiled at her.

The smile took her by surprise. If he said anything she expected more annoyed remarks about her disobeying his orders. She understood his annoyance, it came from concern for his men, but she didn't think that she could take any more today, no more pain or annoyance or anger. So the smile took her by surprise and she smiled back.

He said nothing, but his smile changed his face completely. Despite his pain the hardness and strength faded away, and he looked young again. His blond hair stuck to his brow and the long fair lashes drooped over his cheeks. He opened his mouth as if to speak to her, but he was carried away inside.

She turned and watched him go. She had the strangest feeling, as if he had communicated something to her, something of importance. Ridiculous, she thought, and yet she felt a new feeling, of something like pleasure and hope. His smile seemed to have the future in it, a future where beauty had returned, and joy and laughter.

'That's everybody, Miss Amy,' Bill said beside her.

'Thank you, Bill.' She closed the ambulance doors and Bill drove away.

The old man came to her again. 'Is there any news, *mam'selle*? What is happening?' There was nothing that she could tell him.

She stood for a moment in the cooling day. The birds were beginning to gather in the trees and the soft rustlings and twitterings soothed her. Nature went on, the trees still grew and blossomed, the birds still gathered for the night. She wondered if the lieutenant had felt anything when he smiled at her. Could such a feeling be one-sided? She didn't know. Nothing was normal any more.

She followed the men inside, trying to tuck her hair back into the straggling bun. She almost bumped into the RAMC officer who was standing just inside the door. He took off his cap when he saw her and smiled down at her.

'Do you remember me?' he said. 'Captain Fielding? I was hoping to see you before I left.'

'Yes,' she said. 'I remember.' She was acutely conscious of her dishevelled clothes, the stains and the smell. He looked so clean and well ordered, his Sam Brown polished, and his buttons gleaming.

'You look as if you've been busy,' he said.

Busy? The remark was about to annoy her until she saw the look in his eye, of understanding, of pain.

'Yes,' she said. 'We're always busy. It never stops.'

'I know.' He smiled, a grim, tired smile. His face changed. It seemed to slip, the smile twisting away, his eyes set deeper, hooded and guarded.

He does know, she thought. He's been there.

He looked at her in disturbed silence, his face working as if he were struggling to find his words. His distress was palpable. She knew that he, like her, was battling with images too terrible to forget. She wanted to touch him, to bring him back.

'The men all seem to have been looked after,' she said quickly. The new arrivals had already gone into the wards to be washed, de-loused, assessed. One of the group's surgeons and two nurses hurried across the hall to the operating theatre and the lights were turned on. For a moment she looked at the lights, trying not to feel anything, no anger, no bitterness.

'I shall have to leave very shortly,' he said.

She turned back to him and nodded, with some relief. 'Yes, of course.'

'You must be very tired,' he said, 'But I wonder if I could talk to you for a moment? Perhaps we could sit over there.'

'Captain Fielding,' she said, 'I really am very tired, and very dirty, as you see.'

'I would be most grateful,' he said. 'I have to write a report for the army on what your group is doing. They have directed me to do that. I might not have another chance. I really should have left an hour ago.'

'I see,' she said. 'Very well then.' She led the way across the hall and they sat down on one of the sofas.

'A report?' she said. 'Are you telling me the army is having second thoughts?'

'Possibly.'

'Oh fine. Now that they see how good the women are they will generously agree to accept their help.'

'Miss Osborne,' he said, 'I would like to say that I think the army was wrong. I have never been against women doctors.'

She looked into his face and could see only honesty. 'I'm sorry,' she said. 'It isn't your fault, but it makes me so angry. Women are treated as if we don't really exist. We can't vote. The doctors can't officially even treat our own wounded.'

'I think it's all wrong,' he said. 'My mother went to Oxford. She has a much better mind than mine but some of the top local tradesmen can vote and she can't.'

Amy laughed and relaxed. 'I'm sorry,' she said again.

Across the hall came the sounds of voices, the rattle of instruments being put into the sterilizer, the operating theatre being prepared.

'I spent most of the day in theatre with Miss Hanfield,' he said. 'She seems enormously competent – much more experienced than I am.'

He sounded perfectly sincere. How old was he? Thirty, perhaps? And he could do what he had been trained to do, while she. . . .

Her feelings must have shown in her face. 'Have I upset you?' he asked. 'Have I said something to annoy you?'

She shook her head. 'No, of course not. I just get angry sometimes. The women doctors here are just as competent as any man. It's just the same for them.'

He said nothing for a moment, looking down at his hands, his fingers clenched. That isn't quite right, she thought. It isn't the same. If she decided that she couldn't take any more she could go home and no one would ever blame her. If any man ran away they would be caught, and probably shot. This wasn't the time for recriminations. There were worse things going on in this terrifying world than her own problems, or even of the problems of women in general. The thought made her even more determined to stay, to see it through. After the war, that would be the time to fight. She had no weapons now. The British Army wouldn't accept women surgeons. They certainly wouldn't accept one who had been branded as she had been.

'Perhaps it isn't the time,' she said, 'for political ructions.'

'No,' he said. 'But it is the time to use competent doctors. The army is beginning to run short here, let alone what's going on at home. The hospitals in England are bursting at the seams. They're trying to recruit more doctors but it's getting difficult already, and heaven knows how long this is going to go on.'

'So – maybe they'll change their minds?'

He nodded. 'I hope so.'

'That's good to hear.' She began to get up. 'If you'll excuse me. . . .'

He looked up at her, contrite. 'Please don't go.'

She looked down at him, her surprise clear on her face. The tips of his ears turned pink. 'I would be most grateful,' he said, 'if you would just tell me what you do when you go out with the ambulance. Where do you go?'

She sat down again. 'As I told you,' she said, 'we go wherever the men are. Sometimes they come into Paris on the trains and we go to the station. Sometimes they come from the clearing hospitals, in army ambulances, or buses, or taxis, or whatever kind of vehicle they can requisition. But sometimes they are just lost, lost in the chaos. The army orderlies bring them back somehow, away from the trenches and we pick them up wherever we can. They manage to get word to us about where they are.'

His face was grave. 'Are you ever under fire?'

She shook her head. 'Not so far, but I expect it will happen sooner or later.'

Three men came out of the wards, wearing the blue uniform of the wounded. They sat down on the other side of the hall and got out their cigarettes. One of them had a bandage over his eyes and one of the others lit a cigarette and put it into his hand. They were quiet, subdued, not talking.

'Have you done anything like this before?' he said. 'Nursing, or anything?'

She hesitated considering her words. 'I have never been a nurse.' He seemed to be expecting more. 'I wanted to do something and this group seemed perfect. Dr Louisa Garrett Anderson has formed one too.'

'I know,' he said. 'I believe someone is going to see her too.'

Her head began to droop. 'Captain Fielding,' she said. 'I'm sorry, but I really am very tired and I'd sell my soul for a cup of tea.'

'I'm sorry,' he said. 'I'm a brute. Please forgive me.'

'Not at all,' she said. 'I hope it helps us.'

He stood up, and she stood up beside him.

'I wonder,' he said.

She looked up at him. The tips of his ears were really pink now.

'I shall be back in Paris sometime,' he said. 'I wonder if you might dine with me one evening? They've allowed music in the restaurants since we beat the Germans back at the Marne. We might even be able to dance.'

She was almost shocked. It hardly seemed the time to be dining and dancing, and she didn't know him. It was also not the time to gain any kind of reputation. Her surprise and hesitation must have been very obvious to him. She could feel the colour rising in her face and she stiffened slightly, drawing a little away from him.

'Of course,' he said, 'I would not ask you alone; I would hope that you would bring a friend, and I can find another officer to join us. And I would, of course, ask permission from your matron.'

Amy still hesitated. She was sure that Helen would come. Helen was always ready for a lark, and within the bounds of a certain respectability she was quite prepared to break the social rules. She wasn't sure, though. It was so easy to give the wrong impression. There were some English girls in Paris, happily not in this group, who had very dubious reputations indeed.

He turned his cap in his hands. 'It's so nice to talk to an English girl,' he said. 'I'd never tell them, but I think I must be missing my sisters.'

Amy relaxed and laughed. He was smiling at her, looking impish, but behind his smile she sensed a tension, a longing, a need for something that might have gone for ever. In his eyes she saw the world that they had both left behind. She saw him in white flannels, bounding about a tennis court, laughing, letting the girls win. She saw him poling a punt on the river with a cargo of his sisters and their friends, and a picnic basket, at Henley, perhaps, or Boulter's Lock at Maidenhead. She saw him dancing, waltzing, his tails flying. She realized with a shock of painful nostalgia that he was asking her for the most simple, and perhaps the last gift that she could ever give him. They both knew that he was going back and that he might not return. This might be his last chance to spend a pleasant evening with a girl.

'I don't know when I'm off duty,' she said.

'I don't know when I'll be back,' he said. The words 'or if' were not spoken, but they hung in the air, loud and vivid.

'I'd like to come,' she said.

All his muscles seemed to relax. His words tumbled over. 'That's wonderful of you, thank you so much. I'll really look forward to it. I'll be in touch. Will you shake hands?'

She put out her grimy hand and he enclosed it in his own, dry and warm.

'My name is Dan,' he said.

'Amy.'

'Goodbye then, Amy. I'll hope to see you soon.'

She crossed the hall and climbed the stairs. Halfway up she turned and looked back. He was still standing where she left him and he raised his hand in a brief wave.

I wonder if I've done the right thing, she thought. Still, he was going to speak to Matron, so he seemed quite genuine. She wanted a bath and a hair wash and a cup of tea. Helen would be all for it, she knew, and they didn't get much chance to relax. He seemed a nice man. It was only dinner, and only once – something to look forward to, dining, perhaps dancing. It was a long time since she had danced. A waltz sang into her head – the 'Blue Danube' – a floating dress. With a little shock of surprise she realized that the partner in her mind had blue eyes and blond hair, and an unexpected smile.

Half an hour later, Amy was sitting on the edge of her bed, drying her hair, rubbing it with a rough towel. She let her hair fall over her face; it smelt of soap now. She breathed it in, clean and tangy.

'Are you all right, Amy?' Helen was sitting opposite her on her own bed. 'Was it awful?'

Amy threw her head back, swinging her hair behind her, curling down below her shoulders. 'I didn't think I'd ever get it clean. Thank God for bathrooms and hot water and Lifebuoy soap.'

Helen looked at her, waiting.

'You know what it's like.' Amy bit her lip. 'It was just about as bad as it could get. We had to leave some of the men behind.'

Helen nodded. Amy could see Helen's own memories reflected in her face, in her compressed lips and unblinking eyes.

'You know.'

'Yes, I know.'

Amy wrenched her mind away from the morning; from all the mornings. 'Did you come across that surgeon from the army?' she said, 'Captain Fielding?'

'Yes,' Helen said. 'He came round the wards, poking into everything. Doing a report, or something.'

'Guess what?' Amy's eyes were bright now. 'He's asked us out to dinner – you and me. What do you think?'

Helen laughed, surprised and delighted. 'Has he really? What a lark! Why us? Oh do let's go, Amy. We don't get much fun, do we?'

Amy smiled at her enthusiasm. 'What's fun?'

'Exactly,' Helen grinned. 'How did it happen? Where did you meet him?'

'Dr Hanfield introduced us as I was going out this morning. I think she was trying to make a point about what we do. And then he was in the hall when I got back.'

Helen's eyes danced. 'Was he indeed? Waiting for you, was he?'

Amy laughed. 'Don't get any ideas.'

'Why not? You could do worse than marry a doctor.'

Amy's smile faded. She saw again the women waiting around the hotel doors, their fear and pain. What must it be like to be a mother or a wife? What horror must that be now?

'It isn't any good, is it?' she said. 'What's the use of getting fond of anybody? I don't think I'll ever marry or have children. I couldn't bear this. What on earth must it be like to have your husband or son out there? I'd go out of my mind.'

'It'll never happen again,' Helen said. 'No one would be mad enough to do this again. This has to be the last war there will ever be.'

Amy didn't reply. Her dark thoughts wouldn't go away.

'Anyway,' Helen went on, 'they say it'll be over by Christmas.'

Amy shook her head. 'It won't be over by Christmas. I can't see the Germans just giving up and we won't.' She got up and hung her wet towel over the towel horse. 'We can do our bit to cheer up the troops,' she said. 'We'll go out to dinner with Captain Fielding, and whatever other officer he manages to inveigle into our clutches. That's if Matron says yes.'

'Splendid.' Helen got up and took a comb from the dressing table. 'Here, let me untangle your hair for you.'

Amy sat on the stool and looked at Helen's bent head in the mirror, at her freckled cheeks and brilliant auburn hair. That hair must have stood out like a beacon in a crowd. She had a sudden picture of Helen on a suffragists' march, hitting a policeman over the head with her umbrella. She laughed softly and Helen looked up at her.

'I was thinking about the marches,' she said.

Helen waved the comb in the air. 'Votes for women!'

'Not much chance of that,' Amy said, 'while the war's on.'

'Soon after then.' Helen fingered the badge that she persisted in pinning to her lapel. 'You know our motto; deeds not words. Surely they can't stop us after this. They'll have more deeds than they can count.' She held up a lock of Amy's hair and struggled with the comb. 'It's men, isn't it? They're always fighting, one way or another. If women were in charge things would be different, wouldn't they?'

I don't know, Amy thought. I don't know if it would be better. I don't know anything any more. Trying to understand all the problems in the world was like trying to grasp a handful of water, chaotic, uncontrollable.

Would women be any different? Her mind went home again to a dinner party before the war started. She and her father had been invited to the Poulsons, across the road.

'We must go to war,' Mr Poulson said. Amy remembered him piling his plate with food, dabbing with his napkin at the gravy on his chin. 'Can't let the Hun have his own way. No knowing what that would lead to.'

Her father had been grave and quiet, too polite to disagree, and appalled, as Amy well knew, at the thought of any war, at the thought of his boys at school.

'I think it would be a very good thing,' Mrs Poulson said. The rings on her fingers glittered in the candlelight. 'A war now and again is good for the boys. Stiffens them up a bit. They're getting too soft.'

The day came back to her, the stench, the courage. Too soft! My God! Helen was still talking. 'It's men, men, men,' she said. 'Everything is always men. It's time women had a go.'

There was a knock at the door and Helen went to open it. 'Good afternoon, Sister,' she said. 'Do come in.'

The sister stepped into the room, her cap and apron crisp and shining white. 'I'm looking for Amy.'

Amy got up from the stool. 'I'm here, Sister.'

'Oh Amy.' Sister looked contrite. 'Would you do a couple of hours' duty on the officers' ward this evening? I know you must be tired and I'm sorry to ask but one of the nurses isn't well. We're just hoping it isn't influenza. That would go through the place like wildfire. We've put her in isolation.'

Amy nodded. 'Of course.'

'Good girl. Have you had something to eat?'

Amy shook her head. 'No, not yet.'

'Well have an early supper. It shouldn't be too busy. We've only had one officer admission today – the one you brought in. He's in theatre now, I think. Eight o'clock.'

'Very well, Sister, I'll be there.'

After she had gone Amy groaned. 'I was hoping for an early night.'

Helen grinned. 'Deeds, not words.'

Amy coiled her hair up into a neat bun again. She put on a clean uniform and walked downstairs to the dining-room. She ate her shepherd's pie and drank her tea. There was only one new officer then, her lieutenant. He was in theatre. His leg!

She finished her meal. She had an hour before she was on duty. She felt a need to be outside in the open air, a strange feeling of claustrophobia in this huge hotel. She went upstairs for her hat – Matron was very insistent that a hat should always be worn outside.

She walked slowly down the wide street. The occasional passers-by smiled at her; the men raised their hats. The claustrophobia, the feeling of suffocation, had nothing to do with space, she knew that. It was a constriction of the mind, the absolute denial of everything that she wanted to do. She was caged, pacing, straining at the bars. She should have been in theatre with the lieutenant and all the other men, doing her job. She walked and the feeling eased. The strained faces of the passers by brought her back to the job she had to do. Her own problems were of another time, another place. She would deal with those when the time came. She walked back to the hotel, took off her hat and jacket and walked down to the officers' ward.

Dusk was falling as she went in and the electric light was on over Sister's desk, set at the far end. The little oasis of light reminded her of home. She felt a stab of homesickness, missing her father, missing the house, the garden, the town. Most of all it reminded her of her father, sitting in his study in his own pool of light, marking his students' work, endlessly reading his scientific books.

Someone turned on the overhead lights. It was quiet this evening, and peaceful. Most of the officers were lying on their beds, some reading, some staring at the ceiling. Two of them were sitting on the edge of one bed, playing chess. She looked around quickly but she couldn't see the lieutenant.

Sister smiled at her. 'Could you help with the dressings, Amy? Nurse will show you what to do.'

Dressings, Amy thought. My promotion. She rolled up her sleeves and put on a white apron and cuffs. She and the staff nurse moved from bed to bed, changing the dressings. Many of them were infected, the bandages sodden and foul and the dressings had to be changed every four hours. Some of them made her gag, the pus foul and running. She tried to think of other things, of the scent of the roses in the garden at home, and again, the sweet scent of her father's occasional pipe tobacco.

There were screens around the bed nearest to Sister's desk.

'We don't need to go in there,' the nurse said. 'He's just come back from theatre. He has a nurse with him.'

It must be him, Amy thought. His handsome, ravaged face came back to her. She realized with a jolt that he had been in her thoughts for most of the day. What had happened to him in theatre? Not his leg. Surely he hadn't lost his leg. He was a free spirit; somehow she knew that. He should be running, riding a fine horse, climbing a mountain. Please no, not his leg.

They finished the dressing round and Sister glanced at her watch. 'Dr Hanfield is coming to do a round shortly,' she said. 'We'd better get the men into bed.' The beds were neatened and the men tucked in, jackets buttoned up, hair combed.

Dr Hanfield arrived and Sister took her on a round of the beds. Amy watched their progress. Dr Hanfield looked calm and cheerful, but Amy could see the lines of strain around her eyes and her mouth. She must have been operating all day, Amy thought, ever since she had spoken to her that morning. Captain Fielding should have been impressed. They came at last to the screened bed.

'Excuse me, Doctor,' Amy said.

Sister looked severe. 'What do you want, Amy?' she began, but Dr

Hanfield stopped her.

'What is it, Amy?'

'This officer,' Amy said. 'I brought him in today. I just wondered. . . .'

Dr Hanfield smiled. 'He's been very lucky. The bullet chipped the bone but the femur is intact. We got the bullet out and cleaned up the wound.' Amy knew what that would be like, fragments of clothing and skin and muscle and earth and horse dung.

'He's lost a lot of blood,' Dr Hanfield went on, 'But he's young and strong. He'll be all right as long as it doesn't get infected.'

'What about tetanus?' Amy said. 'They were working on a tetanus antitoxin. . . .' She knew that she shouldn't have said it, but it just came out. She was hungry for news about medicine, cut off from *The Lancet* and the other journals that she used to read so avidly.

Dr Hanfield looked surprised. 'They are,' she said. 'But we don't quite have it yet. Very soon, we hope. How do you know about that? Is your father a doctor?'

Amy was shaken. She had almost made another mistake. 'No,' she said. 'He's a teacher. He teaches science and he's very interested in medicine.'

'I see.' Dr Hanfield looked thoughtful. 'Do you know Lieutenant Maddox?'

'Is that his name?' Amy said. 'No, I don't know him – it was just bringing him in. I was interested.' But I do know him, she thought. In some odd way I do know him. She had brought in dozens of men now and none of them had stayed in her mind like this man. Maybe it was just because he had annoyed her so much.

Dr Hanfield and Sister went behind the screen and Amy could hear a murmur of voices. Sister came out.

'He's awake,' she said, disapproval in her face, 'and he would like to speak to you.'

Amy felt herself flushing. 'Thank you, Sister.'

She stepped in behind the screens to find him lying on his back with a cage over his legs. He was washed and clean. His face was deathly pale, but his blue eyes were bright, as she remembered, and his smile as disturbing.

'Hello,' he said. 'I'm Johnny Maddox. I think I owe you my life.'

'That's all right, Lieutenant,' she began, 'I was glad to help,' but his eyes were already closed.

She slipped out of the screens. Dr Hanfield had already gone. Sister was standing at her desk, still looking disapproving. 'You can go now, Amy,' she said.

'Thank you, Sister.'

She walked wearily up the great staircase, tired out; she had to pull herself up the last few steps by the banister rail, then walked slowly along the corridor.

He hadn't lost his leg. She stopped and looked at herself in one of the big mirrors, looking into her eyes as if she were someone she didn't know. Why him? In the river of men that flowed through this hospital, why had he become so important? Her reflection gave nothing away. I'm just tired, she thought, just very tired.

She opened the door quietly so as not to disturb Helen, but she was still awake, sitting up in bed with a book on her knees.

'I couldn't sleep,' Helen said.

'I think I could sleep on a clothes line.' Amy undressed, almost too tired to bother. She washed and cleaned her teeth and got into bed. For a few moments she stared at the ceiling.

'I brought an officer in today,' she said. 'Leg injury. He was very rude about women doctors.'

'Oh nice,' Helen said. 'You should have left him behind.'

'I think he's changed his mind,' Amy said. 'He actually thanked me this evening.'

'That's all right then.' Helen turned off the light. 'We'll let him stay.'

Amy laughed and was instantly asleep.

CHAPTER SIX

1914

'W E'RE on the general ward this morning.' Helen wound up her glowing hair. 'Sponge baths and changing beds.'

'Nothing new then.' Amy buttoned up her shirt and bent around to do up the side placket on her skirt. 'I wish they'd invent something easier than buttons to do up these things. It's always a struggle.'

'We've got a few hours off this afternoon,' Helen said. 'Had you forgotten?'

'Of course I haven't. We'll do something – that's if I can stay awake.'

The ward was bustling with the usual early morning activity. Sister looked harassed. 'We have ten more coming in today,' she said. 'I don't know where we're going to put them. I really don't want to put the beds any closer together; it all makes cross infection more likely. And I really do wish we could stop all and sundry visiting the men. They seem to think that they can wander in whenever they feel like it.' Visitors to the ward were frequent, often just the local people bringing gifts, fruit and cigarettes and sometimes books in English. The men seemed to enjoy it.

'I expect it cheers them up,' Helen said. 'It makes a break from the usual routine.'

'It won't cheer them up if they get colds or flu,' Sister said tartly. 'And it tires them out sometimes. Get on with the beds, please.'

Amy glanced around the room. It was completely full, as always. The lingering smell of infection would not go away, no matter how much they scrubbed everything with carbolic soap. As soon as a bed was freed because the man had gone home, or died, it was instantly filled again. She felt as if that smell had lodged in her senses for ever, become a constant part of existence. She wondered, often, if it would fade away after the war was over. Would it be overcome by the scents of flowers, new-mown grass, the salty smell of the sea, all the clear, lovely scents of nature? Or would it never, never, go away, fixed in her brain like all the other ineradicable memories?

She and Helen moved from bed to bed, changing stained and soiled sheets, making the beds and washing the men who couldn't look after themselves, and that, Amy thought, was most of them. There had been new admissions overnight.

'The next one looks about twelve years old,' Helen whispered. 'He certainly can't be more than sixteen.'

Amy nodded. 'Lied about his age, I expect. You'd think the recruitment officers would notice, wouldn't you? He looks like a child.'

He was sitting up in bed, talking continuously, whether anyone was listening or not. His young voice was tense, high pitched. 'And then the officer blew his whistle and we all had to go over the top and the Huns started firing at us, shells and machine-guns, and everybody was falling down and I was shouting and then I got mine. . . .'

From across the ward there came a gasp, and then a terrified wailing.

An older man stopped by the boy's bed. 'That's enough, son,' he said. 'We all know what it was like. We don't need tellin'.'

The boy's left arm ended in a large bulbous dressing. As they came to him he held it up. 'Lost me 'and,' he said.

Amy glanced at Helen. She looked stricken. 'I'm so sorry,' she said.

He grinned at her, a smile full of pain, but still the smile of an innocent boy. 'Doesn't matter,' he said. 'I'm right-handed.' Helen made a little sound, a little gasp of mixed sympathy and despair. Panic spread across the boy's face. He began to breathe quickly and the pupils of his eyes dilated. 'It is a Blighty one, isn't it? They won't make me go back? I can't fire a rifle with one 'and, can I?'

Amy shook her head. 'No, of course you can't. Don't worry. They won't make you go back.'

Tears of relief began to run down his cheeks. 'I can't go back, miss. I can't go back.'

Helen took his hand. 'What's your name?'

'Bert. Bert Fizackerly.'

'And where do you come from, Bert?' She helped him off with his jacket and began to wash his back.

'Manchester,' he said. 'Best place in the world.'

Amy smiled. 'I bet your mam will be glad to have you back.'

'That she will,' he said. 'When she's finished telling me off for going in the first place. I thought she might have been glad to get rid of me for a bit; she's got four others to feed and my dad was out of work.'

'She'd never be glad to get rid of you,' Helen said. 'You wait and see.'

'I want to see her,' he said. 'I want my mam.'

Amy could see tears in Helen's eyes.

He was silent for a moment and then he said, 'It wasn't like they said when we joined up. It wasn't saving the country, having an adventure like they said.' Amy glanced at Helen. Was it she who had mentioned adventure when they first met? That was before they knew. 'It was terrible,' he was shaking now. 'I was at Mons, in the retreat. It was terrible. But something happened. Do you know what?' They shook their heads. 'I saw the angel.'

'The angel?' Amy asked.

He nodded, his young face eager. 'We was pinned down.' He gulped, the memory almost too much to bear. 'We was being slaughtered. There was men fallin' everywhere, men screamin'. And then. . . .' He gulped again. 'And then this angel came in the sky, shining like, all lit up. Great big angel, wings and everything.' His face filled with a child-like wonder. 'The Germans ran off and we was able to get away.'

Amy and Helen glanced at each other. 'How wonderful,' Helen said.

'Aye, it was. We're going to win all right.' Amy and Helen finished his bed bath and then moved on, Bert still chattering behind them.

'What do you think?' Helen said. It wasn't the first time they had heard about the angel of Mons.

'I think it was just a silly rumour, or they all imagined it.' Amy said. 'A kind of mass hysteria. Things were so awful that they imagined that some kind of out of this world being would come along to protect them.' She remembered very well that feeling of unreality; that feeling that things were so dreadful that it must all be a dream from which she would wake, or that someone, somehow, must surely come to help and change it. No one had come, that awful day when she had lost everything.

'Perhaps it helped them at the time. Perhaps it gave them some kind of strength. Nobody really saw an angel.'

'But it would be nice to think that the angels were on our side, wouldn't it?' Helen said.

She sounded wistful, Amy thought. She shrugged. 'I should think the angels have all fled.' They moved on. 'I think the next man is French.'

The man was lying on his bed, eyes on the ceiling.

'*Bonjour*,' Amy said, but he was silent, not turning his head until she touched his arm. He began to tremble.

Helen bent down to him. 'It's all right,' she said but he didn't respond. She straightened up, frustrated. 'I wish I could speak better French.'

'It wouldn't help.' Amy stroked his arm, trying to relax him. 'He can't hear what you say and he couldn't answer you. He's dumb too.' His trembling increased so much that the bed began to rattle.

'He obviously can't stand,' Helen took off his jacket.

One of the other men came up to the bed. 'We all talk to him,' he said. 'Shout to him really. He hasn't stopped a bullet or anything; it's shell shock. We'll get him right. We're all going to get together and shout to him, all together. He ought to hear that.'

'It's dreadful.' Helen's eyes were wet. 'Sister told me where he comes from. His village is behind the enemy lines. He can't know whether his family is alive or dead.'

These French soldiers, Amy thought. He had come in filthy and desperately hungry, no socks, his feet blistered and bleeding. As if his own suffering wasn't enough, he suffered for his family as well. Anything could have happened to them. At least the British men knew that their families were safe at home.

They finished the morning's work. 'What shall we do this afternoon?' Helen said. 'In our few precious hours off. Or do you just want to sleep?'

'Oh no,' Amy said at once. 'I'm getting claustrophobic. I need some air. We'll go for a walk, shall we? See what's going on in Paris. We can get about on the Metro.'

'We could go to see where the Germans dropped that bomb,' Helen said. 'Apparently there's a great big hole in the ground. I didn't think they'd ever bomb civilian places. Those Germans will do anything.'

Anything to win, Amy thought. She sighed. 'Let's not. I've seen enough of the war for today.'

Sister stopped them as they were leaving the ward. She gave Amy a sharp look. 'Miss Osborne, apparently there is a young man in the officers' ward who has asked to see you,' she said.

'Oh?' Amy tried to look puzzled, but she knew at once who it was. 'Who is it?'

'A Lieutenant Maddox, I believe,' Sister said. 'You'd better go now. You won't have time later on.' She swept away down the ward, her shoulders stiff with disapproval.

'And who is Lieutenant Maddox?' Helen widened her eyes, her eyebrows raised in amused enquiry.

'He's that officer I brought in the other day,' Amy said. 'The one who was so rude about women surgeons and then changed his mind.'

'Now, now, Miss Osborne,' Helen said in a mock schoolmarm voice. 'We seem to be hearing a lot about him. You know you're not supposed to get involved with the patients. No wonder Sister had a poker up her back.'

'I'm not getting involved.' Amy said. 'What an idea. I've only seen the man a couple of times. Anyway, you know how I feel about that. I expect he just wants to thank me again; he fell asleep last time.'

'I was only joking,' Helen said. 'Honestly.'

Amy smiled. 'I know. I'll only be a minute. Wait for me at lunch.' She walked into the officers' ward and spoke to the sister in charge. Sister also looked disapproving.

'He's over there,' she said. 'He's been asking to speak to you. Please make it quick, we're very busy this morning.'

Amy walked across the ward to his bed with an odd, inexplicable feeling of apprehension, though she couldn't explain to herself why that might be. 'Hello, Lieutenant,' she said.

He was propped up on his pillows, his book on his knees. He looked thin, she thought, and drawn. He looked up from his book and a smile lit up his face. 'Miss Osborne! I'm so glad you've come. I've found out your name, you see.'

She sat down on the chair beside the bed. 'What can I do for you, Lieutenant?' He looked paler than ever, she thought, and tired.

He looked surprised and then amused. 'I think you've done enough for me already. I just wanted to see you again, to thank you properly and apologize for some of the things I said. Obviously I was completely wrong. Very ungentlemanly.'

Amy smiled. 'It doesn't matter, Lieutenant. It wasn't exactly an easy time for any of us, was it? I'm sure you had the best intentions. You were only trying to look after your men. That's what you're supposed to do, isn't it?'

'And you had to do what you were supposed to do,' he said. 'I was very rude to you, especially under the circumstances.' He became unsmiling and serious. He grimaced and moved a little under the sheet. 'I really meant it the other day, you know. You did save my life and I shan't ever forget it. So I apologize.'

'It's all right,' she said. 'It really doesn't matter now.' She put her hand on the cage over his legs. 'I'm very pleased about your leg. That is really good news.'

He nodded. 'I had a good surgeon.' He noticed her knowing smile and grinned. 'All right, I was wrong about that too. A good woman surgeon. Frightening lady. Frightens me more that the Huns. She says I'll be as good as new soon, if I do what I'm told. Might not even have a limp.'

Amy thought of the boy who had lost his hand. 'A Blighty one' he had called it. It didn't sound as if Mr Maddox's injury was a Blighty one. Not a permanent one anyway. 'Will you be going home to convalesce?' she asked. 'Will you go home to your family?'

He nodded. 'Yes, I expect so, for a while. My mother is already barracking about that. She's even threatened to come over here and get me. That should frighten everybody. Then I shall be coming back – back to my regiment. I shall have to go through a Board, of course. They decide whether you're fit enough to come back, but I should have no trouble with them.' He said it casually, as if it didn't matter.

Amy bit her lip and looked away. The thought was almost unbearable, that he would have to go through all that again, the horror and the danger. It was unbearable to her but not, apparently, to him. She looked back at him; his face drawn with weakness and pain, but his eyes were clear and untroubled. He didn't appear to have any fears about it at all. Was that true? Was he really fearless, or did he just expertly hide it. He wouldn't want to look like a coward; none of them did. He wouldn't want to let his men down. He looked back at her so steadily that she flushed a little.

'Miss Osborne,' he said, 'might I know your Christian name?'

'Amy.'

'Will you come to see me again, Amy?'

Incomprehensibly, the feeling of apprehension came back and she hesitated.

'If there is time. . . .' she began.

He saw her hesitation. 'Please,' he said. He looked like a little boy trying to wheedle some treat or other. His nanny must have been putty in his hands. She had no doubt that he came from a family where he would have had a nanny. She laughed and said, 'I'll try, Lieutenant.'

'Johnny.'

Sister walked by and gave her a disapproving stare.

'I'd better go. I'm holding up the work.' She got up to leave and then on an impulse she said, 'Were you at Mons?'

'Yes,' he said. 'Why?'

'One of the soldiers,' she said, 'says they saw an angel in the sky, and then the Germans let them get away.'

He didn't smile. 'You're the only angel I've seen,' he said.

She flushed again. She wasn't used to compliments from men. There had never been time for such things in her life. Some of the soldiers teased the girls, asking them about their boyfriends and pretending to be bowled over by their charms. They all got used to it; these jokes were part of keeping the men cheerful and they were innocent enough. But this compliment seemed to be real – he seemed to mean it.

'All the orderlies go out with the ambulance,' she said hurriedly. 'Not only me.'

'But you were the one who rescued me.' Pain flickered suddenly across his face and his hand clutched at the sheet. 'I think it's nearly time for my next dose of whatever it is they give you.'

Amy looked around her. The nurse with the drugs trolley was starting at the end of the ward. 'The nurse is coming,' she said.

'Good. You will come again, won't you?' His face was strained now, the pain returning.

'Yes, I'll come.'

'I'll look forward to that.'

She smiled and turned away and made her way out of the ward. Sister didn't look up as she walked past her but Amy could read disapproval in her hunched shoulders.

She walked slowly back to join Helen. Something seemed to have happened again, some unspoken communication. Something that stirred and worried her. It'll be all right, she thought. He's going home soon and I won't be seeing him again. I won't know whether he has gone back to his unit. She didn't allow herself to think of the ultimate question: would he come through? Would he live?

She joined Helen for lunch in the dining-room – roast beef, cabbage and potatoes, followed by rice pudding.

'Cabbage again,' Helen said. 'Maybe we'll get some French food when we go out with your captain.'

'He isn't my captain,' Amy began and Helen laughed. 'And how's your lieutenant? You seem to be collecting quite a harem, or whatever the male equivalent is.'

'Now you're getting silly.' Amy finished her rice pudding, carefully avoiding the skin. 'I've never liked the skin.'

'I'll have it.' Helen helped herself. 'It's the best bit. So what about your lieutenant?'

'He seems to be recovering well. He thinks he'll be well enough to go back when he's better.' She didn't go on to voice her thoughts, her horror at the thought of him going back to that hell.

'Oh? So what did he want to see you about?'

'He just wanted to thank me, as I said.'

Helen looked at her seriously for a moment, then she smiled. 'Come on, let's go out. Time is a-wasting.'

They went back to their room to put on their jackets and hats and walked down the staircase and out into the street. As they walked away from the hotel many of the passers-by stopped them with smiles and murmured thanks. Some of them pressed coins into their hands, '*pour l'hôpital.*' Their uniform was well known now in the streets around the hospital.

'Let's go somewhere else,' Helen said, 'or we'll be stopped every minute.'

They took the Metro. All the ticket collectors were women, everywhere women. They walked down the boulevards in the afternoon sunshine. 'There are a lot more soldiers about,' Helen said, 'but not so many refugees.' Two young men passed them, one on crutches and the other with his arm bent up in a splint. They grinned at them as they walked by.

Amy nodded. 'More wounded.'

Some of the street cafés were open again. Most of the shops were closed and shuttered, but here and there one or two were opening, the windows being cleaned and the pavements swept.

'I think some of the people must be coming back since the Marne,' Amy said. 'It all seems to be waking up. They must think the Germans aren't going to get here after all.'

'Do you think they will? Ever?'

Amy shrugged. 'We'll just have to hope they won't. At least they're further away now.'

'Well, we'll soon find out,' Helen said, 'if they start shelling us. The French Government's still away in Bordeaux and the Louvre is still closed. Maybe they know more than we do.'

Amy was silent. The whole of Paris lived with this fear but she was filled with admiration for them – the ordinary people who passed them by in the street, especially those who had stayed, who hadn't run away. There had never been any panic, just a stoic acceptance of what they had to do. They went about their daily lives, knowing that Paris could be shelled or bombed at any time.

She tried to push the images from her mind. She tried not to think of the consequences – getting the men out, cramming them into ambulances, moving south, perhaps having to leave some of them behind to the mercies of the invading Germans. Leaving them behind, as she had to do before, so many times.

'I wish I could have seen it before the war,' Helen said. 'I saw a cinematograph of Paris once and it looked wonderful. All those elegant women in beautiful clothes and gorgeous hats and the men in morning dress, all strolling along, enjoying themselves and the beautiful shops and the gardens. It must have been absolutely fantastic. A magic place. It seems like a hundred years ago.'

A woman passed them, and then another and another, all dressed in black with widow's veils. They hurried by with their eyes down, their shoulders bent and drooping. So many thousands dead, but for these women one special man was dead; one loved, appallingly missed, special man. Helen shivered.

They walked past a pavement café. The waiters with their big white aprons tied under their armpits were carrying trays among the tables, but the tables were half empty, and the waiters were old men. The people in the café seemed to Amy to have an unsettled, temporary look about them, as if they were ready to fly off at any moment. They sat on the edges of their chairs, looking out over the rims of their cups and wine glasses, their eyes shifting and wary. As they walked by a motor car backfired in the street – a sharp, loud bang. There was a flurry of movement and sharp cries as the people started up, and then settled back again, for all the world, Amy thought, like the pigeons in Trafalgar Square. Here and there an old man drank his wine or pastis in a single gulp. There was a young soldier, who didn't stir. He sat at his table, rigid and staring, his hands shaking and tears running down his face. Amy couldn't pass him by. She walked over to him and patted his shoulder.

'It's all right,' she said. 'It's all right. It was only a car. *Seulement un automobile.*'

He didn't move, didn't seem to have heard her.

'Come on, Amy,' Helen whispered. 'There's nothing we can do.'

Amy closed her eyes for a moment, filled with rage and pity. 'Will it never end?'

'Come on,' Helen took her arm. 'Let's have a drink.'

They sat down at a table and ordered coffee. The evocative smells rose around them, coffee and garlic and Turkish cigarettes. 'I'm going to come back after the war,' Helen said, 'When it's all back to normal and full of beautiful clothes and sit right here and watch all the beautiful people walk by.' Amy suddenly remembered the young soldier she had met with the ambulance, the young farm worker, so sure that he could come back after the war. Already there were thousands of fine young men who would never leave. The old waiter brought their coffee, shuffling under his white apron.

'What about this officer,' Helen said, 'the one with the leg.'

'Lieutenant Maddox,' Amy said. 'Nothing about him. He's just a grateful patient.'

'As long as that's all.'

Amy laughed. 'Of course that's all. What else would there be?' Is that all, she thought again? Of all the dozens of men she had cared for, why was this one in her mind so much? There was something about him, something so alive, so vital, so hard to ignore. She sipped her coffee. The soldier, still crying, got up and limped away down the street. 'I'm not interested in men or marriage or anything to do with it.

And now certainly isn't the time.'

Helen smiled. 'I don't think it works quite like that, Amy.'

'What do you mean?'

'I think that sometimes it overtakes you, unless you nip it in the bud. I wouldn't want you to be hurt.'

'Overtakes you? The bolt from the blue? Love at first sight?'

Helen nodded. 'So they tell me.'

Amy laughed. 'Has it happened to you then? Are you harbouring a secret infatuation?'

'No. What about you? Have you ever been in love?'

Amy shook her head. All those years of work and study. She'd never had the time or the inclination to even think about getting involved. The horrible memory of Bulford came back to her again, of his gross intrusive body, his thick fingers. He was enough to put anyone off men for ever. She laughed. 'I think you've been reading too many novels, Helen. Too much of the Bröntes perhaps. I can't say that I fancy a Heathcliffe in my life.'

'What about your captain? When is he coming back?'

Amy laughed again. 'I have no idea, Amy. Come on, finish your coffee and let's walk.'

Sister caught them as they came back. 'Would you do the officers' ward this evening, Amy? We've now got two nurses off sick with colds. I'll be the only nurse on duty but there's another orderly and it's fairly quiet. We'll manage.'

Amy had dinner and then made her way to the ward. Some of the officers who were up and about were out in the main hall, smoking cigarettes. Sister wouldn't allow smoking on her ward. Some of the officers had had words with her about it, but she was adamant. She maintained that smoking was bad for you.

She glanced around but she couldn't see Johnny Maddox. He was obviously one of the figures asleep, hunched under the bedclothes. Sister was standing beside her desk. 'I have to go out for a moment, Amy,' she said. She took off her white working cuffs and rolled down her sleeves, buttoning them up at the wrist. 'Can you manage, just for ten minutes or so?'

Amy nodded, 'Of course.'

'Good. I'll just be in the office if you want me. We desperately need some more sheets and pillow cases. I'll have to go down on my bended knees.' She bustled out.

Amy sat down at the desk. The patients' reports were stacked tidily in a box. She slid out Johnny's notes. Lieutenant John B. Maddox, she read. Age twenty-eight. Home address Faring Hall, Winchley, Berkshire. Next of kin Sir Henry Maddox, father. She read quickly through his operation notes – it was much as Miss Hanfield had said. She turned the page. His temperature was registered in red ink. He had a fever. No! She almost spoke it aloud. He must have had a fever when she saw him earlier in the day; he had not looked well then, tired and in pain. He had come through so well, surely now he wasn't going to suffer the pain and horror of infection, the infection that they all dreaded. If it took hold it was relentless, first the wound, then perhaps septicaemia, certain death.

She put the notes back in the box and walked down the ward to Johnny's bed. As she came towards him she could see that he was motionless, lying on his back. Then she was standing beside him, looking down at his face, as white as paper against the pillow. 'Johnny,' she said. 'Johnny.' He didn't respond, didn't move, his breathing rapid and shallow. She pulled back the blanket and caught her breath. Blood was seeping steadily from his wound, soaking through the dressing, staining the sheets. She knew at once what was happening, a deadly haemorrhage, the infection eroding through a blood vessel. He was bleeding to death. 'Help,' she shouted. 'Help me.' She pulled up his jacket and with both thumbs pressed as hard as she could into his groin, closing off the femoral artery. The other orderlies and an officer ran towards her. 'Get Sister,' she shouted. 'Get Dr Hanfield. Tell her it's a secondary haemorrhage.' In a few moments Sister was beside her, putting on a tourniquet. 'Dr Hanfield is in theatre now,' she said. 'Come on.' They lifted him on to a trolley and ran with him to the theatre. He was moaning now, his hands clutching and scrabbling at his jacket.

Dr Hanfield was waiting. 'You'll have to assist us, Amy,' she said, 'He needs an anaesthetic. He mustn't struggle about like this.' The anaesthetist stationed herself at his head, put a gauze-covered mask over his face and slowly dripped chloroform on to the mask. 'We haven't time to scrub up.' Dr Hanfield took off the soaked dressing, cut through the stitches. 'Release the tourniquet, Amy,' she said. 'Very slowly.' The blood welled up again. 'There it is.' Amy heard the familiar crunch of the clamp as Dr Hanfield closed off the bleeding artery,

exposed a little of its length and tied it off. 'Release a bit more, Amy.'
Slowly Amy took off the tourniquet. There was no more bleeding. Dr
Hanfield stood up, sweat standing on her forehead. 'I think we got it,'
she said. Amy watched as she put in a drain and closed the wound.

For a moment tears stood in Amy's eyes. Emotions overwhelmed
her. She realized that it wasn't just the relief that Johnny was, for the
moment at least, saved; to be back in theatre, to be doing what she
longed for, what she had struggled and trained for, was like waking
from a bad dream. Now she had to go back to reality.

They took him back to the ward and Sister put screens around him.
Amy looked down at his white face. He was desperately ill. She
suddenly felt overwhelmingly tired, swept with a feeling of utter futil-
ity. What were they achieving here? The beds emptied and filled,
emptied and filled. They got men better, only for them to go back, to
risk it all again. What was it for, this life? Had he been born, loved and
cared for and nurtured, for this – Johnny and all these men, these boys,
who had found in themselves a heroism and stoicism that they never
knew existed? Not just the British and French boys, she thought,
Australians and New Zealanders and Canadians and Indians and the
whole world and, no matter how much they were hated, ordinary
German boys were horribly dying. And what was her life for, deprived
as she had been of her reason for living?

Johnny was struggling for his life. She could see it in the blanched
face, the shallow, laboured breathing, the beads of sweat on his white
forehead. She tried to blink the tears away.

'You did well, Amy.' Dr Hanfield was smiling at her, looking faintly
puzzled. 'You seemed to know what to do.'

Sister interrupted, saving Amy from replying. 'When I was in training a secondary haemorrhage was the only time we were ever allowed
to run in the corridors.'

'I wish to God we had something to use against infection.' Dr
Hanfield looked exhausted. 'We could save so many more young lives.
Sometimes I feel so helpless.' She rested her hand on Johnny's shoul-
der for a moment, and then left the ward.

'Amy,' Sister said, 'you look dreadful. Go and get a cup of tea and
then go to bed. You've done enough. The night staff will be here soon.'

Amy went to the little kitchen where they could make tea and coffee.
She sat down at the table, her hands shaking. She had seen dozens of

men die, but in a strange way Johnny seemed to embody them all. He seemed to hold in himself everything that was best from home; he was young, strong, handsome and fearless. It was such an appalling waste. It seemed to be more than that. His death would in some way be the end of something that had hardly begun; something that she couldn't, or wouldn't, admit to herself.

She finished her tea and dragged herself up the marble staircase to her room. Helen was sitting up in bed again, reading. Amy sat down on her bed and began to cry, soft tears running down her face. Helen got out of bed at once and sat beside her and put her arm around her shoulders.

'What is it, Amy? What's happened?'

Amy rested her forehead on her hand and then wiped her tears away with her fingers. 'It's everything,' she said.

'What exactly?'

For a moment Amy was tempted to tell her, to pour it all out, her horror at what was happening, her bitter frustration at what had happened to her. But she drew back. If it ever got out she might not be allowed to stay and do the little that she could. Her own troubles were buried under a mountain of pain.

'It's Johnny Maddox,' she said. 'His wound's infected. He had a secondary haemorrhage tonight. He's very ill.'

'I'm so sorry,' Helen said.

Amy looked into Helen's questioning, troubled eyes. 'It's not what you think, Helen. It just seems so awful, so wicked, such an evil, horrible waste.'

Helen hugged her closer. 'He might be all right. We'll just have to hope.' She helped Amy into bed and looked down at her. 'He might be all right,' she said again. 'Don't give up hope.' She gave a little smile. 'The Frenchman can hear. The men all yelled at him at once, and it seemed to break through. He can hear now, anyway, and talk. I wish I could understand what he was saying.'

Amy closed her eyes. Perhaps it's just as well that you can't, Helen, she thought.

CHAPTER SEVEN

1914

AMY opened her eyes the next morning and her first thought was of Johnny. Was he still alive? She bathed and dressed, unable to get him out of her head. Was he still in the ward, clinging to life, or had he been taken out in the night, moved out in the dark from the back of the hotel, sent home to his suffering family? She had to know, but she had to go to the general wards immediately after breakfast.

More ambulances had arrived in the early morning, bringing in wounded from the railway stations. They were all dirty and hungry. One of them, wounded in the leg, was reluctant to let Amy take off his clothes.

'It's all right,' Amy said gently. 'Don't be embarrassed. We wash the men every day. We do it all the time.'

'It's not that, Sister,' he said. Amy smiled at the 'Sister'. 'It's because me uniform's so filthy.' He coloured. 'And covered in lice. I don't like to think of you young ladies touching it.'

He hasn't even mentioned his wound, she thought. 'It's all right,' she said again. 'We do it all the time.' She cut off his trousers, trying not to disturb his leg. His socks were almost fused to his feet, rotting and stinking.

'I've not had any clean clothes since I got here,' he said. 'Weeks and weeks. I don't even know how long.'

Amy stripped and washed him and put his tattered clothes into the basket for burning.

'That's wonderful, Sister,' he said. 'Being clean again. It's wonderful. God bless you.'

'The nurse will be along very soon,' she said, 'to see to your dressing.'

She went to the store to ask for more socks. The hospital was getting regular parcels from England, from English women at home, knitting socks and scarves and gloves. They would never know, she thought, how much they were appreciated. She remembered, grimly, how determined she had been not to stay at home knitting, and how grateful she now was to those who did. Sometimes French soldiers came to the hospital asking for socks – the word seemed to have got around about the parcels from England – and went away with a few pairs, highly pleased. Why on earth couldn't the armies provide a simple thing like socks? Such little things, she thought, and so hugely important that the men's feet were looked after. 'For the want of a nail the shoe was lost.' The old rhyme came into her head. 'For the want of a shoe the horse was lost, for the want of a horse the rider was lost, for the want of a rider the battle was lost, and all for the want of a horseshoe nail.' Why couldn't the army take better care of the men? 'More socks please,' she said.

Mechanically she stripped, washed, dried, powdered feet, helped to change dressings. And all the time the question repeated in her head. Johnny. Is he dead? The thought was constant, insistent. Is he dead? Had he been sent back to England to be grieved over and laid to rest in some quiet country churchyard? She hesitated to go to the officers' ward. Such visits would be heavily frowned upon, and she was afraid to ask, afraid of what the answer would be.

She met up with Helen at lunch. They sat down at the table with their steak and kidney pudding.

'How is your lieutenant?' Helen said.

Sometimes, Amy thought, Helen had a strange way of knowing what she was thinking. 'I don't know,' she said. She toyed with her pudding, separating out the kidney.

'Don't you want the kidney?' Helen speared a piece from her plate and popped it into her mouth. 'It's the best bit.'

Amy smiled, 'Help yourself.'

'You're a fussy eater, aren't you?' Helen took another piece. 'Don't like rice pudding skin, don't like kidney.'

'No I'm not,' Amy said. 'It's only the rice pudding. I'm just not very hungry today.'

Helen looked at her. 'What's wrong?'

Amy put down her fork and pushed her plate away. 'I don't know if he's alive or dead. I haven't had time to breathe this morning and I don't suppose I'd be very welcome on the officers' ward, asking questions.'

'Go and see,' Helen said. 'You won't settle until you do.'

Amy hesitated, unwilling to admit, even to herself, that she couldn't get him out of her mind.

'Go on,' Helen said. 'I know you're worried about him.'

'I don't know why I am, about him specially.' Helen gave her an arch look, but she ignored it. 'I suppose it's because I was there when he bled and nearly died. It all seemed so terrible, so pointless.'

'Go and see.'

'You're right.' Amy got up. 'I'll go now. Sister can only tell me to go away.'

Sister was sitting behind her desk, making up notes. She glanced up. 'Yes?'

'I wanted to know about Lieutenant Maddox,' Amy said, 'the one who had the secondary haemorrhage.'

'I know who he is.' Sister looked at her for a moment or two and then her face softened suddenly. 'It was you who looked after him, wasn't it, Amy? He's very ill, but he's fighting hard. You can go and see him if you like, but don't disturb him. He needs all the rest he can get. He's behind the screens.'

Behind the screens again. She glanced down the ward. Most of the patients were resting now after lunch and it was very quiet. One of the nurses was still feeding a man whose arms were both in splints. She noticed with a chill that Johnny's bed was near the door. They put the men who were the most ill near the door. It was thought better not to take them all the way through the ward if they died. It was just another dreadful reminder for the men.

She slipped behind the screens. He was lying on his back, his face pale and sweating. He began to mutter and twitch, his eyes rolling under the lids, and then he lay deadly still again, his eyes still closed. She touched his hand. 'Johnny,' she whispered, but he didn't move or answer. He didn't seem to be aware of her presence. Once, for a second, his lids flickered open and he stared at her for a moment, his eyes empty, and then they rolled back in his head and the lids closed again. She stayed with him for a few moments, touching his hand, wishing that she could do something, anything, to bring him back, and then she left him and walked back to Sister. 'He didn't know me,' she said. 'He opened his eyes, but he didn't know me.'

'He doesn't know anyone.' Sister looked grave. 'He is very ill. We have sent a message to his family, but I don't know if anyone will be able to come.'

'I hope so. He might recognize someone in his family. It might help him.'

Sister nodded. 'If they can get here at all. The Germans have submarines in the Channel now, attacking the shipping. It might not be safe for civilian passengers any more.'

Amy shook her head. 'Is there nothing they won't do? May I ask again tomorrow?'

'Do you think you should?' Sister's voice sounded concerned, not angry. 'All the men need your attention. The war is going to go on and they are going to keep on and on coming. It isn't wise to become too attached to one. Especially one who is so ill.'

Amy looked at her, into a now sympathetic face. 'I'm not – I mean it's just that I brought him in and was there when he haemorrhaged.'

'You can ask again tomorrow, Amy. I'll let you know if – if he's still here.'

Helen was waiting for her in the hall, the question in her eyes.

'He's still alive,' Amy said. 'Just. They've sent for his family.'

Helen took her hand. 'Come and have a cup of tea. You didn't even finish your lunch.' They went back into the dining-room.

Helen collected their tea and sat down opposite her. 'You really mustn't get involved, Amy. Not with a sick patient. It isn't wise. It can only lead to heartache.'

Amy made a sound, half a laugh, half a sigh. 'I'm not involved, Helen. How could I be? I don't know him. He doesn't know me.' She paused, trying to explain it to herself. 'It's just – he seems somehow to represent them all, all these young men, all the dying and the dead.' Tears started in her eyes. 'He shouldn't be here like this. None of them should.'

'Don't,' Helen whispered. 'You'll set me off. You've always been the strong one.'

Amy smiled briefly, a humourless smile. 'And you. I'm glad you're here, Helen.'

Helen clasped her hand. 'If you want to have a good cry, wait till we get back to our room. Goodness knows, I've cried all over you often enough.'

'It's all right,' Amy held back her tears. 'I'm all right now.'

They went up the marble staircase to their room and both lay down on their beds to rest before the afternoon work. Amy lay, staring at the ceiling. She wondered how much her feeling about him was simply due to the fact that at this one time she had been back handling the familiar instruments, stemming Johnny's blood loss, doing her job. Perhaps her interest in him was just part of the joy of being in theatre again, and he had been the man who happened to be there. They had been there together. Perhaps it had all become mixed up in her mind. Or was she trying not to admit what she really was feeling? Any kind of feeling for him was utterly pointless. He would go, one way or the other. He would get better and go home to convalesce and then he would go back to the trenches. Or he would die, here and now. Either way she would never see him again.

She visited the officers' ward again the next morning.

'He's still fighting.' Sister actually seemed pleased to see her. 'Perhaps you can help him, Amy. He's barely conscious most of the time. We're having quite a job getting fluids into him. If he knows you he might respond to you.'

When she went behind he screens he was lying so still that for a dreadful moment she thought that he was dead. Then he began the restless muttering and twitching. 'Johnny,' she said. She took his hand. 'Johnny.'

His muttering stopped suddenly and he opened his eyes and looked at her. Slowly his eyes focused on her, as if he were coming back from a great distance.

'Amy,' he whispered. His eyelids fluttered. 'Water.'

'Johnny,' she said again. 'I'll get help.' She called Sister and between them they propped him up and he drank, too weak to stop the water dribbling down his chin.

They lay him down on the pillows. 'Thank you,' he whispered, and then his eyes closed again.

They went back to Sister's desk. 'You could come back tomorrow,

Amy,' Sister said. 'He seems to respond to you. If we can just get him to take more fluids, and perhaps some nourishment, he might have a chance.'

'Yes, of course, I'll come back.' She left the ward. Did he have a chance? She desperately, fiercely, wanted him to live. She felt that his life would somehow be a fist shaken against fate, a gesture of defiance in the face of overwhelming odds.

'How is he?' Helen said.

'He knew me today. But I don't know. He's still very ill.'

Helen said nothing more, but Amy could see the concern in her eyes.

The next day he knew her at once. He even managed a weak smile. 'Hello,' he said. 'Come to save my life again?'

'It's not me this time,' she smiled down at him. 'The doctors and nurses have saved your life this time, and I suppose you might have had something to do with it. There's such a thing as the will to live.'

'The Hun can't get me,' he said. 'Their aim isn't good enough.'

It wasn't the Hun this time, she thought. It was the bacteria, the staphylococci and streptococci or whatever organism had taken over his body, those tiny creatures that left them helpless, almost hopeless. It all depended on the patient, on his ability to resist the infection, to fight those invisible killers. Things were changing, but so slowly. They had a vaccine now against typhoid, and an anti-toxin was coming against tetanus, but there was nothing that would kill the deadly bacteria. The advances were coming too slowly to help these men, just when they needed it most.

She went to see him every day. Slowly, day by day, he seemed to be getting better. His temperature was erratic, but was coming down and he was drinking and taking soup. Even Sister made no comment now when she went to see him; she even smiled at her.

At last, she could be sure. He wasn't going to die. As he got better and it seemed that he would live, her concern for him increased again. But now it was a different concern. One day he would probably be well enough to go back to his regiment, back to that hell. All that effort to save him, all his strength and spirit, and what for? So that he would have to risk it all again? It was not fair. He should not have to go back. There was no justice.

Amy was sitting in their room reading *Pride and Prejudice* for the umpteenth time. Jane Austen was almost like a drug, soothing and calming. For a short time she could escape into a world of elegance and pleasant, easy living. Those had not been the best of times, perhaps, for intelligent women, but Jane Austen seemed to have beaten the restrictions. And the best thing about her writing was that she was very funny. Anything that could make you laugh was precious.

Helen poked her head around the door. 'Your captain's here,' she said. 'He's downstairs in the hall.' She bounced into the room and sat down on her bed.

Amy put down her book. She was surprised; she had not really expected Dan Fielding to come back, or at least, not to contact her if he did. She had almost forgotten about it. Promises were not promises in a war. 'Are you sure it's him?' she asked. 'The place is full of soldiers.'

'Absolutely. He was talking to Dr Hanfield and then I heard him ask if he could speak to you.' She was smiling broadly. 'Do go and see him, Amy. We might get that dinner out.'

'Well I can hardly go down there and drift about until he notices me, can I? If he really wants to speak to me they will send someone up.'

Almost at once there was a knock at the door. Helen laughed. 'There you are then.'

Amy opened the door to one of the ward maids. 'There's a soldier downstairs,' she said. 'He says he wants to speak to you.'

'Thank you,' Amy said, and closed the door. She sighed. 'Oh dear, I expect it'll be all over the hospital in five minutes. I suppose I'd better go down and see him.'

'Oh yes, do.' Helen's eyes were dancing. 'And if he asks you, say yes.'

Amy brushed her hair into place and put on her jacket. 'Don't get too excited. Matron might very well say that we can't go.'

Helen sighed. 'I don't know why we have to be treated like children. Surely if we're responsible enough to do all this they could trust us to go out in the evening now and again.'

Amy could only agree, but she could see the reason for it, under the circumstances. 'I suppose it's the war. Even if they've partially lifted the curfew I suppose Paris isn't as safe at night as it used to be. There are a lot of odd characters about.'

'But we wouldn't be alone. We'd have two British officers with us.'

Amy smiled at Helen's frowning face. 'It would be just the same at home, wouldn't it? Ladies don't go out with men unless they have a chaperon. Your mother would be scandalized.'

'It's such nonsense,' Helen said, still annoyed. 'What on earth do they think we are going to do? Run amok? It ought to be changed. It's just another thing that men can do and women can't.'

'After the war, Helen. Perhaps things will be different then.'

Dan Fielding was standing in the hall, looking towards the stairs. He looked thinner, she thought, leaner, the planes of his face sharper, his eyes dark and brooding. He saw her and walked towards her, smiling. 'Miss Osborne,' he said.

'Captain Fielding.'

'I've come back,' he said, 'as you see. It's good to see you again.'

She smiled. 'I'm very glad to see that you are well.'

'And you. Last time I saw you, you were a little – overworked, shall I say?'

She laughed. 'Yes, I was a bit dishevelled.'

'You were doing a wonderful job, as I recall. The dishevelment was truly honourable.'

She didn't reply at once. His look was warm, and she noticed that the tips of his ears had gone pink again. She remembered that now. It must mean that he was a bit unsure, a bit embarrassed, perhaps. They would always give him away. 'Have you come to report on the hospital again?' she asked.

'Yes,' he said, 'but I wonder if you remember that I asked you if you might come out to dine with me, with a friend, of course.' She hesitated, and he went on hurriedly, 'Of course, if it's inconvenient. . . .'

She could almost feel Helen poking her in the ribs. 'No,' she said. 'It's not inconvenient, but it rather depends on Matron.'

'I know, but if you would like to come I'll try to speak to her today or tomorrow. Is she a dragon?'

Amy laughed. 'No, not really, but she is rather a stickler for appearances. Any disrepute to the hospital and it would be instant dismissal. If she says no, I'm afraid it's no.'

'I'm really not that disreputable,' he said with mock seriousness. 'I'm quite well behaved. What day would suit you?'

'Helen and I are free in the evening on Friday,' she said. 'Where were you thinking of taking us?'

'Some of the hotels are still functioning. One of them has a good restaurant, I believe, despite the shortages, but I'm not sure about dancing.'

'That doesn't matter. I don't think I can remember how to dance, but it would be nice to go to a restaurant again.'

'Fine. If we can go I shall be bringing a friend, Peter Turner. He's another doctor in the RAMC. He's quite well behaved, too.'

Amy laughed again. 'I'm glad to hear it. I'll hear from you after you've seen Matron, then.'

'Yes.' He held out his hand and she took it briefly. '*Au revoir* then – Amy. I hope to see you on Friday.'

She walked back up the stairs. At the top she turned and looked back. He was still standing at the foot, and he waved to her before turning away.

'Well?' Helen was sitting where she had left her, obviously waiting. 'What did he say?'

'He still wants to go. He's going to ask Matron.'

Helen pouted. 'I bet she says no.'

'We'll just have to wait and see.'

'What's he like, Amy? Is he nice? He's quite good-looking.'

Amy laughed. 'I don't think that's anything to go by. Yes, he seems nice, quiet and sensible.'

'So we won't be having a night of wild excitement.'

'I sincerely hope not.'

Helen opened her wardrobe. 'I've no idea what to wear. I haven't brought anything.'

'I've got a tea dress,' Amy said. 'That will have to do. Surely none of the hotels will insist on evening dress in the present circumstances. I don't suppose we can go in uniform.'

'Certainly not. We'll have to go shopping. Some of the shops are open again.' She got up and looked at herself in the long mirror. 'Won't it be lovely to wear a dress again.'

Amy went to visit Johnny again the next day, and he was definitely better, definitely gaining strength, and his temperature was nearly down to normal. He sat up in his bed as he saw her.

'Sit down and talk to me, Amy,' he said. She drew up a chair and sat beside him.

'I've had a letter from my mother,' he said. 'Apparently my father is coming to take me home. I can be looked after there until I am well enough to go back to the war.' He said it quite cheerfully, as if it didn't matter.

'I'm glad you're going home,' she said.

'Are you?' He looked at her with a half smile. 'Won't you miss me?'

'Of course.' It's just banter, she thought, just a bit more of the joking that went on with the men.

'Where do you live, Amy, at home?'

His question surprised her. It was more personal than she had expected. 'I live in Bromley,' she said.

'With your parents?'

'With my father. My mother is dead. She died when I was a child.' He seemed to be waiting for more. 'My father is a teacher, at a local boys' school.'

'I see.' He was looking at her closely, not smiling, not joking. 'I live at home too, in Berkshire. I'm lucky enough to have both my parents. My father looks after the estate with my elder brother.'

'Isn't he in the army too?'

'No. He's in a reserved occupation. He looks after the farms. It's very difficult at the moment, apparently. Many of the men have gone. They've even got some women working on the farms, doing quite heavy work, I'm told.'

She smiled. 'It's amazing, isn't it, what woman can do when they're allowed?'

'*Touché*,' he said. 'I've already apologized for what I said about the surgeons. I couldn't have been looked after better anywhere.'

'It must be a lovely place to go home to.' She was careful not to say that she already knew where he lived.

'It is,' he said, animated now. 'A real piece of old England. Worth fighting for. Do you hunt, Amy?'

She shook her head. 'Oh no. We could never afford that sort of thing. Anyway, I'd always feel sorry for the poor fox.'

He laughed. 'It's great sport,' he said. 'The best, and foxes are vermin. But there's better hunting now.'

She raised her eyebrows in question.

'Huns,' he said. 'Big game. I'd rather hunt the Hun than the fox. Far more fun.'

She thought of the men in the trenches. 'It isn't fun, Lieutenant Maddox,' she said. She used his title, her voice rising in distress. 'How can you say that? You've been through it, you know what it's like, and you're going to have to go back. . . .'

'It's the only way to look at it, Amy,' he said. 'And won't you please call me Johnny? Make it a game, a challenge. It's the only way to get through.'

She said nothing, bent her head so that he wouldn't see her distress.

'Anyway,' he said, 'I may not go back into the army. I'm going to apply for the Flying Corps. I shall hunt them in aeroplanes. That would be more my kind of thing.'

I can believe it, she thought. That would be more like him, to have his own flying machine, to be facing danger with no one to help him, testing himself, facing that peril alone. He's a bit wild, she thought. He likes danger; he courts it. She also knew what was happening, that most of the pilots lasted about a month. Young Frensham!

'I see,' she said. 'Do you think they will take you?'

'I'm pretty sure they will,' he said. 'They want more pilots.' Amy suppressed a shudder. It was obvious why they wanted more pilots. 'And my father knows a few people.'

Sir Henry Maddox, she thought. She could imagine that he might know a few people. 'When is your father coming?'

'He's on his way now.'

'I see,' she said again. 'So I will be saying goodbye to you soon. Take care of yourself.'

He laughed and took her hand. She looked down at his hand, enclosing hers. It was the first time that he had ever deliberately touched her. 'I'm not saying goodbye to you, Amy. I want to see you again. I want you to give me your address in England.'

She tried not to feel the burst of pleasure that he should want to see her again. She couldn't forget the rules, the warnings: 'Don't get too attached to anyone. Not now.'

He saw her hesitation and grinned at her. 'You can't go about saving a chap's life a few times and then just walk away. You have a responsibility towards me now.'

She relaxed and laughed. What harm could it do? 'Very well,' she said. 'I'll write it down for you, but I don't know when I will ever be back in England.'

'They'll have to give you some leave, sometime. I'll give you my address too, and you must promise to let me know.'

She gently removed her hand. 'I will, but I've no idea when that will be, possibly not until after the war.'

'Oh, I'll see you before then.' He was smiling into her eyes.

'I have to get on,' she said. 'I'll see you before you go.'

She went back to their room to find Helen waiting for her. 'I've got nothing to wear,' Helen said at once. 'I'll have to buy something. There must be somewhere I could buy a dress.'

'I suppose there is.' Amy was still thinking about Johnny. 'But why don't you wait until we know whether Matron will let us go?'

Helen waved a paper. 'There's a note for you here. It's probably from her.'

The note was indeed from Matron, asking Amy to go to see her.

'Go now,' Helen said. 'Then we can start planning.'

Amy smiled at her enthusiasm. 'Very well.'

She walked down to Matron's office. To be honest with herself, she wasn't as wild to go as Helen seemed to be. Her pleasure at Johnny's wanting to see her again was worrying and was occupying her mind too much. I won't do it, she said to herself. I don't, and won't, have feelings for him other than friendship.

Matron was more amenable than she expected. 'I shall give you permission to go, Amy,' she said. 'I'm sure you need a little relaxation, and Captain Fielding seems a very respectable young man. You are very sensible, I know, and you will look after Helen, won't you?'

'Of course.' Amy tried to sound as sensible as she possibly could. Otherwise Helen would never forgive her. She gave an involuntary smile, wondering what Matron would have said if she had asked to go out with Johnny. Johnny, from a very respectable family, but perhaps a bit wild. The answer would probably have been no.

'I would prefer it if you do not wear uniform,' Matron went on. 'I'm sure you can find something else, can't you?'

'Yes, I'm sure we can. Thank you, Matron.'

'The restaurants close at nine-thirty. Be back by ten, Amy.'

Helen was even more excited. 'We can go out shopping tomorrow afternoon.' She was almost dancing. 'There'll be something. I think there was a dressmaker near that milliner we saw.'

The next afternoon they went out. 'I think Printemps is open,' Amy said, 'but I think they are mainly selling stuff for the military. We might be able to get a couple of plain cloaks though. We'll need those. We can't use our uniform coats.'

'Let's find that little dressmaker,' Helen said. 'She might have something.'

They found the shop. There was now a single dress in the window, a discreet afternoon dress in pale green. 'It's the right colour,' Amy said. 'Green would look good with your hair.'

They went inside, to a delighted dressmaker who was only too eager to help them. Helen tried on the dress. 'It's perfect,' Amy said, 'but it needs taking in.'

The dressmaker bustled about with her pin cushion. 'Ask her when it will be ready,' Helen said. 'Your French is better than mine.'

'*Quel jour?*' Amy began.

'*Demain,*' the dressmaker beamed. '*Demain.*'

'Tomorrow,' Amy said.

Helen beamed. 'Wonderful. I'll rush out at lunchtime.'

'We'll go to Printemps then,' Amy said, 'and get the cloaks.'

Amy and Helen walked down the marble staircase. 'This is more like it,' Helen said, 'Sweeping down this staircase in a dress, going out to dinner.'

Dan and Peter were waiting in the hall, and Dan introduced Peter. Amy was watching Peter as he met Helen, and noticed the slight widening of his eyes. She wondered if Helen had noticed.

'We've even managed to get a cab,' Dan said.

They climbed into the carriage and the horse clattered off. 'Where are we going?' Helen asked.

'We've found a hotel that has a good reputation,' Peter said. 'About food, I mean.'

'Whatever it is it will be better than the food at the forward hospital,' Dan said. 'It tends to be rather monotonous.'

They drove through streets that were dimly lit and empty of people. Amy gazed out of the window as they passed, imagining these streets as they used to be, bright with light, the tables outside the cafés thronged with people, conversation and laughter. She glanced up to see Dan looking at her.

'You look very thoughtful, Amy,' he said.

'One day,' she said, 'I'd like to see Paris at its best, as it used to be.'

'So would I,' he said. 'Perhaps we'll be able to do that one day.'

She smiled briefly and looked out of the window again, not quite sure what he meant.

They arrived at the hotel and it was like stepping into another world, the world of old Paris; low-lit tables, flowers, the unaccustomed scents of French food, that unique cuisine. An ageing waiter showed them to their table.

Peter put his nose into the air and sniffed deeply. 'Fabulous,' he said. 'Real food. We've had nothing but bully beef stew for weeks.'

'We've had cabbage,' Helen said.

There was an orchestra; four middle-aged ladies playing Strauss. 'So much for dancing,' Dan said, laughing. 'No ragtime.'

'I like waltzing,' Helen said, looking at Peter. They were both gazing at each other then, not speaking. Dan smiled at Amy and slightly lifted his eyebrows.

They ordered dinner from a limited menu, consommé, roast leg of lamb in a wine sauce and a lemon tart.

'How do they make it taste so different?' Amy said, putting down her knife and fork after the lamb.

'Garlic and herbs and wine,' Dan said, 'And whatever wonderful secret ingredient the French are keeping to themselves.'

'This poor, beautiful country,' Amy said.

Around them the other diners ate and chatted. 'These are the real Parisians,' Amy said. 'The ones who stayed after Mons, the ones who wouldn't give up.'

'You both stayed,' Peter said. 'I think you ladies are very brave.'

'Not as brave as you,' Helen said, gazing at him. 'And there are women at your hospital, aren't there? They are the really brave ones.' There was a tremor, an excitement in her voice.

Now what is she up to, Amy thought? She had obviously found something with Peter. It was beginning to look like the bolt from the blue, love at first sight, a *coup de foudre*, whatever you wanted to call it.

The orchestra began to play a slow waltz. Peter stood up and held out his hand. 'Would you like to dance, Helen?' She went off with him to the little dance floor.

The waiter brought coffee. Dan laughed. 'They appear to have hit it off,' he said.

Amy nodded. 'Quite amazing. I've never seen anything like it.' She dropped her eyes before Dan's steady gaze.

'He's a good man,' Dan said.

She looked up again. 'And she's a great girl, straight and honest. I wouldn't like to see her hurt.'

'He wouldn't hurt her,' he said. 'I know him well. We were at Cambridge together. I think he's rather shy with women. A bit like me, I suppose.' She noticed that his ears were pink again.

'But the war,' she said, 'it doesn't seem the right time to – to get involved.'

She sensed his withdrawal. He looked down and stirred his coffee and when he raised his head his look had changed, become detached, impersonal. 'Perhaps you're right,' he said.

Helen and Peter came back. They all lingered over coffee until half past nine, talking of family and home; Dan and Peter telling stories about their clinical training at St Bartholomew's. Amy listened, asking innocent questions, careful not to make a mistake.

At half past nine promptly the restaurant closed and the cab was waiting for them at the door. They were back at the hospital well before ten, and said goodbye just inside the door. Helen and Peter stood apart talking, leaning towards each other, almost touching.

'Will you go on writing to me, Amy?' Dan said. 'It makes such a difference, getting normal, friendly letters.'

'Of course,' she said. 'And thank you for the evening.' They shook hands and the men left, out into the night.

Amy called in at Matron's office to say that they were back, and they went up to their room and undressed and got into bed.

'Wasn't that absolutely marvellous?' Helen said.

'Yes, it was. 'Amy lay on her back, looking at the shadows on the ceiling.

'I'm going to write to Peter,' Helen said. 'He asked me. Isn't he nice?'

'He seems very nice indeed,' Amy said. Helen sighed happily and turned over.

I should be there with them, with Dan and Peter, Amy thought. I should be doing what they are doing.

CHAPTER EIGHT

1914

A s Amy crossed the hall on her way to the dining-room, the main door of the hotel was hurriedly opened and a man, an older man in civilian clothes, stepped inside. He was tall, very upright, but he passed her so quickly that was all she could see. He spoke urgently to one of the nurses, and she led him away. Another official from the War Office, she thought, come to see what they were up to. But, as she was leaving the dining-room after lunch, one of the orderlies stopped her.

'Sister wants you,' she said, 'On the officers' ward. She said to come when you're ready.'

She had time, then, to wash her hands and put her hair up again into its neat bun.

Sister smiled at her when she went into the ward. 'Lieutenant Maddox's father is here,' she said. 'Sir Henry Maddox. He wants to see you.'

She sounded rather overawed, Amy thought, with some amusement. Sir Henry must be quite something. It took quite a lot to overawe the sisters. She was glad that she'd had time to do her hair and change her apron.

'He's with Lieutenant Maddox now,' Sister went on. 'I've put the screens round to give them a bit more privacy. Just go in.'

He was the man she had seen earlier in the hall. He had been given a chair beside his son's bed, but he stood up as she went in behind the screens.

'Amy,' Johnny said. He was sitting up in bed, his blue eyes bright.

'I'm so glad you've come. I would like you to meet my father, Sir Henry Maddox.'

Sir Henry put out his hand. 'Will you shake my hand, Miss Osborne?' Amy took his hand. He put his other hand over hers, holding her in a warm grasp. He looked into her eyes and smiled. 'I believe I have to thank you, for saving my son's life. Not just once, he tells me, but twice. So I am doubly grateful.' His eyes were the same bright blue as Johnny's and he had a neat, grizzled beard, a bit, she thought, like King George. He was a lot taller than the King, though, six feet at least. He had an unmistakable air of confidence, of command, but added to that was a pleasant, friendly air. He seemed like a man who was approachable – kind even.

'I'm just glad that he is better,' Amy said. 'He's been through a lot.'

He let her hand go. 'So has every man,' he said. 'And so have you, from what my son tells me. And the other ladies here.'

'I just do my job,' she said quietly, 'As we all do. We are all in this together, men and women.'

'You are very courageous young women,' he said, 'All of you. Unbelievably so.' He put his hand on Johnny's shoulder. 'You have given my son back to me, Miss Osborne, and I shall be eternally grateful.' He paused, emotion working in his face. 'I can't tell you. . . . ' For a moment he seemed near to tears, and then he recovered himself, and smiled. 'If there is ever anything that I can do for you, anything that you need or want, I hope that you will feel that you can come to me. I really mean that.'

'Thank you, Sir Henry,' she said. 'You are very kind.'

She looked at Johnny, expecting his usual bright, carefree smile, and was startled, almost shocked. He was staring at her, unsmiling, his eyes fixed on her face so directly, so urgently, that she was transfixed and couldn't look away. He stared at her for several seconds. He seemed to be giving her some kind of message, a deep, personal message, drawing her to him, reaching out to her. She felt her body stir, contract, in a way that was new to her, sensual and overwhelming. She wanted to touch him, to hold him, for him to touch her. She looked back at him, disturbed and puzzled. Then he smiled suddenly. His face softened and he went back to his usual carefree, cheerful self. Sir Henry coughed gently beside her. She glanced at him and saw that he also had intercepted the look and that he was surprised. For a few seconds he looked at his son and raised his eyebrows in question and then he too smiled and the moment of tension passed.

'I shall have to leave you now, Johnny,' he said. 'I have a few things to arrange.' He held his hand out to Amy. 'I'm taking him home, Miss Osborne, home to his mother. He'll soon recover there; he'll be well looked after. Don't forget, if ever I can be of service to you. . . .' He left and she could hear him talking to Sister. 'Very soon, Sister, I hope. I am trying to arrange a place for both of us on a hospital train.'

'If he says very soon,' Johnny said, 'it'll probably be tomorrow. He wants to travel on the train with me.' He laughed. 'He usually gets what he wants.'

'I can believe that,' Amy said. He seemed to have forgotten, or was ignoring what had happened. She did not mention the way he had looked at her, and neither did he. She could only imagine what his message had been, and the thought was very disturbing. But to do that in front of his father, knowing that he would see – what did that mean?

'You haven't given me your address,' he said. 'There's a notebook and pencil on the locker there. Is your home on the telephone?'

'No,' she said. 'Not yet.'

'Write it now, please, Amy. If I know anything about my father we really will be going tomorrow.'

She wrote her address in his notebook. 'I don't know when I'll be in England again. Nothing is certain these days.'

'I'll probably be back in France anyway,' he said, 'Sooner or later. In an aircraft, with any luck, or else back with my regiment. I'll find you. You can rely on that.' He took her hand in his. 'And thank you again, for everything.'

She left the ward, anxious and confused. Something seemed to have changed, though she couldn't define it. He had changed. There had been that moment of a different kind of communication, but she didn't really know what it meant. Yes, she wanted to see him again and he obviously wanted to see her. She felt as if she had placed her foot on a road that was new to her. But what was the point of it? What future could anyone rely on?

She was aware, or thought she was, that there was a moment, balanced between two states of mind; a moment of which she thought she had control. It was a kind of watershed. She could still decide. She could go one way or another. She could overcome her feelings. She could go back, albeit with a heart pang or two. She could forget him, or place him only among the memory of hundreds of other patients, hundreds of other men. That would be the safe way. Or she could go forward, see him again, accept the fact that she was attracted to him and he, apparently, to her. That way would lie enormous risk. She would be taking the chance of loving someone, of the pain of fear and longing and perhaps of agonizing loss. She told herself that she wasn't a young girl any more. She wasn't going to be swept away by emotion, just because she had never felt this way before.

Perhaps he would forget her, anyway, as soon as he got home and back into his own world. There must be girls at home who knew him and his family and who were eligible and eager. She tried to comfort herself with that thought; she probably would never have to decide which path she would take. He would forget her.

There were, of course, other problems. He did not know her past history – she had told no one. Her determination to get her licence and her life back was as urgent as ever. If it ever came to the point, how would he react to that?

She went back to her duties on the ward. There were more urgent problems to deal with.

'I hear your lieutenant's father has been speaking to you,' Helen said.

Amy laughed shortly. 'I was going to tell you myself, Helen, but you can't do anything here without everyone knowing about it. Yes he did. He just wanted to thank me for looking after him. He's come to take him home.'

He was gone the next day. He must have left very early in the morning to catch the hospital train that would take him to the hospital boat for England.

'He's gone, hasn't he?' Helen said, in their room, that evening.

Amy nodded. 'Early this morning.'

'Are you upset?'

'No,' Amy said firmly. 'I'm glad he's gone home. He will get better quicker there.'

'Are you going to keep in touch?'

'I don't know. He's taken my home address.' Amy sat down on her bed. 'I don't know whether I want to or not. I think perhaps you are right – one shouldn't get involved.'

'I don't think I quite said that.'

'Yes you did, very clearly.' Amy smiled. 'And you could very well be right.'

'Did I?' Helen paused and looked sheepish. 'I've told Peter that I'll write to him, and he is going to write to me.'

Amy looked at her, her eyebrows raised. 'You've changed your tune, haven't you?' She laughed. 'It only took the appearance of Lieutenant Turner, didn't it?' she teased. 'Love at first sight, Helen?'

Helen blushed. 'Well, I did say that, yes, but sometimes it just happens, and there isn't much you can do about it.'

'Are you telling me that you are in love?'

'No,' Helen said. 'I don't know. We've only just met, but he's so. . . . Well he certainly isn't boring.'

'Don't you think you should take your own advice?'

'It isn't that easy, Amy. I'm so worried. You know where they are, he and Dan, back at that Clearing Station. It's near a road and a bridge and the Germans won't think twice about bombing it, even if it is near a hospital.'

Amy sighed. 'Johnny says he's going to join the Flying Corps.'

Helen's eyes widened. 'Oh, Amy, that's so dangerous.'

'It can't be worse than going back to the trenches.'

Helen sighed. 'It's all so terrible. There's just nowhere to turn, is there? What a pair we are.'

Amy lay awake. She imagined Johnny boarding the train, being carried from the train to the boat, crossing the Channel. She could only hope that there wouldn't be any German submarines. Then the train home, the carriage or motor car to meet him, his family waiting, his mother beside herself with joy and relief. He would be back in his own world.

What did she really feel for him? Here, she knew, she was in a completely new situation. She had little or no previous experience to go by. She had been so intent on her studies and her career that she had never even thought about having a relationship with a man. Perhaps if her mother had lived she would have been better informed, better prepared for such relationships; but perhaps not. Mothers didn't usually discuss such things with their daughters. The sexual side of marriage was simply not mentioned. A new bride was supposed to be educated in this regard by her husband. Marriage was just accepted as the normal way of life for a woman. Spinsters were regarded with pity. She was lucky in one way, she supposed. She had studied reproduction as part of her medical training, so she knew about the mechanics of sexual congress. But she had no idea about the feelings that went with it, that preceded it. She had never wanted to know. She had resisted or ignored any advances from any man who might have been interested. She did not want to be involved. She did not want to be deflected from her main purpose. But now this feeling – this was something new. She couldn't just brush Johnny aside. Her age and the experience of her career had not prepared her for this.

Once, one Christmas, some of the women students had been invited to a dance at St Bartholomew's Hospital – heavily chaperoned, of course. She remembered a conversation with one of the male students, a hearty, red-faced young man. 'I don't know why you all bother,' he said. 'You'll probably get married and then it will all be a waste of time.'

'Why?' she said, surprised. 'Why should it be a waste of time?'

'Because you'll give it up,' he said. 'You can't work after you are married.'

She had been indignant. 'Elizabeth Garrett Anderson didn't give it up,' she said. 'She went on practising. There are a lot of women doctors who are married and still practising.'

'Well I wouldn't let my wife work,' he said.

And that seemed to be the usual attitude. Men seemed to regard it as some kind of slur on themselves if their wives worked. It implied that he wasn't able to support her.

Then she sighed to herself in the dark. What on earth was she doing, even thinking about marriage? Johnny had never given the slightest sign that that was in his mind. She was worrying about nothing. There were much more important things to worry about than that. This war was going on and on. In the face of such disaster her worries were nothing. She turned over and went to sleep.

A letter arrived from Dan.

Dear Amy
I want to thank you for your kindness in dining with me. I can't tell you how much I enjoyed it. I hope that we shall be able to do it again one day.

There isn't much to say about life here, you know what it is like. It gets more and more difficult to cope. We have large numbers of German wounded as well as our own. Still, we struggle on.

Please write back as promised.

Best wishes

Dan Fielding

PS Peter is well.

No, she thought, I don't really know what it is like. It was difficult enough here in Paris, but to be working under those conditions, shelling, attacks by aircraft dropping bombs, numbers they could hardly cope with. She didn't know what that was like. Not that Paris was immune. While autumn had crept into Paris and the poplars by the river had turned to golden glory, the Germans had dropped bombs near Nôtre Dame and several people were killed. Nôtre Dame! Why did they have to try to destroy all beauty?

She found Helen. 'I've had a letter from Dan,' she said. 'He says Peter is well.'

Helen coloured. 'I've had one from Peter. He says it's just possible that they might get to Paris at Christmas.' She bounced away down the ward. Amy smiled after her. Helen was so ... uncomplicated. She seemed to have clean, clear paths in her life. Apart, that was, from risking loving someone.

The weeks went by, unchanging, relentless. Amy received four letters from Johnny, reporting on his progress: *I am on my feet now, with a crutch; I am walking with a stick and feel about ninety; I am walking without a stick, almost back to normal; I have been riding.* His letters were brief, factual, without any kind of emotion, and for that she was grateful. She was torn, wanting him to be well again, and not wanting him to be well enough to go back.

'Christmas is coming,' Helen said. 'The goose is getting fat.'

Christmas, Amy thought. What would that be like this year, this terrible year? What would it be like for all those families at home whose sons were not coming back? So much for it all being over by Christmas.

She had a card from Johnny that she kept in the drawer beside her bed. It had a beautiful scene in watercolour of the English countryside in the snow. Inside, under his name, he had drawn a small biplane, and

106

beside it the word 'soon'. Did he mean that he would be flying soon, or that he would see her soon?

'Amy.' Dr Hanfield looked contrite. 'We've had an urgent message about some men in one of the villages, wounded, I hardly need say. There's only one way to get them out. Someone will have to go. I realize it's near to Christmas, but I know I can always rely on you.'

'It's all right,' Amy said. 'Of course I'll go.'

'But we'll need two ambulances. I wonder if Helen. . . ?'

'I'm sure she will,' Amy said. 'She'll mark it down for votes for women.'

Dr Hanfield smiled. 'She'll have my backing as soon as all this is over.'

'When do we go?' Amy asked.

'Tomorrow, first light. The village is very close to the front, Amy. It may not be easy.'

Amy sought out Helen. 'Of course I'll come,' she said.

They were given the evening off to go to bed early. Helen seemed to drop off at once. Amy lay awake for a while. Near to the front, Dr Hanfield had said. How near? Not that it mattered. They would go anyway.

They set off before dawn, Amy with Bill and Helen with another driver in the other ambulance. As they left Paris behind them the sun rose in the east, painting the countryside with gold.

'Lovely morning,' Bill said. 'Cold though.'

Amy nodded, thinking of the men in the trenches, the freezing snow and frozen mud. Christmas must mean very little to them.

The morning star shone in the indigo and golden sky. 'Venus,' Bill said. 'Beautiful, isn't it?'

They drew up at a crossroads and Bill got out his map. The other driver and Helen came to the door and the two men conferred.

'It's cold,' Helen said, 'But I needed to stretch my legs. We have to find these men before they freeze to death.'

'The villagers will help them,' Amy said. 'They always do.'

The drivers seemed to have reached a decision and they climbed back aboard and set off again. The daylight slowly revealed the ravaged countryside: abandoned farms, shattered and broken trees, trees that had grown for decades, perhaps a hundred years. Now they were just jagged stumps in the blasted earth.

107

They joined a road where the army was moving, lorries and horses and mules struggling in the snowdrifts and frozen mud.

'This'll slow us down,' Bill said. 'Perhaps I can find a side road.'

Wherever it could the traffic drew aside to let them through and they crept along.

'What's that?' Bill said.

Amy peered out of the window. A speck on the horizon grew bigger.

'It's a plane,' Bill said. He stared out of the window for a few moments. 'It's a bloody German plane. Sorry for the language.' The plane came on. 'Get out, Miss Amy,' Bill said suddenly. 'Get out and get in the ditch, now. Some of those planes have started carrying a bomb.'

They jumped out of the doors, together with Helen and her driver. Many of the men got out of the army lorries and began to fire their rifles at the plane. They crouched in the ditch. The plane flew over them and then circled to fly over them again. 'He's coming back,' Bill said. 'He's probably just reconnaissance, but you never know. Keep down.'

They heard another sound, another plane. 'Oh my God, 'Amy whispered.

They watched it approach and then Bill cheered. 'Look, it's one of ours. It's a BE2.' The plane pounced upon the German. They watched, fascinated, as they circled one another in the sky above them. They were so low that they could see the pilots firing at each other with pistols. Then suddenly, the German plane slipped and dipped and a stream of smoke spiralled out behind it. It seemed to fall so slowly, sliding and turning, and then it hit the earth with an explosion of sound and flame. Amy closed her eyes, thinking of the man inside it, but Bill jumped to his feet, cheering and waving his arms. 'He got him,' he shouted. 'He bloody got him.' Amy could only think of the pilot, dead, without a doubt. It could be Johnny, was all that she could think. It could be Johnny.

They climbed out of the ditch and back into the ambulance and set off again. 'Those planes,' Bill said. 'They should put something on them so you know which is which. Those boys in the trenches mostly don't know. Half the time they're firing at their own side.'

They found the village at last and the four of them stepped out into the village street. The men were in the church again, lying in straw in the bitter cold. The villagers had brought in some charcoal burners, but they had made little difference. The men seemed too sick to greet them, half conscious with the effort to fight the cold and the pain of their wounds. Amy and Helen automatically tried to breathe through their mouths. The stench was overpowering, but at least they were used to it now; they knew what to expect.

They moved among the men, giving morphine, applying new dressings over the blood and pus-soaked dressings that were already there. One of the nurses on a hospital train at the station had said that they now thought it was better to leave on the old dressing until they got the men to hospital. There appeared to be less infection and less shock.

'I think we can take them all,' Helen said. 'Even him.' One of the wounded – a bullet in the shoulder – was a German. He was lying alone in a corner. 'Or shall we leave him behind?'

'No,' Amy said sharply. 'Of course not.'

'I didn't mean it,' Helen said. 'It's just a bit strange, that's all – saving the enemy.'

We don't choose who we help, Amy thought. Medicine doesn't work that way. We do the best we can, whoever it is, whatever we feel about them. 'Love your enemies,' she said.

Helen pulled a face. 'We don't have to love them, do we?'

They loaded the men into the ambulances and drove away, the villagers behind them smiling and waving.

They stopped on the way to give the men water. Amy bent over one of the men on a stretcher. She looked down at him and closed her eyes in pity and sadness. They were too late; he was already dead. She said nothing and did not cover his face, not wanting to upset the other men. Not that they had not seen a corpse before. They lived with them every day, under their feet, half concealed in the walls of the trenches, lying in the mud in no-man's land. Death was all around them.

They arrived at the hospital in the dark, too late for the usual group of Parisians. The men were unloaded from the ambulances and were led or carried away to be assessed, given more pain control, washed, de-loused. The lights were already on in the operating theatre; there were the busy sounds of preparation, the staff hurrying in and out. The young German looked terrified, Amy thought. He probably thought that they were going to torture him and kill him. Heaven knew what lies they had been told.

She and Helen bathed and went early to bed. Amy lay awake for a while, thinking about the young German. She had noticed a strange schism in her own mind. If an allied victory was reported and she heard that a few thousand Germans were dead, she would rejoice with everyone else, but if the report said that a few thousand men were dead, she would be filled with horror and pity, even though the men were German. What has happened to us, she thought? We have lost our humanity. That very word, 'German', 'Hun', seemed to have taken on a life of its own, conjuring up menace, cruelty and barbarism. That boy downstairs was just a boy, after all, a boy just like the British boys, caught up in something they didn't want and didn't understand. Dying for some crazy useless power struggle invented by their leaders. She hoped the boy was sleeping now and had realized that he was going to be taken care of.

In the wards a kind of Christmas fever was beginning. The men were making paper chains with a lot of glue and muttered language and laughter. Flags of all nations were fixed to the beds. Two of the doctors were organizing a short pantomime, *Little Red Riding Hood*, and Helen was selected to be the heroine. 'Can't get much redder than that,' one of the sisters said, pointing to her hair. A very large sergeant was chosen to be the wolf and kitted out with huge cardboard teeth and ears and a great false beard. Someone had provided a spiked German helmet for the wolf to wear, much to everyone's amusement.

'Well he certainly frightens me,' Helen said.

M. Le Blanc promised that he had found some turkeys, and a consignment of Christmas puddings was on its way from England. Just for the day they were determined to help the men to forget what had happened – what was still happening.

Christmas morning started bright and early. Many of the men had parcels from home and the beds were littered with socks, gloves, scarves, books and cigarettes. Breakfast was good old British bacon and eggs and pints and pints of tea. Amy worked in the general ward. Some of the men that she and Helen had brought in needed their dressings changed. The young German boy had had the bullet removed from his shoulder and medically was doing well. He was lying with his face to the wall. Amy watched as one of the older men went up to him and touched him gently on the shoulder but the boy shrugged him away. So much for 'love your enemy', Amy thought. The boy didn't want to be loved, not by the English anyway. She wondered what they were told by their officers – that the British were vicious and cruel, perhaps? Did he think he was being disloyal, just to join in with Christmas? They had no alternative but to leave him be.

Breakfast over, the men who could leave their beds assembled in the hall and the ward doors were left open so that everyone could hear. A group of choirboys from the local church had come to sing carols. They were singing in French, of course, but it was such a reminder of home that many of the men had tears in their eyes.

Lunch was a great success. M. Le Blanc had turned up trumps with the turkeys and the puddings had arrived on time from England. M. Le Blanc had also found enough beer to go round. All the staff, including the doctors, waited at table. Then a cab arrived with the gifts from Princess Mary. The gifts were just a small brass box with a card and some pipe tobacco and cigarettes and a writing case for the non-smokers, but they were highly appreciated by the men. A young corporal, wounded in the knee, tucked his into his pocket. 'It shows they haven't forgotten us,' he said. 'I'm going to send mine home to my wife. A present from Royalty! She'll be that pleased.'

Most of the men had a sleep after lunch and an unusual quiet fell on the hospital.

'I did hope Peter and Dan would come.' Helen had been looking pensive all morning, looking often at the main door as if willing them to walk through it.

'I suppose we shouldn't look forward to anything too much,' Amy said, 'But the day's not over yet.'

Helen smiled. 'I wish I had your optimism.'

At five o'clock they all gathered in the hall again for the concert. Matron played some Chopin on the piano, which was very politely received. Then came some recitations and a large sergeant major with a fine bass voice led the men in a sing-song, 'Pack up your troubles' and 'Good bye Dolly' and all the popular songs. There was a stir of anticipation as the curtains, (two sheets) opened on *Little Red Riding Hood*. All the men were familiar with pantomimes and there were constant cheers and boos and shouts of 'oh yes you are', and 'it's behind you'. Helen got loud cheers and whistles and the wolf in his German helmet got boos that rattled the windows.

Amy was sitting at the back, near the main door. She heard the door open and turned around. Dan and Peter were standing just inside muffled up in their greatcoats. She got up at once and went to meet them, smiling. They both took off their caps and grinned broadly.

'We got here,' Dan said softly. 'Just.'

'It's nearly over,' she whispered. 'Let me take your coats.' Peter looked around the hall, obviously looking for Helen, and not finding her. Amy touched his arm and pointed to the stage. 'Up there.' His look of relief was almost comical and he laughed loudly at the wolf. 'If he touches her I'll kill him,' he said. He got as close to the stage as he could, clapping loudly whenever Helen appeared.

'How are you, Amy?' Dan looked down at her, brown eyes smiling.

'I'm very well. And you?'

'Well,' he said, 'but tired, I have to admit. We don't get much sleep.'

He looked even leaner, she thought, sharper. 'Have you had anything to eat?' she said. 'I'm sure we can find you something. There must be a lot left over from lunch.'

'A sandwich would be nice,' he said. 'We've been travelling most of the day.'

'I'll go and talk to cook.' Amy came back after a few moments. 'Turkey sandwich do? And perhaps some cold Christmas pudding?'

'Excellent.'

The pantomime ended with a burst of applause and the men began to move from the hall. She and Dan sat down on one of the settees.

'How long will you be in Paris?' Amy asked.

'Just this evening,' he said. 'We'll have to go back early in the morning. We're staying at a hotel we found that still had some rooms. I'm really looking forward to an uninterrupted sleep.'

Amy was almost shocked. 'You've come all this way?' she said. 'Just for one evening?'

He smiled at her, a slow, warm smile, looking into her eyes. 'There was no way to keep Peter back,' he said. 'So of course I had to come too.' His smile turned into a speculative, amused look. She knew then perfectly well what he was saying without words – 'I wanted to come too; I wanted to see you.' She didn't know what to say, she just gave him a brief smile. 'I don't suppose you and Helen can come out, can you?' he said.

She shook her head. 'I'm afraid not, but I'm sure you'll be welcome to spend the evening here. There'll be dozens of people here till all hours. Lots of the local people have come in and brought things for the men – a lot of it alcoholic.'

He laughed. 'Maybe we can help them get rid of some of it.'

Peter came back to them. 'Helen's gone up to change.'

When Helen came down they all went into the dining-room while the men ate their sandwiches.

'I'm going to ask Matron if I can go out for a walk,' Helen said. She and Peter looked at each other. They were obviously very eager to be alone, even if it was cold outside.

After they had gone she and Dan sat on a settee in the main hall. Later on, in bed, she couldn't really remember much of what they had talked about. He told her a bit more about himself, his GP father, his sisters, his ambitions for his career in surgery after the war. She had told him about her father, and her lost mother. They had been joined by other people, staff members and some of the French visitors. Peter and Helen came back, Helen looking a bit flushed, and eventually they said their goodbyes.

Helen was humming, brushing her hair before bed.

'You sound very happy,' Amy said.

'Oh, Amy.' Her eyes were shining. 'I know we've only met twice, but he's so nice. And I'm going to see him again, somehow.'

'Are you sure it's not just a wartime fling?'

'I'm not sure of anything,' Helen said. 'But what's the point in holding back? There isn't time for all the usual things.'

'I suppose not.'

'What about Dan?' Helen said. 'How do you feel about him?'

Amy was surprised. 'He's just a friend.'

'That's not what he thinks,' Helen said.

'I'm sure he does. He told me before; he misses his sisters and the girls at home. He just wants a bit of female company.'

Helen got into bed. 'I think you're wrong about that.'

They put out the lights. It's all too complicated, Amy thought. My life is too complicated to be thinking about any kind of relationship. She could only see the immediate future, not beyond.

The next day the young German was still refusing to speak to anyone. Then, over the next few days the rumour started coming in that some of the soldiers, British and German, had met in no-man's land on Christmas day, and had talked, had a drink, played football together. And then, two days later, they were killing each other again. The whole world, Amy thought, has gone stark, staring mad.

CHAPTER NINE

1915

IN January a letter arrived for Amy from her father.

Dear Amy

I do hope you had a pleasant Christmas and that you got the money I sent you. I didn't know what to buy and thought you could probably get something in Paris.

I haven't been too well – a chest infection, the doctor says. I have been in bed for a while. Our Mrs Jones is still coming in every day to look after the house and she has been very good, getting my meals. Don't worry, I shall probably be better soon. Let's hope that 1915 sees the end of this dreadful conflict and you are able to come home.

Happy New Year.

Your loving father

She was immediately very worried indeed. Her father had never been one to complain. The fact that he had written at all was a cause for concern. She hardly remembered him being ill at all, apart from an occasional cold. I must go home, she thought, and find out what is really going on. It certainly wasn't like him to stay in bed and to miss school.

Matron was sympathetic. 'Of course you must go, Amy,' she said. 'But I hope very much that you will come back to us. You do a good job, dear. We'll miss you.'

Dr Hanfield stopped her in the hall. 'Come into my office for a moment, Amy.' Amy followed her in. 'I hear you are going home,' she said.

'Not permanently,' Amy said. 'I'm sure my father will be all right. He's never been really ill before. I'm probably worrying about nothing. I shall come back.'

'Sit down, Amy.' Dr Hanfield perched on the edge of her desk. 'I was wondering,' she said, 'whether you had ever thought of doing nursing training. You seem to have a real bent for this kind of work. You are very efficient and you seem to be really interested. I'm sure you would do very well.'

Amy was so startled that for a moment she didn't know what to say. 'I – I don't know,' she said. 'I hadn't thought about it. I don't think I can plan further than the end of the war, whenever that may be.'

'We need good people in medicine and nursing,' Dr Hanfield said. 'It's not an easy life though, Amy. You would have to be aware of that. You would have to deal with a lot of problems, other people's difficulties and pain. . . .'

'It can't be worse than this,' Amy said. 'Nothing could be worse than this.' She looked at Dr Hanfield's face, full of strain and fatigue. She was so tempted to tell her, so tempted to say, simply, I know. I am Amy Richmond. I am a doctor. Let me help you.

Dr Hanfield got up and looked out of the window, choosing her words. 'It can be just as hard. There may not be the wounds of war but there are other equally dreadful things, even in England, that just seem to get swept under the carpet – squalor, hunger, bad housing, horrible poverty. Not even clean water in some cases. The children are undernourished; they get almost no milk or meat, little fresh fruit, hardly any sunshine. It's hardly surprising that they have anaemia, rickets. . . .'

Amy heard the echo of her own thoughts. She knew Dr Hanfield only as a surgeon, a good surgeon, but she obviously had the same feelings, the same anxieties. There were many men at home, doctors and politicians, who voiced these concerns, but perhaps women doctors in particular had sympathy with these desperate families. After all, many of them were wives and mothers. Charity was not enough. These men, fighting and dying, deserved the right to a decent life for their families.

Dr Hanfield came back to her desk. 'And then there is disease,' she went on. 'Diphtheria, pneumonia, scarlet fever, meningitis, TB; I could go on and on.' She rubbed her forehead with her hand, as if to remove a headache. 'We have no tools, Amy. We have nothing that will kill the bacteria that kill and maim.'

'There is research,' Amy began. 'There's a typhoid vaccine. . . .'

'I know.' Dr Hanfield said. 'But we need something that will kill the bacteria without killing the patient. Almroth Wright and young Alexander Fleming are doing great work at St Mary's and they are running some laboratories in France. But oh, how I wish we had something now. We could save so many young lives.'

'It'll come,' Amy said. 'I'm sure it will come one day. Things are advancing all the time. We've got some vaccines. I believe the Americans are doing blood transfusions and they have a method of grouping the blood. My father says,' she added hurriedly.

Dr Hanfield smiled. 'I like your positive thinking, Amy. Perhaps you will live to see it, the great breakthrough. Perhaps even I will.'

'One of the sisters tells us that Madame Curie is going to take her X-Ray machine around the forward hospitals,' Amy said.

Dr Hanfield nodded. 'Yes, isn't it wonderful? Being able to see exactly what has happened to the bones and where the bullets and shrapnel are. What a wonderful help that would be.' She smiled again and visibly relaxed. 'What a lecture,' she said. 'But I do think you should stay in medicine, Amy. You seem right for it.'

Amy had difficulty in hiding her feelings, holding back angry, frustrated tears. If only you knew, she thought. If only I could tell you. Even if she did tell her, she wouldn't be allowed to practise. Dr Hanfield couldn't risk her own career.

'I hope you find your father well and that you come back to us.'

Amy wrote a note to her father to tell him that she was coming home. With any luck it should get there before she did.

'I'm really going to miss you,' Helen said. 'You do really mean to come back, don't you?'

Amy nodded. 'Unless my father is really ill.'

She packed a small case. She deliberately left most of her possessions behind. She was coming back. She took the train to Boulogne. The train was crowded; worse than crowded, but she managed to get a seat in a corner next to a very large woman, with a baby who cried most of the way. Most of the passengers were military, and many of those seemed to have wounds of some kind; bandages and crutches and sticks were everywhere. She supposed that they were on their way to the hospitals in Boulogne, and from there, perhaps, to England and home. At Boulogne she boarded the boat alongside streams of men who were being repatriated. Eventually, as darkness fell, they steamed slowly out of the harbour. She stood for a while on the deck in the dark, watching the dimmed lights of France fade into the distance.

She had a strange feeling, as if she herself was on the way to a foreign country. She had no way of knowing what had happened to England in the past months. She felt lost, as if she might not even know her way about any more. It was a foolish thought, she knew. All the familiar streets and buildings would still be there, but what had happened to the people? Did they know, could they even imagine what was happening in France? Yes, they saw the wounded coming home in their thousands, but they didn't see what they had left behind. They didn't see the piles of dead, or worse, the scattered, shattered pieces of the dead. They didn't have to hear the cries of suffering and deadly pain. They didn't see the ever growing rows and rows of crosses in the graveyards.

She went below. The ship moved steadily through the night. The passengers were quiet and subdued; the thought of German submarines was never far away.

Dawn was breaking by the time they arrived in England. She took the train to London, and by the time she got there it was light. She made her way to Ludgate to take the train for home. It was very cold, colder than Paris. The people looked much the same, but there were black armbands everywhere. Still, the wheels seemed to be turning, the omnibuses and trains running, the usual bustle of London.

She walked down the familiar street, with the same feeling of strangeness, of unfamiliarity. She let herself into the house, into the hall. Nothing here seemed to have changed; the same rugs on the floor, the same pictures on the walls. It's me who's changed, she thought. Nothing will ever seem the same again. Nothing will ever be the same again. She could hear Mrs Jones, busy in the kitchen.

Her father was sitting in his chair in the sitting-room, a blanket over his knees, reading *The Times*. He gave a cry when he saw her, 'Amy, my dear,' and his newspaper dropped to the floor as he held out his arms.

She put her arms around him and kissed his cheek. 'Here I am,' she said. 'Safe and sound. How are you, Father?'

He had tears in his eyes. 'I'm much better,' he said, 'And very much better now that you're here.'

She took off her hat and coat and sat down beside him and took his hand. 'Are you really better?'

He nodded. 'Yes, I shall be back at school in a week or two, the doctor says. It took a little while. It turned into pneumonia, for which there seems to be no cure, just time and hope.'

'And the fact that you are a very healthy man,' she said. 'I'm sure you cured yourself.' He looked better than she had expected, to her relief. Chest infections could so easily become purulent and killing. Dr Hanfield's words came back into her head; 'We have no tools, Amy.'

She spent the day at his side, answering his questions about France as well as she could without telling him about her sorties with the ambulance. The less he knew about that the better.

'Dr Hanfield, our senior surgeon, called me into her office before I left,' she said.

He looked alarmed. 'Why?'

'She wanted to ask me whether I had considered doing nursing,' she said drily. 'She said she thought I had a gift for medicine.'

'So you do,' he said. 'It's going to be all right, Amy.'

'One day.'

His relief that she was there was palpable. 'I was so worried,' he said. 'After Mons the Germans were said to be within twenty miles of Paris, or even nearer. The newspapers were very frightening.'

She could imagine him, sitting here, terrified for her safety, unable to help her. 'It's all right now, dear,' she said. 'You don't have to worry any more. Paris is safe.'

'Nothing is safe,' he said. 'All those boys at Ypres, thousands of dead. You know that German ships shelled Hartlepool and Scarborough? What is happening, Amy? It's almost impossible to believe it.' There was nothing she could say, no comfort that she could give him.

He went to bed early. She knew that feeling; the exhaustion of relief. At the door he turned. 'Oh, Amy. I quite forgot in the pleasure of seeing you. There is a letter for you. It came a couple of weeks ago, addressed to Miss Amy Osborne. You'll find it over there in my desk.'

After he had gone she took out the letter. 'To await return to

England' was written across the top. She knew immediately who it was from.

Dear Amy
I have sent this letter to your home to be sure that it reaches you if you are coming to England. I have sent another letter to France but Heaven knows when it will get there, or if. I shall be here in England until the end of January. I am on leave until I get a squadron. Please let me know if you are coming home before then. I want to see you. Telephone or telegram.

Johnny

She took the letter up to her room. She was undecided what to do about it. At least, her rational brain was undecided but, underneath all that, the rest of her had no doubts at all. She lay in bed, the letter on the table beside her. She read it again. What am I afraid of, she thought? I'm being childish. She wasn't afraid of taking her ambulance close to danger, but she seemed to be afraid of getting too close to some person – some man. Her past history was another deep concern. Johnny didn't really know anything about her, nothing about her history. He probably thought she had been an ordinary girl, living at home with her father until the war had changed all that. What does he see in me, she wondered? He didn't seem to be the kind of man who would be attracted to a quiet little home body, but who knew, with families like these? Perhaps that was what they did want, a capable wife in the home, a healthy mother for their children, while the men went off to do whatever they wanted. Or did he actually see in her some mysterious quality that he didn't quite understand and that intrigued him? Did he sense that she was holding something back? She couldn't work out her own feelings, let alone his. It's all chaos, she thought. The whole world and my brain alike. How could anyone make decisions on such shifting ground? How could one trust mere feelings? I'll sleep on it, she thought.

She slept on it for a week. She spent the week with her father, talking, playing chess, taking him for little walks around the garden. He seemed to get better every day, comforted by her presence. At the end of the week she was satisfied that he was well on the way to recovery and she began to think about going back to Paris. She felt as if she were living in a fairy tale, that this world, the peace and safety of home, was unreal. Reality was the brutality of what was going on in France.

She didn't telephone Johnny's home; she didn't want to talk to anyone else in the household. It seemed too close, too intimate. She sent a telegram: *I am at home in England. Amy.* She received a reply at once: *Splendid. Have tea with me on Thursday. I'll be at the Ritz at four. Come if you can. Johnny.*

Over dinner she said, 'I thought I would go to Town on Thursday, Father, if you don't mind. There are a few things I need.'

'Of course, my dear,' he said. 'You must have a lot of shopping to do.'

She debated what to wear. Her uniform? No, not that. Even her best one that she had worn home was looking rather weary. She rifled through the clothes that she had left behind. She decided on a grey coat and skirt and a pink high-necked blouse and a waterproof overcoat. Her hat was small, neat and unadorned. She had come home in winter boots.

She travelled up to London on Thursday morning and spent some time looking in the shop windows in Oxford Street and Regent Street. They were all decked with flags of the allied nations and streamers in red, white and blue. She went into Selfridges and looked around the store. There were still many very prosperous looking women strolling the streets and the shops, dressed in the latest fashions, muffled in furs against the cold and with large, extravagant hats. Some people, she thought, seemed to be untouched by the war. She bought a few necessities, toilet soap and cologne, handkerchiefs and writing paper, enough for herself and Helen. She had a simple lunch in the restaurant in Selfridges. The other customers were mostly women, loaded with bags of shopping, chatting to each other, gesticulating and laughing. It's another world, she thought, another planet. France might not exist.

At almost four o'clock she walked down Piccadilly towards the Ritz. This would be only the second time she had ever been there. Her father had brought her to tea to celebrate when she qualified. She stopped outside the Royal Academy, wondering again what she was walking into. Nothing, probably. Johnny's last letter had been friendly, that was all. It had been filled with his enthusiasm about flying: *It is wonderful,* he wrote. *It's the most terrific thing I've ever done. I've finished my basic training and got my wings so I'll be getting a posting to a squadron soon.*

A posting? Doing what? Shooting down German observation balloons? Being shot at over the German trenches? Air battles with German airmen? Danger, all the time.

Now that she was about to see him again she knew precisely what she was going to do and what she was going to say. 'It's so nice to see you, Johnny, looking so well. I'm so glad you're enjoying the flying. I do hope your father is well. No, I don't think we should meet again.' She half thought of turning away, of telephoning a message to him at the Ritz to say she wasn't able to come after all. But that would be extremely ill-mannered and wouldn't achieve what she wanted.

She crossed the road and walked on and went into the hotel. She paused just inside the door. The foyer was busy, beautifully dressed women and a scattering of male uniforms. She was glad that she hadn't worn her own uniform; she would have stood out like a sore thumb. She walked on inside, but she couldn't see him. Perhaps, she thought with some relief, he hasn't been able to come.

'Hello, Amy.'

He was standing beside her, looking down at her, smiling. She felt a momentary shock. In all her memories and imaginings of him she was standing over him; he was lying down in the filthy straw, or his bed in the hospital or sitting in a wheelchair. She drew in her breath. She realized that she had never seen him standing upright before. He was as tall as his father, at least, and broad in the shoulder. She had almost forgotten how blue his eyes were, how bright. He was wearing his new uniform, the close-fitting jacket, jodhpurs and boots of the Royal Flying Corps, and the wings gleamed on his breast. As he looked down at her she felt that same moving, disturbing, pleasurable contraction of her body, that same urge to touch him. Did he know, she wondered? Did anything show on her face?

'Johnny,' she said. Her mouth seemed to have gone suddenly dry and her brain bereft of words.

He held out his hand. 'It's good to see you, Amy. Thank you so much for coming. You look very well.'

'So do you.' She took his hand, now firm and strong. 'I hadn't realized – you aren't even using a stick.'

'Totally back to normal,' he said. 'Thanks to you and a talented lady surgeon.'

She smiled. 'I'm glad we managed to change your mind about that.'

'Absolutely,' he said. 'I've booked for tea. Shall we go in?'

They were shown to their table. As they walked by women looked up from their tea and smiled at him. The older women gave him proud, maternal glances and some of the younger women blushed faintly and looked away. A young boy whispered loudly, 'Look Mother, look. He's a pilot. I'm going to be a pilot when I grow up.' Amy was amused. He seemed to be making quite a stir.

The waiter held out her chair for her and she sat down. 'Tea, madam?' the waiter asked.

'Yes, Assam for me please.'

'And me,' Johnny said. 'I don't care for the China stuff. Tastes like cheap perfume.'

She smiled and looked away from him around the room. She thought it highly unlikely that he had ever smelt cheap perfume. The women were taking their tea, chatting, appearing to be unconcerned about anything.

'A bit different from France, isn't it?' he said.

She looked back at him. 'I feel as if I've been away for years. In a way I was surprised to see it all looking the same. I know it isn't the same – the shortages and all the people with armbands, and you know what they have lost – but London seems the same, everyone doing the same things.'

'That's the British way,' he said, smiling. 'Stiff upper lip.'

She thought of the people streaming out of Paris, and of the many brave souls who had stayed. 'I wonder what it would be like if the Germans were twenty miles from London and no sea and navy to protect us.'

'We'd beat them, of course.' He sounded surprised at her question. 'Whatever they did we'd beat them.'

The waiter brought their tea and tiny sandwiches and cakes on a stand.

'So you've got your wings,' she said.

He touched his badge briefly. 'It's terrific, Amy. I can't tell you what it's like, being up there. It's as if you've left the world behind you; all the nasty bits anyway. It's so clean and clear. And you can see England spread out below you, so green, or shining white, where it's been snowing. You can see what you're fighting for.' He laughed. 'I'll have to be careful or I might turn into a poet and get a bad reputation.'

123

'It sounds wonderful,' she said.

'It is. Perhaps I'll be able to take you up one day and show you.'

One day, she thought? What about her resolution to tell him that they mustn't meet again? It seemed to be retreating out of reach.

'Have you just come home for leave,' he said, 'or are you staying?'

'Just leave. My father has been ill but he's much better now. I shall be going back soon.'

'So shall I, when I get my posting to a squadron. I'll probably go to Maubeuge first, then it might be anywhere.' He ate another two sand-wiches. 'Are you not eating, Amy?'

'I had lunch,' she said. 'I'm not very hungry.'

He ate a cake. 'I seem to be hungry all the time.'

She laughed. 'You're a growing boy.'

His look changed from amusement to an intense study of her face. He was suddenly serious, his words measured. 'I'm not a boy, Amy.'

She flushed a little. 'No, of course not.' She drank her tea so that she didn't have to look at him.

'When exactly are you going back?' he said.

'I've booked a passage for next Friday – a week's time.'

'Good. We've got some time then. What shall we do?'

She looked at him, surprised. She wasn't sure what she had expected, but not this direct approach, not this automatic assumption that she was going to see him again.

He saw her hesitation. 'Times have changed, Amy. We've got to take what we can until the war is over. We won't have much chance of doing nice things once we go back.'

She thought suddenly of Dan, of his quiet pleasure just to have dinner with her and Helen. Times had certainly changed, contracted, every minute of life important. There was an urgent sense that if you didn't do it now, whatever it was, you may never do it at all. Conventions had changed too. She had noticed many young men and women out together in the streets and restaurants, unchaperoned.

'I shall have to spend most of my time with my father,' she said, 'but perhaps we could meet – perhaps have lunch?'

'I'll be in touch,' he said.

They left the hotel and he insisted on coming with her to the station and hailed a cab. He bought a penny platform ticket and waited with her until the train came in. She watched out of the window until they rounded a bend and she couldn't see him any more. She leant her head back against the seat and closed her eyes. So much for not seeing him again. It had been a foolish thought anyway. She couldn't possibly have meant it; she was just deceiving herself.

Her father was waiting for her in the sitting-room when she got home. 'You haven't got much shopping,' he said. 'I thought you would be laden with parcels.'

'I don't need much,' she said. 'Not clothes or hats. We wear our uniform all the time.' She sat down on the sofa.

He was looking at her expectantly, as if he knew exactly where she had been. She knew perfectly well that he was waiting for her to tell him what was in her letter. She was going to have to tell him anyway if she was going to see Johnny again.

'The letter was from a lieutenant I looked after in France,' she said. 'A grateful patient. He's better now and he's joined the Flying Corps.' Her father was smiling broadly. 'He said he would like to see me so I thought I might have lunch with him one day.'

'Yes, do,' he said. She didn't respond and he sat beside her. 'Did you see him today, dear? Is this young man special to you, Amy?'

She sighed and then smiled ruefully. 'I can't hide anything from you, can I? I don't know, Father. There are so many difficulties now. He doesn't know that I'm a doctor or anything about what happened. I haven't told anyone, not even Helen. And there's this terrible war, the danger. Everything is so uncertain.'

'Amy,' he said, 'I have always been so proud of you, you know that. But I have often wondered whether there wasn't something missing from your life.'

'I know what you're going to say,' she said.

'Marriage, Amy. Someone to love you and take care of you and perhaps one day the blessing of children.'

'I don't need anyone to take care of me. . . .' she began.

'I'm talking about someone to share your life with,' he said. 'I'm talking about love, Amy. To love someone and for them to love you back. Someone to rely on and help you through all the difficulties that can come along. It adds so much to your life.'

'Surely it's not the time, Father,' she said. 'What's the point of letting yourself love someone when you know' – she paused for a moment, distressed – 'when you know they might very well die.'

'I lost your mother, Amy,' he said, 'but I still have that; I still have her love. I wouldn't have missed it for the world.'

'I've never needed it,' she said. 'I've found my career to be enough, everything I ever wanted. It's been all absorbing. I've never needed anything else.'

He smiled and patted her hand. 'When you do need it, you'll know,' he said. 'Loving someone like that is a positive, living thing. It could even make you a better doctor, more understanding, more deeply aware of your patients' feelings. Don't be afraid of it, dear. Love is never wasted.'

She put her head on his shoulder and burst into tears, crying at last for so many things that were lost.

On Sunday a telegram arrived: *Wednesday? Will collect you from home at ten-thirty. Wrap up very warm. Johnny.* She telegraphed back: *Yes, Amy.*

'Do you mind, Father?' she asked. 'Seeing that I'm leaving on Friday?'

'I'm delighted,' he said, smiling.

'Father,' she said, 'stop matchmaking. He's just a friend, a grateful patient.'

'Of course, dear,' he said, but he was still smiling.

Over dinner she said, 'Father, you do remember that he will call you Mr Osborne, don't you?'

He sighed. 'I'd forgotten about that. I wish we didn't have to have all this subterfuge. Can't you just tell him?'

She shook her head. 'No, dear, certainly not yet. And you mustn't say anything. Please.'

He patted her hand. 'Of course not, Amy, if you don't want me to.'

What does he mean by wrap up warm? She was going through her clothes again. She had a thick skirt, stockings and boots, a thick coat, scarf and gloves. Perhaps he was thinking of a long walk. She wished he had been a bit more explicit.

She was ready at a quarter past ten. The doorbell rang. Mrs Jones went to open it and Amy followed her into the hall. Johnny was muffled up in a greatcoat and scarf. He unwound the scarf and grinned at her.

'Ready?'

'Yes,' she said. 'Where are we going?'

'It's a surprise.'

Amy's father came into the hall. 'Father,' she said. 'This is Lieutenant Maddox.' They shook hands. 'How do you do, sir,' Johnny said.

'Where are you off to,' her father asked, 'all bundled up like that?'

'It's a surprise,' he said. 'But I'll take good care of her.'

'Did you come in a cab?' her father said.

'No, sir. I have a car outside, a two-seater AC.'

Her father smiled. 'No wonder you need to wrap up.'

'It's a lovely day,' Johnny said. 'A bit cold, but the sun is shining.'

Johnny helped her into the car and they set off. He had put up the hood but it was still draughty and cold. 'We're going to a little place called Beddington,' he said. 'Not too far away; near Croydon.'

'And what is so special about Beddington?' she asked.

'You'll see when we get there.'

They drove through the countryside in bright, cold sunshine, the trees bare of leaves and patches of snow here and there. She looked around her. Even in winter England was beautiful, orderly and peaceful; no trenches, no guns, no noise. The drive was a delight, well worth wrapping up for. She had no idea why they were going to Beddington. As far as she could recall she had never heard of it.

They turned into what looked to Amy to be a long empty field and they bumped across the grass. At the far end of the field stood an aeroplane. A young man in uniform was walking around it, examining it, touching it here and there, kicking at the tyres.

'It's an Avro,' Johnny said. 'Isn't it great? It's a two-seater trainer. And there's Jim.' They drove down the field.

She turned to him, astonished and excited. 'An aeroplane! And who's Jim?'

He grinned. 'A very good friend of mine. He's borrowed it for an hour or two.' He parked the car and helped her out and they walked towards the plane.

Jim came to meet them. He grinned. 'Here you are,' he said. 'I've done an external check and she's running like a bird. No more than an hour, Johnny. I've got to get it back or they'll start looking for me.' He smiled at Amy. 'Have a good time.'

She stared at Johnny, her mouth open.

'I want to show you,' he said. 'I want to show you how splendid it is. Will you come?'

'Yes,' she said, her eyes shining. 'Oh, yes.'

Jim handed her a close-fitting helmet. 'Put this on instead of your hat.'

They helped her into the front cockpit, showing her where to put her feet so as not to damage the fabric of the plane, and then Johnny climbed into the rear.

Jim pulled away the chocks. The engine started, roaring in her ears. They began to race over the grass, bumping a little; then there were no more bumps, just a serene smoothness, the earth falling away. She realized that she was holding her breath and let it out in a sigh of pleasure and excitement. The cold wind blew into her face, or the little of it that was exposed after she had wrapped her scarf around it, up to her eyes, following Johnny's instructions.

They rose higher, over the trees at the end of the field, up into a dazzling blue sky. Beneath her England unrolled, just as Johnny had described it, snow-dusted fields, bare branched woods, a farmhouse with a plume of smoke rising from the chimney. She caught her breath as the plane banked into a gentle turn, clutching at the sides of the cockpit. Then she relaxed, caught up in the wonder of being in the air. It was indeed a lovely day, blue and cloudless. The air seemed to have a sparkle, a radiance that she had never experienced on the ground. They banked gently again. She looked behind her and Johnny pointed downwards. Below them, at Sydenham, the many windows of the Crystal Palace glittered in the sunlight. It looked like a castle from fairyland, a palace made of diamonds. She began to feel that she was truly separated from the earth, that all her difficulties and trials were unreal and unimportant. They flew on.

She became very conscious of Johnny sitting behind her. She imagined his gloved hands, firm and strong on the controls of this wonderful machine, moving the stick and the throttle to his will. And as if it was as natural as flying, imagined his hands on her shoulders, drawing her to him. Here, separated from the earth, anything seemed possible, clean and clear, without complications or difficulties. She tried to capture the moment, fix it in her imagination, so that she could bring it back whenever she needed it, this freedom and the clear blue sky.

They flew in a wide circle and too soon they were back over the field. The earth came up to meet them and they rolled to a stop. They taxied back to where Jim was waiting, sitting in the AC, smoking a cigarette. He got out and flicked the cigarette away. He helped her down, and she returned the helmet, shaking out her hair.

'Have a good time?' he said, grinning.

'Wonderful,' she said. 'Unbelievable.'

'Got to get back before they miss me,' he said. 'I'll see you tomorrow, Johnny.' He climbed aboard, took off into the wind and disappeared into the distance.

Johnny turned to her. 'How was that? Did you enjoy it?'

'Incredible,' she said, breathless. 'Wonderful. I can't tell you. . . .'

'You don't have to,' he said. 'It has that effect on me, too. There's something about being up there – something so free.'

She looked up into his face and, just as she had imagined, he placed his hands on her shoulders and drew her to him. His kiss upon her lips was warm and dry and sweet. He drew away and looked into her eyes and smiled. 'Do you mind?'

She shook her head. 'No, I don't mind. I don't mind at all.'

He folded her in his arms, his lips against her hair. 'I've got to go back tomorrow,' he said. 'New orders. It's a mad world, Amy. Perhaps when it's all over. . . .'

He kissed her lightly again, then settled her into the car and drove her home. 'I won't come in,' he said. 'Got to pack. Will you write to me, Amy?'

'Yes,' she said, 'Of course I will.'

'Give my respects to your father.' He drove away and she watched the car until it disappeared.

She went into the house. Her father was waiting for her in the hall. 'I heard the car,' he said. 'Where is Lieutenant Maddox?'

'He had to go. He has to go back tomorrow.'

'And where did he take you today?'

She smiled and kissed his cheek. 'Flying,' she said, her eyes shining. 'He took me flying.'

CHAPTER TEN

1915-1916

'AMY! I'm so glad to see you back.' Helen put her arms around her and hugged her. 'I wasn't sure you'd come.'

Amy threw her hat on her bed. 'I'm glad to see you too, Helen. I said I'd come back, didn't I? My father is much better, so here I am.' She sat down on her bed, her shoulders drooping. 'I'm tired out. The journey back was awful – very rough in the Channel and the train was packed. So how is everything here?'

'Much the same,' Helen said, resignation in her voice. 'The war doesn't get any better, does it? We're still bogged down at Ypres. What's it all for? We move forward a few yards and then back a few yards and the boys are all dying for nothing. We've had to put up some more beds in the rooms.' She took a deep breath and sighed. 'So how was England?'

'It looks much the same, on the surface,' Amy said. 'Smart women in the shops, people in the restaurants. You walk about and you might think nothing has changed, but you know it has. The atmosphere is different; people are doing the normal things but they look tired and stressed and you can't walk down a street without noticing the black clothes and the armbands. It's all so sad.'

'Oh dear,' Helen said. 'Poor old England.'

'I suppose the main thing you notice is the lack of men,' Amy went on. 'Young men anyway, just like here. There are women everywhere; ticket collectors on the tube, bus-conductors, shop assistants, factory workers. They're doing everything. It's as if thousands of women have suddenly come out of the woodwork.'

Helen's eyes brightened. 'Good. Now perhaps we can show them what we're made of.'

'I suppose so,' Amy said, 'but dear God, why did it have to be at this dreadful cost? What's going to happen after the war? If this ghastly killing goes on what are we going to do for men? There'll be so many women who can't find husbands, so many children without fathers.' She bent her head for a few moments and then began to unlace her boots.

'I'm not being hard, Amy.' Helen said. 'Truly I'm not. We see the cost every day, don't we? But maybe one good thing can come out of it. They'll have to give women jobs, all kinds of jobs, and then they'll have to give us the vote and some political power and then maybe we can stop this ever happening again.'

Amy looked up and smiled. 'Perhaps you'll be the first woman prime minister, Helen.'

Helen laughed. 'I can't ever see that happening, a woman prime minister, but you never know.'

Amy yawned and stretched. 'It was so nice to see my father, but I'm glad to be back.'

'Didn't he try to persuade you to stay in England? My parents are always hinting.'

Amy shook her head. 'Not really. He'd like me to, but he knows I won't.'

'There are some letters for you,' Helen took them out of her drawer.

There were three. One was from Johnny; she knew his hand now. No doubt this was the letter he had told her about when he was trying to locate her. She read it briefly and put it away in her bedside table drawer. The other two were from Dan; she knew his hand too. She felt a faint reluctance to open them and put them aside until Helen had gone.

'I'm on duty in five minutes,' Helen said. 'I expect you'll be asleep by the time I get back.'

Amy stretched again, straightening her back. 'I need to have a bath and wash my hair. I'm covered in smuts from the train. I hope I haven't picked up anything worse. No little visitors.'

After Helen had gone she had her bath, rubbed her hair dry and combed out the tangles. No lice or fleas, as far as she could see, in spite of being cheek by jowl on the train. She put on her nightdress and got into bed. She picked up Dan's letters and held them in her hand, wondering in a strange way whether the letters themselves, the paper and the envelopes, could convey to her what he was thinking when he wrote them. She wondered if Helen was right and Dan had feelings for her that were more than just friendship. She knew that Johnny had changed her. She was more aware now of such feelings in herself and in others. She was aware that Helen was in love, or nearly in love, with Peter. And she? She was still trying to persuade herself that she wasn't sure, that she could hold back, turn away, retreat. But something was different now. Johnny had kissed her. She felt as if a door inside her had opened, as if a new, unsuspected part of her had come into the light. But it was a light that she was afraid of, a light that might lead to dark, painful places of loss and pain.

The envelopes told her nothing, of course. She smiled wryly at herself. There were so many foolish fancies about now – angels, men who carried lucky charms into battle, men who had told her of their strange little rituals before going over the top. It seemed the real world was so impossibly dreadful that sensible people were falling back into worlds of fantasy.

She opened Dan's letters. They were much the same – his pleasure in seeing her at Christmas, his hopes to see her again. There were no protestations of love but the words again seemed to have a certain warmth, a kind of yearning. Was that for her, she wondered, or just for the past, the way things used to be? He did once say that he missed his sisters, missed the life that was gone. Was that all it was?

She put the letters down. She was fond of Dan and didn't want to hurt him. She realized that she knew more about him than any other man she had ever met. He had told her all about his family. More than that, he shared her world, the world of medicine. Even though he didn't know about her past, they understood each other. In many ways she knew him better than she knew Johnny. Helen was wrong, she was sure. Dan had never approached her in that way.

Helen came back at ten. 'I thought you'd be asleep.'

'Mind going round and round,' Amy said.

Helen undressed and washed and got into bed. 'What's it going round and round about?'

'I saw Johnny in England.'

Helen sat up. 'Amy! How?'

'He wrote to me. He took me to tea at the Ritz.'

'Goodness! How smart! And was he well, has he recovered, was he on his feet?'

'Very much so. You know, I'd never seen him standing up before. It was quite a shock. He's so tall. He's in the Flying Corps now and he's got his wings already.'

Helen's eyes sparkled. 'Tell me all. What happened? Did you see him again?'

Amy laughed. 'You're as bad as my father. Yes, I saw him again. It was absolutely marvellous. He took me flying.'

Helen's mouth dropped open. 'What? In an aeroplane?'

Amy laughed again. 'Of course in an aeroplane. What else?'

'How wonderful! You lucky thing! What was it like?'

'Wonderful is the word. Like nothing I've ever felt before. Out of this world. Being up there, away from everything, being separate from everything, the war seems so stupid, so ridiculous. It's as if you're on another planet. England looked so beautiful, so calm and peaceful.'

Helen looked at her expectantly, waiting for more. 'And are you going to see him again?'

Amy felt a kind of withdrawal, a touch of fear. 'I don't know,' she said quietly. 'Who knows? You know what it's like now.'

Helen lay down and pulled up the covers. 'Yes. I know.'

Amy lay back, looking at the ceiling. 'Are you going to see Peter again?'

'Yes,' Helen said, 'When he comes back to Paris.'

The word 'if' hung in the air.

There was a buzz of excitement the next day. 'What's going on?' Helen asked.

Sister was mysterious. 'Dr Hanfield will tell you all shortly.'

There were three new admissions on the general ward – men with complicated injuries. They had all been scythed down by the same exploding shell and their legs were so peppered with shrapnel it had been impossible to find all the pieces. All three had numerous entry wounds, already suppurating. Amy helped one of the nurses to swab and re-dress them. When they were out of hearing the nurse shook her head. 'They're going to lose their legs for sure,' she said. 'We can't stop the infection without getting the shrapnel out. And even that probably wouldn't save them.'

'It's awful,' Helen said, on the way to lunch. 'Sister says they are all critical. Dr Hanfield has got some of the bits out but she just can't find them all.'

Amy was all too well aware of what would happen. Each piece of shrapnel carried in dirt and mud and bits of filthy clothing. Each piece was a focus of deadly infection. If they were not removed the men had little hope. They were not even men; they were boys with anxious mothers at home waiting for news.

She realized with a kind of shock that she was back again in reality. The time she had spent in England now seemed like the dream; undisturbed sleep, the quiet peace of home, the smells only of lavender furniture polish in the house, and winter bonfires in the gardens. Had she really been flying? Had Johnny really kissed her?

Dr Hanfield came into the dining-room. She tapped a glass with a spoon to gain silence. 'I have some news,' she said. 'I am delighted to tell you that Madame Marie Curie is coming here to the hospital tomorrow with her Rontgen machine. She is going to help us to locate the shrapnel in the three young boys in the ward. It could make all the difference in the world. It could save their lives.'

There was a murmur of excited conversation and Amy looked around her. It seemed that very few of them had ever seen an X-ray photograph before.

'Perhaps you know,' Dr Hanfield went on, 'That Madame Curie takes her machines to the forward hospitals at great risk to herself and has been of enormous help to the surgeons. She has saved many lives. So please give her every welcome and respect.' There was a little outbreak of applause.

'That's amazing,' Helen whispered. 'I hope we get a look at the films. Fancy being able to see someone's bones.'

As she left, Dr Hanfield noticed Amy and smiled. 'Nice to see you back, Amy.'

Amy had seen X-ray photographs before but they were certainly rare here in France. The Rontgen Machines only existed in a few of the larger French hospitals. But she was truly excited at the prospect of perhaps meeting Madame Curie, the woman who had won the Nobel Prize, the only person in the world who possessed a gramme of radium. She had read in a newspaper that when the French Government had decamped to Bordeaux she had taken her precious radium in a lead box to Bordeaux to prevent it from falling into the hands of the Germans, and when Paris seemed safe again, she had brought it back. Meeting her would be a great privilege, a once in a life-time.

The doctors and nurses and most of the staff were waiting in the hall when Madame Curie arrived the next day. She came into the hall with her driver.

'Goodness,' Helen whispered. 'She's so famous and you wouldn't look at her twice, would you?'

Her grey hair was drawn back neatly over pale grey eyes and her clothes were quiet, dark and unremarkable – serviceable clothes and boots for the work she was doing. She smiled and touched hands with Dr Hanfield. Dr Hanfield had warned them all not to shake Madame Curie's hand if they were introduced. Apparently her hands had been damaged during her researches, and were tender. Her driver and some of the men carried in her equipment.

Dr Hanfield led her to the operating theatre and they all watched as the men carried in her Rontgen machine and the baths and chemicals for developing the films.

'You have electricity, I see,' Madame Curie said as she followed them in. 'How convenient. I usually have to take my own dynamo and run it off the car engine.'

The first of the three young soldiers was wheeled in. Dr Hanfield put her head out of the door. 'No one is to come in for the moment,' she said, 'until Madame Curie has taken her pictures.' Amy was about to walk away but Dr Hanfield called to her. 'I shall want you, Amy. We'll need another pair of hands.' Amy was surprised, and delighted, delighted to be in theatre again, and to see such modern equipment being used. She was missing so much, she thought, so much experience, so much learning.

After a while the door opened and Dr Hanfield gestured to the theatre staff to come in. Amy followed them. Madame Curie displayed her films, holding them up to the light, showing the pieces of shrapnel scattered through the muscle. The anaesthetist placed a mask over the young soldier's face, and began the chloroform. 'I want you to hold this dish, Amy,' Dr Hanfield said, 'to take the pieces, and hold the bucket when I irrigate the wounds.' Guided by the films, she removed the first piece of shrapnel, inserting long forceps through the wound, and then inserting a tube to wash out the pus and dirt. 'Hypochlorite solution,' she said. 'Sir Almroth Wright prefers saline. He says that harsh antiseptics can damage the tissue without killing the bacteria, but we'll be on the safe side, I think, for the time being. But things might change. He and Alexander Fleming are working on infection all the time.'

Amy watched, fascinated. The films made it so easy. Without them one could poke about blindly in the wounds and still not find the pieces. A task that had seemed almost impossible was completed in a very short time. At least, she thought, this was one modern invention that could not be used to destroy. One by one the bits of steel dropped into her dish, the dressings applied, and the young soldier taken back to his bed. They worked through the morning and into the afternoon until all three men were free of the killing splinters.

'I think we all need a cup of tea,' Dr Hanfield said. She led them to the dining-room.

Madame Curie was eager to get away. 'I have so much to do,' she said. 'I cannot stay.' After tea they went back to the theatre to help Madame Curie pack up the machinery. Dr Hanfield touched her hand again. 'Thank you so much,' she said. 'It has been wonderful. Those boys have a chance now.'

Madame Curie's eyes filled with tears. 'I hope so,' she said. 'I am glad to help.'

Amy looked at her, at this compassionate woman who looked so ordinary and was so extraordinary. She was one of the great, one of those exclusive few whose name would never die, who had done so much for the greater good of mankind. Madame Curie had already suggested that radium might be used in medicine – might even be able to treat cancer. Amy felt humbled in her presence. She felt a new surge of determination, to get her licence back, to help where she could. Marie Curie had never given up, and neither, she determined, would she.

Some of the men carried the equipment to the door and Amy followed to say goodbye. An officer in uniform was standing just inside the door, his cap in his hand. 'Madame Curie,' he said. He bent down to her and she stopped and smiled and listened to what he was saying so earnestly. She took a notebook out of her pocket and wrote in it. She nodded and patted the officer on his arm. He turned around, and Amy saw with surprise that it was Dan.

Madame Curie left the hospital and Dan looked around him. When he saw Amy his face lit up in a surprised smile and he came quickly towards her. 'Amy!' he said. 'I thought you were in England. How very nice to see you.'

She smiled and took his outstretched hand. 'I've just come back.'

'How is your father?'

She was surprised he knew that her father had been ill. 'He's much better,' she said. 'But how did you know. . . ?'

He grinned. 'Helen writes to Peter, so I get all the news. I've got my spies, you see. I'm keeping track of you. I know what you're doing.'

She looked at him. I hope you don't, she thought. Not everything.

He smiled down at her. 'I'm only joking.'

'What are you doing here?' she said. 'More army business?'

He shook his head. 'Not this time. I heard that Madame Curie was going to be here and I wanted to ask her to come to us. She says she will. If only we had more X-ray machines. It would be infinitely useful. Sometimes it's almost impossible to see what you're doing.' He turned his cap around in his hand. 'I don't suppose it's possible for you to come out tonight?'

'I don't know,' she said. 'I'm off at eight, but I'd have to ask Matron.'

He nodded. 'Could you ask her now? I'll wait.'

Matron sighed but gave her consent. 'Be back by ten, Amy.'

Dan gave a huge grin. 'Well done. I'll pick you up just after eight. We'll go to the same hotel we went to before. I'll get a cab if I have to hold one up like Dick Turpin.' He put on his cap and left the hotel, waving briefly from the street.

He's changed again, she thought. Every time she saw him he looked, not older, but harder, leaner, more predatory. She could hardly remember the fresh-faced young man she had first met. His ears didn't turn pink now when he spoke to her. He was different. We're all changing, she thought. This war is changing us all: Dan becoming stronger, tougher, implacable; Johnny becoming perhaps more reckless. And she? She didn't know. Life now for everyone was a jumble of emotions, of fear, and strength and superhuman courage. Nothing and no one would ever be the same.

'What are you going to wear?' Helen said that evening. 'You can borrow my green dress if you like.'

Amy was sitting in front of the mirror, putting up her hair. 'Thank you, but no. I'll wear my pink thing again.'

Helen leant over her shoulder. 'What are you going to do?'

Amy took two long hairpins out of her mouth. 'What about?'

'You know.'

Amy laughed. 'You're just a little old-fashioned romantic, Helen. I don't have to do anything. They are both just friends.'

'You can fool some of the people all the time,' Helen said. 'You seem to be determined to fool yourself.'

'We have more important things to think about,' Amy said. She took her cloak out of the wardrobe, said goodnight, and walked down the marble staircase to where Dan waited.

The waiter settled them at their table and handed them menus.

'I don't know how they do it,' Dan said, 'producing food like this under these circumstances.'

Amy nodded. 'The French can make anything taste good. It makes one wonder what it would be like in normal times.'

He was studying his menu. 'Perhaps we'll be able to find out one day,' he said.

She glanced at him sharply. It was the second time he had said something like that, something about the future. But he didn't raise his head, didn't look at her.

The waiter came back and they ordered, potage and a Chicken Marengo.

'How were things at home?' he said.

'Lots of shortages, especially anything that has to be imported – sugar, oranges, bananas. There was even a shortage of onions for a while. We used to get the French onion sellers on their bicycles. They've gone now, of course.'

'And how was your father?'

'He's well now, physically at least. But I know he's filled with dread. I can see it in his eyes and hear it in his voice. It's his boys at school, fine boys, seventeen or eighteen years old, and they almost all volunteer as soon as they can, as soon as they leave school. Several of them are already dead. He knows them all so well. He can hardly bear it. It can't do his health any good.'

He put his hand over hers. 'Oh Amy.'

Tears started in her eyes but she blinked them away. 'I'm sorry,' she said. 'Other people have worse things to deal with. I'm just being weak.'

He pressed her hand gently. 'You're just being human, Amy. There's nothing wrong with caring, even though it hurts sometimes. We can't become automata, without feeling. If we lose the ability to care we lose everything and this dreadful evil has won.' His hand on hers felt strong, comforting.

'I know,' she said. He was almost repeating her father's words.

The waiter came with their soup and Dan took his hand away slowly. 'You look very nice,' he said. 'Is that a new dress?'

She looked at him and laughed. 'It's the same one I wore last time.'

He looked sheepish. 'Is it really? I'm afraid I'm not very good at . . . fashion.'

She laughed again and he smiled back. 'You still look very nice.'

'Thank you,' she said. 'We do our best.'

They finished their soup and the waiter brought the chicken, and then a fruit pudding. Dan ate everything before him as if he'd been starved. The waiter cleared the table and brought their coffee.

'Wonderful,' Dan said. 'Real food.' He stirred sugar into his coffee, looking at her. 'Amy?' he said. 'What do you intend to do after the war?'

She was taken by surprise and for a moment didn't know what to say. 'I don't know,' she said eventually. 'How can anyone know? I'm just getting through every day.'

'Don't you have any dreams? Anything you really want to do?'

He seemed so calm, so reliable and sensible that she was almost tempted to tell him, but that wouldn't do any good. He couldn't help her. 'I'm not going to think about it,' she said. 'I don't know what the world will be like then.' She didn't want to talk about herself. 'What about you?'

'Back to peacetime medicine,' he said. His voice was filled with enthusiasm. 'It's going to get better and better, Amy. We've learnt so much already in this dreadful war – so much about surgery and infection and hygiene and nutrition. Science is moving on.'

She smiled. 'You sound like my father,' she said. 'He's mad about science.'

'I'd like to meet him,' he said. 'He sounds like a man after my own heart.'

She smiled briefly and looked down, away from him, saying nothing.

'And, of course,' he said, 'I'd like to marry and have a family one day.'

She glanced at him, but he was looking at his cup, stirring his coffee again. When he looked up his expression was bland and casual. 'How is Helen? Peter will certainly ask me.'

'She's very well.' She was relieved that he had changed the subject. 'She's a great girl, a good friend. Still very much a suffragist, though that's been shelved for the time being.'

'I think,' he said, 'Peter is in love with her.'

'Is he?' she said, warily. Apparently he hadn't changed the subject after all.

'Has Helen said anything?' he said. 'Is she in love with him?'

'I don't know,' she said. 'Why? Has he asked you to find out?'

He looked embarrassed. 'No, of course not. I just wondered.' He was silent for a moment, and then he said, 'I'm not sure it's a good idea, in a war like this one, to say too much, to get too involved.' He paused again. 'I'd hate to think that I might leave a wife, perhaps a child on the way, and not be there to look after them. I couldn't do that.' He looked at her, into her eyes. 'Do you understand?'

'Yes,' she said. 'I do. I quite agree with you.'

He nodded slowly. His expression seemed to her to be a strange mixture of relief and disappointment. What had he expected her to say? 'Helen will do what she thinks best,' she said. 'She is sensible and independent. I would trust her decisions.'

'Of course.' He looked at his watch. 'It's time I got you back to the hospital or Matron will be after my blood.'

The cab was waiting outside. He helped her in and followed her. They clopped back to the hospital. 'I hope you won't tell Helen about that conversation,' he said. 'Peter must make his own decisions, too.'

'Of course,' she said. 'I understand. I won't say anything.'

He handed her out at the door. 'I won't come in,' he said. 'I must be on my way back. Thank you so much for the evening, Amy. I'll keep in touch.' She held out her hand. He took it and held it in both of his. He smiled down at her, then turned abruptly and got back into the cab.

'Gare du Nord,' he said to the driver, and the cab clopped away down the street.

She went into the hotel and stood for a moment inside the door. She imagined him reaching the station, taking the train packed with men, getting off the train into an army lorry, bumping along those ravaged roads, reaching the field hospital. She saw him, masked and gowned, operating while shells and bullets screamed around them.

She walked wearily up the great staircase, tired out by the evening, by the strain of Dan's conversation, by unspoken emotions, so many things not said. Were all those remarks about marriage and relation-ships directed at Helen and Peter? She didn't think so. Dan seemed to be giving her some kind of message. She had to admit now that Helen was probably right and Dan did have feelings for her. But he was also a man in control, who would say nothing until he thought the time was right. He wasn't facing her with decisions or declarations. He was content, for the moment, to be a friend. He had not attempted to kiss her. He was not Johnny.

Helen was asleep. Amy was glad about that. She wasn't ready to give the expected account of the evening. She could be flippant tomor-row.

Amy knew that she would never forget that April as long as she lived. The English newspapers were late, but got to them eventually. Her father's letters reported the same things – Zeppelin raids on Newcastle, German aircraft bombing the East Anglian towns, civil-ians dead, women and children. Nowhere was safe any more. Then, on 22 April, the Germans unleashed chlorine gas on the totally unpre-pared Allied troops in the trenches. The reports came in. The foul cloud had rolled over the trenches, the men had screamed and clutched their throats, coughed up blood and tissue and died in agony.

'Those Germans signed the Hague Commission in 1907,' Helen shouted in rage. 'They agreed never to use poisonous weapons.'

Amy blanched, unable to reply.

Soon the men began to come in, blinded, coughing up their lungs, dying. Amy had thought that she had seen everything, but she had never seen anything like this.

Then the men came in from the battle for Hill 60 and for some reason there were more abdominal wounds than they had seen before. Amy ached to get into the theatre, to anastomose the shattered intestines, remove tattered organs, make the necessary colostomies to save their lives. The surgeons worked hour after hour, day and night. Often Amy was asked to help in theatre, to count swabs, carry away dishes of amputated tissue, apply dressings to dreadful wounds. She watched the surgeons, missing nothing.

Then, at the end of April, came the disastrous news from Gallipoli, where the ANZACS were dying in their thousands, in a hell of heat, flies, dysentery, skin sores and, of course, the relentless Turkish bullets.

May, then, and Helen running into their room with a French newspaper. 'Look Amy. Oh look!' The Lusitania, a civilian liner on its way to America, had been sunk by German submarines. Over a thousand innocent people were drowned, including more than a hundred Americans who weren't in the war at all.

The months ground by, one wearied day after another. The wounded poured in, shot, shelled, gassed; with typhoid, typhus, shell-shocked, exhausted. Time seemed to stand still, unchanging, and yet it flew by; summer, autumn again and the trees turning gold in the boulevards. Neuve Chapelle, Ypres, Loos. One useless battle after another, and thousands dead for nothing, Nurse Edith Cavell, put up against a wall and shot as a spy by the Germans, a woman, a nurse. Christmas again, and New Year's Day, 1916; the effort to be cheerful for the men, knowing that there was no end in sight.

Amy dressed, ready for the day, for the endless chores and forced cheerfulness. For a moment she sat back on her bed, her eyes closed. She felt suddenly chilled, as if her blood had turned to ice. She did not want to feel anything, ever again, no pity, no compassion. Feeling was too painful. She could not. They had to go on, day after day, wading through one horror after another, hoping in a kind of foolish fantasy that one day it would end.

'Are you all right, Amy?' Helen sat on the bed beside her.

'No,' Amy said. 'I'm not. I feel as if my heart has been taken out of my body. I don't think I will ever feel anything again.'

Helen took her hand. 'You need someone to put it back,' she said. 'You need someone to love you and care for you and put back all the feeling that you've lost. I don't think I could go on if it wasn't for Peter.

142

Even though I don't see him very often I know he's there, thinking about me.'

'I don't know how you do it, Helen,' she said. 'I don't know how you can risk it – loving someone like that.'

'It's worth the risk,' Helen said. 'It keeps me alive. Let it go, Amy. Take the risk.'

There was a knock at the door and Helen went to answer it.

'There's someone downstairs for Miss Osborne,' the maid said. 'It's an officer.'

'An officer,' Helen said, smiling. 'I wonder which one it is. I wonder which one you want it to be.'

Amy shook her head at her. She went to the dressing-table and checked the neatness of her hair and straightened her cuffs.

CHAPTER ELEVEN

1916

WHICH one was it? Both of them wrote to her from time to time. Dan's letters were the same as ever, warm but non-committal. Johnny's were full of flying, of new aircraft, of sorties over enemy lines and being shot at from the trenches. Sometimes she could hardly bear to read them. He didn't mention the kiss. She wondered if he even remembered it.

She walked down the staircase. Johnny, tall and in his Flying Corps uniform, stood out among the uniforms below. He was standing with his back to her, looking out of the window. She felt a glow that rose through her body and flushed her cheeks. It's been a year, she thought. I haven't seen him for a year. For a year she had wondered every day whether he was alive. She had waited every day for a letter, telling her that he was well. His letters had arrived at irregular intervals, sometimes two or three together. They were always full of life. He even sounded as if he were enjoying himself. She had wondered often whether she would ever see him again, not because he was dead, God forbid, but because he may not want to see her, because the kiss might have been one of those passing things that happen in wartime, impulsive and meaningless. The memory of the day he took her flying had, for some time, seemed unreal, like a dream, but unlike a dream, retaining clearly every detail. She paused for a moment on the stairs. She just wanted to look at him, to reassure herself that he was really there, and to compose herself. He had not seen her yet.

She went on down the stairs and walked to him across the hall. 'Hello Johnny.'

He turned to her, a smile lighting his face. 'Amy!' She held out her hand and he took it in both of his and held it, enclosed in his own. He looked down at her, laughter in his eyes. 'You do remember me, don't you?'

She laughed back up at him. 'Of course I do.'

'I'm very glad to hear it.' He looked at her in silence for a moment. 'It's been a long time. Too long.'

She nodded. After a few moments she gently took her hand away, conscious of the many pairs of eyes around them. The hall was thronged, nurses and men and visitors and a man from the post bringing in letters and parcels.

He grinned at her. 'A bit like Piccadilly Circus.'

She nodded and smiled. 'Even more crowded than that. It's lovely to see you, Johnny.'

'I'm sorry to just appear like this,' he said. 'I couldn't let you know I was coming. All a bit of a rush. I'm just glad you were here.' He grinned. 'Not out with your ambulance rescuing some other admirer.'

'It doesn't matter,' she said. 'It's so lovely to see you.' She led him to one of the sofas. 'How long have you got? How long will you be in Paris?'

He made a rueful face. 'About half an hour. I've got a new posting. I'm between trains.' He was looking at her intently as if trying to remember the details of her face. 'I wanted to see you, even if it's only for a few minutes. Do you realize I haven't seen you for nearly a year?'

'Yes,' she said, 'I know.' She glanced around at the busy hall. It was impossible to have more than a casual conversation, or one that appeared to be casual. She looked into his eyes, looking for any sign of strain, of that slow, gradual breaking down that so many of the men carried in their eyes, the wearing down of constant danger and stress. It did not seem to be there. 'How are you?'

'I'm fine,' he said. 'Enjoying myself, actually. Flying's still the greatest thing in the world. I'm flying a BE2. It's a nice machine and the observer has a machine-gun, but I think there is something better in the pipeline – single seaters with guns for the pilots.'

Amy chose to ignore the guns. She didn't want to think about it. She nodded. 'It was wonderful wasn't it, that day? I never thought I'd be going up in an aeroplane.'

'So you remember?' His look settled briefly on her mouth. 'All of it?'

'Of course I do,' she said. 'All of it.'

He looked around him and laughed, a short, humourless laugh. 'It's like a bear garden here. I can't even touch you.'

She blushed and glanced around her. 'No.' One of the sisters walked by, starched apron rustling. One of the patients, balanced on crutches, winked at her.

'How have you been?' he said. 'What have you been doing?'

She gestured with her hand around the hall. 'Just the same, day after day. It never stops, does it? It never shows any sign of coming to any kind of end. I don't know how long the men can go on taking this – this carnage.'

'What about you?' He touched her hand again briefly. 'Can you go on taking it?'

'Of course,' she said. 'I'll go on till the end, as long as I'm needed. We all will.'

He took out his cigarette case. 'Do you mind if I smoke?'

'No,' she said. 'Nearly all the men smoke.' A year, she thought, and we can't say anything that we really want to say.

He lit his cigarette and leant back against the sofa. 'I think about that day a lot,' he said. 'When I'm up there on my way home over our territory and there's nothing interesting going on. It's a favourite memory.'

'All anybody has now is memories,' she said. 'Normal living has gone. When will it end? How long. . . ?'

'God knows.' He drew deeply on his cigarette. 'You can see it all from up there. You can see the shells exploding, men running and men falling and bodies hurled into the air. The noise is incredible, even over the engine. Sometimes you can even feel it, the plane shaking and vibrating. Sometimes you think that everybody down there must be dead. You wonder how anyone could survive it. I can fly away from it when I've done my job. Those men have got to stay there.'

'I'm glad you're flying, then,' she said. 'At least you can sleep in a bed at night.'

He said nothing and for the first time she saw a fleeting glimpse of that look in the eye, that horror, that wasteland. He looked around for an ashtray and stubbed out his cigarette. He wouldn't fear death, she knew that. For him and probably all of them, there could be worse things than death. A month ago they had admitted a pilot, rescued from his crashed, exploding aircraft and horribly burned. She dragged her mind away from it. Johnny seemed to be looking into some kind of empty distance. He lit another cigarette.

She smiled brightly. 'Look at us,' she said. 'We've only got a few minutes and we're talking about the war.'

'I'm sorry,' he said, and smiled the smile that so touched her. 'No more war. I'm due some leave, probably in June. I don't suppose there's any chance of you getting leave then too? I want to see you in England again. We could go out, have some fun. We might even be able to go out in the evening on our own. I believe the insistence on chaperons has gone by the board.'

'That would be wonderful,' she said. 'I've almost forgotten what fun is. Send me some dates, and I'll try.'

He glanced at his watch and stubbed out his cigarette in the ashtray. 'I'll have to go, Amy. Write to me.' He looked down into her eyes. 'And promise me you'll be in England in June.' They stood up together and he solemnly shook her hand and laughed. 'Very formal,' he said. 'I'm guarding your reputation, you see.'

She had a sudden image of the aircraft she and Helen had seen, no one knowing whether they were friend or enemy.

She put her hand on his arm. 'Johnny, have you got something on your aircraft now, some sign, so that everybody knows you're British? We've heard of our aircraft being shot at from our own lines.'

He grinned. 'We've got a big bright circle of red, white and blue. We've had it for some time. The Germans have got a big black cross. Appropriate, don't you think?'

'That's one worry less then. But I see you're carrying a pistol.'

He nodded. 'A Webley. Just in case.'

In case of what, she wondered. She didn't have to voice the question, it was written on her face.

'Don't worry so much,' he said. 'I'll be fine. And if I'm downed, the Germans are being very decent to pilots.' He glanced at his watch again. 'I've got to go.'

'Look after yourself,' she said.

He put on his cap and looked down at her, and then, very briefly, touched her face. He left then, striding out into the street, and away.

She hurried back into the ward to help with the dressings. Dr

Hanfield was in the ward talking to Sister.

'Amy,' she said, 'could you come to my office this evening after dinner? There's something I want to talk to you about.'

Amy's heart missed a beat. Now what? Surely Dr Hanfield couldn't have found out. If she had, what would she do about it? Make her leave? Amy tried to read her face. She didn't look disturbed or annoyed, but she wouldn't show her feelings. Maybe it was something else.

'Of course,' she said. 'I'll be there.'

She met Helen for lunch in the dining-room, worried now about Dr Hanfield; thinking and worrying about Johnny. It was busy, as usual, the maids bustling about with trays and plates.

'Meat and potato pie today,' Helen said. 'And carrots and swede. It's very good.'

The good smell of the food was underlined by that inescapable odour of the hospital. The staff seemed to carry it about with them, no matter how much they bathed or washed their clothes. Amy sat down and Helen looked at her, bright enquiry on her face.

'Well?' she said.

Amy couldn't control her broad smile. 'It was Johnny.'

'I know that.' Helen laughed. 'Everybody knows that. He caused quite a stir. Apparently Dr H. and Sister spotted him before you went down and said hello. He's one of their great successes.'

The maid brought Amy's lunch.

'Well?' Helen said again.

'He was just passing through,' Amy said. 'He only had a few minutes.'

Helen looked at her in silence for a moment, then she shook her head, eyes cast up. 'Most women would give their eye teeth.'

Amy laughed. 'Not in public they wouldn't. The place was seething. Dozens of pairs of eyes.'

'In private then.'

Amy ate some of her pie. 'This is good.'

'In private then,' Helen persisted.

'He wants to meet me in England.' Amy said. 'He's got leave in June. I don't know if I can get leave then.'

'You can try,' Helen said. 'God knows we're all due for it. I want to meet up with Peter. . . .'

Two nurses crossed the crowded room and sat down to share their table.

'Talk to you later,' Helen mouthed.

After dinner Amy went to Dr Hanfield's office. She tried to prepare herself for what she presumed was the coming embarrassing discussion about her future. Would she be thrown out, or would Dr Hanfield believe her, accept that Bulford was a misogynist and a power-mad bully. And how had she found out? She supposed, wearily, that she would have been found out sooner or later. She would just have to face it out.

Dr Hanfield smiled as she came in. 'Sit down, Amy.' Amy sat down in front of her desk. It reminded her sickeningly of sitting in front of the General Medical Council. 'I wonder,' Dr Hanfield said, 'whether you would be prepared to take on some more duties in theatre. Two of the nurses are leaving – problems at home, I believe, and there are staff needing leave.'

Amy stared at her trying to disguise her surprise and relief.

'You do seem to have a talent for this kind of work,' Dr Hanfield went on, 'And I'm sure you could do the job. What do you think?'

Amy wanted to lean across the desk and hug her, give three rousing cheers, dance around the room. 'I'd be very happy to do that,' she said calmly.

'Good. I thought you would.' Dr Hanfield paused. 'You do realize that it would mean handling other parts of the body, severed limbs, perhaps?'

Amy nodded. 'I know. That wouldn't be a problem at all. I'd like to do it very much.'

'Excellent.' Dr Hanfield smiled, a tired, weary smile. 'We'll start you in a few days then. We'll have to give you some training – how to scrub up, sterilize instruments, do swab counts, that sort of thing. We'll see how you get on, what you can do. Is that all right?'

Any nodded. 'Of course.'

'Thank you, Amy.' Dr Hanfield looked relieved.

Amy stood up. 'Thank you, Dr Hanfield. I shall look forward to it.'

Outside the door she gave a huge sigh of relief, and not only relief. Not by a long way. She was going to be in theatre again. She would be part of it again, eyes and ears open to observe and learn every new fact and technique that came along. And there were many. Hideous though it was, the injuries and diseases that raged through a war were an unequalled stimulus to medical advance and change. She made her way slowly up the stairs. New things were happening all the time. American doctors had enormously improved blood transfusion techniques and they were already being given in some of the Regimental Aid Posts or Clearing Stations. One of their patients had been transfused at an Aid Post and it had saved his life. There was a tetanus antitoxin, a typhoid vaccine, Madame Curie with her X-rays. So many things. Now perhaps she'd be able to keep up with at least some of the changes. She might even be able to read some of the medical journals without arousing suspicion. It really was a huge change for the better, and a huge joy to her. And today, she had seen Johnny. Her heart began to lift.

Helen was waiting in the hall. 'What did she want?' she said.

Amy took her arm. 'Let's go upstairs.' They sat down on their beds. 'She wants to know if I'll do more work in theatre. Apparently they're a bit short of staff.'

'Do you really want to do that?' Helen looked doubtful. 'I'm not sure I would, handling all those things. It's bad enough on the wards.'

'I want to do it.' Amy tried not to sound too enthusiastic. 'It'll be much more interesting.'

'It'll be a change, anyway.' Helen stared out of the window. She looked and sounded unsettled, restless.

'Are you getting sick of it, Helen? Or just dreadfully all round tired? Are you thinking of giving up?'

Helen shook her head vigorously. 'No, of course not. It's just. . . .' The words seemed to burst out of her. 'I want to see Peter. We hardly ever see each other. It's not fair!' Her mouth twisted. 'It isn't fair for anybody, is it?'

'No, it isn't. Perhaps he can get leave at the same time as you. 'Amy thought immediately of Johnny. 'Why don't you get him to send you the date, and then we'll have a go at persuading Matron.'

'Perhaps,' Helen said. 'But it's never enough, a few days now and again. I want to be with him all the time.' Her eyes filled with tears. 'We're going to get engaged, Amy.'

'Oh, Helen, how lovely!' Amy moved over and sat beside her and took her hand. 'Congratulations. I should say that to Peter really, shouldn't I, and wish you every happiness? Have you told your family?'

'Not exactly.' Helen smiled and dried her tears. 'Peter wants to speak to my father first. He's a bit old-fashioned – Peter, I mean. I do hope they like him, and I hope his parents like me, but I'd marry him anyway.'

'There's nothing wrong with being a bit old-fashioned,' Amy said. 'Keeping up the standards. I'm sure your parents will love him, and his will adore you. It'll be wonderful.'

'What about you and Johnny?' Helen said eagerly. 'What are you going to do?'

'I really don't know.' Amy looked away from Helen's eager face. 'We haven't got that far. We're just friends.'

'No you're not,' Helen said. 'Or he wouldn't have come to see you.'

Amy sighed. It was all so easy in Helen's eyes. You fell in love and you got married. There was no problem. 'I just don't know, Helen,' she said. 'I hardly know him really. I don't really know how he feels.'

Helen smiled. 'I think you do. You just won't let yourself admit it.'

Amy sighed. 'Perhaps you're right.' But there are problems, she thought. So many problems.

Amy started her work in theatre. She helped the surgeons and the sisters into their gowns and gloves, she sterilized instruments, she held bowls to take the shattered parts of the human frame that had to be discarded, she carried away severed limbs and soaked, stinking swabs. All the time she watched and remembered, and she obtained permission to read the medical journals. She began to feel alive again.

February came, and the battle for Verdun. They watched and worked in horror as the new batches of wounded arrived, many of them burned, sometimes beyond recognition. 'The Germans are using flame-throwers,' Dr Hanfield said. 'They've got these ghastly machines that burn them where they stand.' Amy spent day after day in theatre, watching the surgeons clean up the burns as well as they could, removing dead tissue, sometimes down to the bone. Infection raged through the burns and many of the men died of toxic shock.

Alongside the others Amy laboured through the days. Now and again when staff shortages were at their worst she was allowed to assist Dr Hanfield. To scrub up, to handle the instruments again, was a satisfaction that went deeper than even she had anticipated. Coming back into theatre after the months away was like coming home. She had that feeling of utter contentment, knowing that she was in her rightful place. She had missed medicine as one might miss a lover and the reconciliation was deep and true. She lay awake in bed at night, the old resolution rising more surely. She would get it back. She would.

But she had another love. She wanted Johnny with the same yearning. She wanted his arms around her. She wanted to rest her head on his broad shoulder, on the shining wings on his breast. She wanted his smile and his fearless optimism and his boundless energy. She couldn't answer the question as she tried to get to sleep. Could she have them both, or would she have to make a dreadful, painful choice?

A letter arrived from Johnny. 'I've got three days in England,' he wrote, 'starting on 20 June. Promise me that you'll be there. Tell your matron that if she doesn't give you leave I'll come after her in my BE2.'

Amy bearded Matron in her office. Matron sighed and shuffled her papers and consulted her roster but in the end she said yes. 'I hear that Helen wants to go too,' she said. 'We can't spare you both at the same time. Helen will have to go when you come back.' After a flurry of letters they both managed to organize their dates.

'I'm a bit disappointed,' Helen said. 'I wanted you to be there when I got engaged.'

'I'd rather be there when you get married,' Amy said, 'If leave is going to be rationed like this.'

Helen hung a calendar up in their room and crossed off each day when they went to bed. 'I'll have to get some clothes,' she said dreamily. 'I can't turn up to Peter's parents in a shabby uniform. I shall go to Woolands in Knightsbridge and get something really nice.'

'Good idea.' Amy was reminded of her own lack of wardrobe. The clothes she had left behind were so utilitarian. Johnny had never seen her in really nice clothes. If she were going to see him, certainly lunch and perhaps dine with him, she would need something to wear. Her own battered uniform still wouldn't go down very well in London restaurants. The very thought was cheering – something feminine and pretty and something with colour. How she missed colour, after the endless khaki and dark blue and grey. Just to see pastel pink and green and pale blue and lilac would be a tonic. She had been given a week's leave, so she would have a day or two before Johnny arrived. She could shop, have her hair done, have a manicure. . . .

Helen interrupted her daydreams. 'What are you going to do about these letters from Dan?' she said. 'They still keep coming.'

'I don't know.' They had brought the post up with them and a letter from Dan was lying on Amy's bed. 'There isn't any harm in writing to him, is there?' she said. 'Lots of women at home are writing to soldiers, even ones they don't know. It's a link with home.'

'I think you'll have to tell him about Johnny,' Helen said. 'Peter said he talks about you. Quite fondly, apparently.'

'There isn't anything to tell yet, Helen. Anyway, Dan told me very carefully that he didn't want to get involved with anyone until the war is over. He's not interested in that way.' Helen merely smiled and shrugged.

Amy arrived home in England on a warm, sunny day. Her father hugged her with delight. 'You look well, Amy. Tired, but well.'

'I think I could sleep for a week,' she said.

'You can do that if you want to. Your room's all ready.'

'Johnny's coming in a few days,' she said. 'I want to do some shopping.'

He smiled. 'I thought he might be.'

After dinner they walked to the top of St Martin's Hill. 'Look,' her father said, 'you can see the grounds of the Crystal Palace from here and it's all of three miles away.'

I've flown over that, she thought. I've seen it from the air. Johnny will soon be here.

That night she looked at herself in the mirror in her bedroom. She was thinner than she used to be. Her old clothes wouldn't fit her now. Her hair needed the attentions of a good hairdresser – she would leave it long so that she could put it up, but have it trimmed a little, and a really good wash and a rinse with camomile. Her hands needed a manicure and lots of soothing hand cream. All that washing had roughened them. I need everything, she thought, from the skin outwards, new underclothes, a coat and skirt and a hat, an afternoon dress, a dress for dining, new shoes. She was going to enjoy herself.

She went to town the next day and toured the shops, D.H. Evans and Selfridges and Woolands, revelling in the colours and the fine fabrics. In D.H. Evans she held a silk petticoat up to her face. The softness and smoothness were an almost forgotten and sensuous delight after two years of cotton and rough linen and worsted. She bought a fine cream linen summer coat and skirt and a brown felt hat, a lilac silk afternoon dress and a black taffeta dinner dress. Then she went to Dunlops and bought a pipe for her father. She went to Savory and Moore's to buy some scented toilet soap. She had almost managed to forget the war until she heard an army officer buying some morphine. I'm not going to think about it she thought. Just for a few days, I'm not going to think about it.

The next day a telegram arrived from Johnny: *Can you meet me tomorrow for lunch? The Ritz. One p.m. Johnny.*

The Ritz again, she thought. Thank goodness she'd been shopping. She telegraphed back: *Yes.*

'Johnny?' her father asked and she nodded.

'He wants to meet me in Town tomorrow. You don't mind, do you, Father? He's only got a couple of days.'

'Of course not, my dear. I'll have your company for a day or two after that.'

She walked down Piccadilly the next day, remembering the last time she had met him here, when she almost turned back. Now she had been drawn into a relationship that she was almost afraid of, but she knew now she couldn't resist. The thought that she was going to see him now, in a few moments, made her almost tremble.

He was waiting for her in the hotel, looking splendid in his uniform. No gun this time, she noticed. He came to her at once and stood very close, holding her hand and looking down at her. 'Hello, Amy.'

'Hello, Johnny.' For a few seconds they looked at each other, not speaking, until she became aware again of the other people moving around them and moved away a little.

'It's so lovely to see you,' she said. Such a trite remark, she thought. She had longed to see him and all she could do was to say that. She should be able to throw her arms around him. Chaperons may have been dispensed with, but the restraints were still there. He took her hand, though, as they walked into the restaurant. The waiter settled them at a table.

'You look wonderful,' he said. 'You've done something to your hair.'

'A little,' she said. 'It's nice to do a few frivolous things again.'

He ordered champagne. 'Not quite *de rigueur* for lunch,' he said, 'but

I feel in a champagne mood.'

Over lunch he talked about flying, as if he were just doing it for fun. She almost told him about Helen's engagement; he had met Helen at the hospital, but then she didn't want to talk about engagements.

'I will have to leave you after lunch,' he said. 'My mother has arranged a dinner party for the family and half the county.'

'I expect she wants to show you off,' Amy said. 'She must be very proud of you.'

'She's glad to see me home,' he said. He took a small box out of his pocket. 'I thought you might like to have this.'

She opened the box. Inside, on a silk cushion, was a brooch, a small replica of his wings in gold, with a diamond at the centre. 'It's beautiful,' she said. 'I love it. Thank you so much, Johnny.'

'I thought you might like it.'

'I shall treasure it.'

After lunch he took her to the station in a cab. 'I'm sorry to leave you so soon,' he said, 'but I'll see you tomorrow. I'll pick you up from home in the car. About ten.'

He arrived promptly the next day. She brought him into the house to see her father.

'Hello, sir,' Johnny said. 'I hope you are keeping well.'

'Very well, thank you. All the better for having Amy at home.'

Johnny smiled. 'I quite agree, sir.'

'Let's hope you will all be home for good soon.'

'Yes, sir. We all hope that.'

Her father came to the door to see them off. 'Enjoy your day,' he said.

Johnny started the car and they drew away. 'Where are we going?' she said.

He touched her hand briefly. 'I'm taking you home to meet my mother.'

CHAPTER TWELVE

1916

THE house came into view at the end of the drive, much as she had imagined it. It was large and rambling and settled among the lawns and trees with the serenity of old age. She thought she could recognize the additions that had been made through the years – a bit of Jacobean, Queen Anne and certainly mid-Victorian – but melded by the years into a charming mellow whole. She smiled to herself. It could only be an English country house. She could understand why his family would cling to it, why they kept to their traditional ways, why they didn't want anything to change.

'It's a lovely house,' she said.

'Been in the family for a few hundred years.' Johnny drew up in a crunch of gravel.

The door opened and the butler came out on to the porch.

'Hello, Barnes,' Johnny said. 'All well?'

'Yes, sir.' He held the door open for them. 'Good afternoon, miss. Her ladyship is waiting in the drawing-room, sir.'

He took Amy's coat and she glanced around her. The beamed entrance hall, perhaps the original part of the house, would have been warm and welcoming if she hadn't been slightly apprehensive. Johnny's ancestors, she supposed they were, looked down at her from the walls; unchanging, unbroken continuity. She was not, she thought, apprehensive about the woman she was about to meet; she wasn't afraid of anyone. If she could face the thought of meeting the Germans, she could face Johnny's mother. She was apprehensive about the situation, about the influence his mother would undoubtedly have, one way or the other. She was also worried that the coming social exchange might prove difficult. She was not used to this any more. Some of the old social rules had begun to seem more and more foolish and exaggerated. She was used now to the very lowest, most primitive situations that anyone could be in, to nerves stripped raw, grunted exchanges and strangled cries. That she could be judged now by some casual word or minor action seemed unreal. She hoped that her impatience with traditional social niceties would not show. Lady Maddox knew nothing about her – thankfully.

The butler showed them in. Lady Maddox was standing by her chair, her hands clasped in the long skirt of a grey silk afternoon dress. She was small, smaller than Amy, but she held herself so ramrod straight that she was still imposing. Amy determined not to be intimidated. This little woman lived in a different world, one where Amy was no longer at home, where perhaps she had never been at home. She met Lady Maddox's direct gaze.

'Mother,' Johnny said, 'may I introduce Miss Osborne. Amy, this is my mother, Lady Maddox.'

Lady Maddox did not offer to shake hands. She indicated an upright chair. 'Please sit down, Miss Osborne. Johnny, would you ring for tea?'

Amy sat. Lady Maddox looked at her from guarded grey eyes. 'I believe that I have to thank you for saving my son's life.'

'Twice,' Johnny said.

She inclined her head. 'Twice.'

Amy smiled. 'I was very glad to be able to do it.'

Lady Maddox sat down and regarded her carefully. 'It must be very difficult for you young women.' Her lips compressed in an expression perhaps of puzzlement, or perhaps of distaste. 'The things you have to do now. Things you have certainly not been brought up to do.'

Oh dear, Amy thought. There isn't much doubt about her opinions. 'We live in difficult times,' she said.

The butler brought in the tea. Lady Maddox poured it out into delicate china cups, a far cry, Amy thought, from the tin mugs and thick cups and plates she was now used to. The butler handed it round. 'Thank you, Barnes,' Lady Maddox said, and he left the room. 'Yes,' she went on, 'we have all had to make sacrifices. Several of our servants have enlisted and two of them, sadly, have already lost their lives. So we are very short-handed. My elder son tells me that he has had to employ two women on the home farm. They belong to the Women's Defence Relief Corps, apparently.' She pronounced the words in capital letters. 'Whatever that may be. Two young women from the East End of London.' She made it sound like the end of the earth.

'He tells me they are doing very good work,' Johnny said. 'Women are doing amazing things now, Mother. I think they're splendid.'

His mother glanced at him and then back at Amy, a look of quick suspicion, of interrogation, and thinly disguised disapproval. 'One hopes,' she said, 'that the young women will go back to their normal lives and duties at home when the war is over. I'm sure they will be very glad to do so. Such things can surely not be tolerated for ever.'

Amy glanced at Johnny, but he just smiled. She would not pretend to agree. 'I think perhaps some things have changed for ever,' she said.

Lady Maddox sat up even straighter. 'I trust not, Miss Osborne. I think that well-brought-up girls will be thankful not to have to see – not to have to do these things. One hopes it will all be forgotten.'

It isn't any good opposing her, Amy thought. She could not, or would not, understand what was happening. She glanced around the room, at the marble fireplace, the heavy hangings, the furniture of such varied periods that it must have been passed down in the family for generations. This woman was fixed here, part of the house, part of the past. She would regard it as her sacred duty to keep things as they were. She would not change.

Lady Maddox smiled at her, a wintry smile. 'I don't think I know your father, Miss Osborne? What does he do?'

'He is a schoolmaster,' Amy said. 'He teaches science at a boy's school in Bromley, where we live.'

Lady Maddox raised her eyebrows. 'Science? Not the classics, then? I would have thought that he would teach the classics.'

Amy smiled. She could, she thought, have predicted this attitude, that Greek and Latin were more fitting for a gentleman's education. What would a gentleman have to do with science?

'He thinks that science is the way of the future,' she said. 'That it is something that people should think about and understand.'

Lady Maddox shrugged. 'I should think that those things could safely be left to the tradesmen.' She picked up her cup and looked at Amy over the rim.

Amy could see Johnny raising his eyebrows at her from across the room. He shook his head briefly, but she couldn't let this go by. 'Science has given us so many wonderful things, Lady Maddox,' she said. 'Steam trains and electric light and motor cars and aeroplanes.'

'Especially aeroplanes,' Johnny said.

Amy continued, 'And all the advances in medicine and surgery.'

Lady Maddox frowned, and carefully put down her cup. 'That is something I prefer not to think about.'

'It saved Johnny's life,' Amy said.

Lady Maddox looked across at her son and for the first time Amy saw a real emotion in her eyes – a deep and horrified fear. She is human after all, Amy thought. She might be set in this aspic of out-moded habits and values but underneath that she is just like everyone else; she is a loving and frightened mother. She felt a deep connection with her. Deep down, suppressed and unacknowledged, they both had the same raw fear.

Lady Maddox looked back at her, that fleeting look now gone, controlled. 'Do you have brothers or sisters?'

'No,' Amy said. 'I am an only child.'

'And your mother?'

'My mother died a long time ago, when I was a child.'

'I am sorry.'

For a few moments there was silence. I am being interrogated, Amy thought. Johnny's mother would surely not be like this with girls that she knew, girls who fitted into the pattern. She would be smiling and relaxed, knowing how these girls lived, what they thought and felt and expected. Johnny had brought a possible cuckoo into the nest and she was worried and suspicious. A schoolmaster who taught science? What kind of a man was that? After all, he could well be a revolutionary.

The thought of her father being a revolutionary made her smile and she hurriedly changed the subject. 'You have a beautiful garden,' she said. 'A perfect English garden.'

Lady Maddox relaxed visibly. 'Yes, it is one of my greatest interests. Perhaps Johnny will show you around it before you go.'

The door opened and Johnny's father came in. He came directly to Amy and took her hand. 'Miss Osborne,' he said. 'How very nice to see you again.' His presence changed the atmosphere, made it lighter, more positive. He took a cup of tea and sat down next to her. 'How are you? Are you still working in Paris? Still saving lives?'

'Yes,' Amy said. 'It's all much the same.' There was a guarded look in his eyes and he glanced briefly at his wife and then back at Amy. She understood at once. He didn't want any real, factual discussion or description of the war or of the horror, or of the wounded. 'Paris is a lovely city,' she said. 'Very well planned with the wide boulevards and pretty gardens. And the people are very' – she almost said brave – 'pleasant.'

'I have never wanted to go to France,' Lady Maddox said. 'A very dirty country, I believe. No proper sanitation.'

'The hotel we live in is excellent,' Amy said. 'Very modern. We are very fortunate in that respect.'

There was another silence. 'I was just saying to Lady Maddox,' Amy said, 'that the garden is lovely.'

Sir Henry put down his cup. 'Perhaps you would like to see it,' he said. 'I would be delighted to show you.'

She glanced at Johnny and he raised his eyebrows again and gave her a quick smile. 'Thank you,' she said. 'I should like that very much.'

He led her into the garden. She wondered what kind of conversation Johnny and his mother were having behind her.

'Let's go to the rose garden.' Sir Henry led her across a trim lawn and past well-stocked herbaceous borders. An ageing gardener was piling weeds and clippings into a wheelbarrow and he touched his hat as they went by.

They went through a wrought-iron gate in a mellow brick wall. 'This is my wife's special interest,' Sir Henry said.

The roses were a mass of colour and perfume. Amy breathed it in, trying to capture the scent, to remember it so that she could bring it back to the wards and the operating theatre. She took a deep breath. 'It's beautiful.'

'My wife has done it all,' he said. 'She likes to develop new roses. Look at this one.' The rose was flame red, exotic, springing free in a mass of blooms. 'She has called this one "Johnny".'

She met his eyes and he smiled. 'It's like him,' she said. 'A free spirit.'

He nodded. 'She is very fond of him. His elder brother, James, is very different, very solid, very reliable, married to the daughter of a local landowner. Johnny was always a bit of a worry, climbing the highest tree, falling in the lake, riding slightly risky horses.'

Amy laughed. 'I can imagine it.'

'She still feels that she has to protect him,' he said. 'I think she sometimes forgets that he is a grown man now, and must make his own decisions.' He looked back at the roses. 'I don't think she quite realizes as yet how much the world is changing.'

He is saying something to me, she thought. She remembered the intense look that Johnny had given her that day in the hospital when his father was there, the look that his father had intercepted, the look that must have told him something of Johnny's feelings.

Amy gently touched one of the flaming roses. 'I imagine one never grows out of being a mother.'

They walked on, through the massed colour and fragrance. The old house stood behind them, solid and secure. She could understand why Lady Maddox didn't want anything to change.

'She just wants him to be happy,' he said.

Looking into his kind, understanding face she felt a stab of conscience. She wanted so much to confide in this man, to ask his opinion and advice, but what could he tell her? The decision, if any were to be made, was hers, and Johnny's.

They strolled back to the house. He stopped before they went in. 'Don't forget, Amy,' he said. 'If I can ever be of service to you, you only have to ask. You have given us the greatest gift. I don't know how my wife. . . .'

Impulsively she put her hand on his arm. 'No!' she said, more loudly than she meant. He seemed to understand. He smiled at her and patted her hand. As they went into the house she was thinking how much he loved and cared for his family, his sons and his wife. He also just wanted them to be happy.

Johnny drove her home through the countryside in the soft, warm evening. They drove past fields of buttercups and daisies where lazy-eyed cows stood immobile in the late sunshine. They drove down narrow country lanes where meadow-sweet and purple vetch and red campion flowered in the hedgerows and the last petals of may blossom drifted from the trees.

Amy watched it all go by with a painful nostalgic sadness. It seemed to her that a new kind of change, like a giant dark cloud, was gathering in the distance. Her country, and the world, had weathered storms and threats for a thousand years but were threatened again now by a war that was different from all others, and would change everything. The world was being ravaged in a new and terrifying way. New horrors blackened the future, new brutalities, new attitudes of cruelty and perverted power. How could they be defeated? This war could only fight horror with horror. There was no escape, no place for compassion or humanity. She looked out on the tranquil, beautiful English countryside and felt as if she were watching a dying old friend.

They stopped at Maidenhead to have a drink at Skindles Hotel on the river by Boulter's Lock – lemonade for Amy and half a pint of bitter for Johnny. They sat in the garden, watching the Thames idle by. The evening held that particular kind of opalescent light that seemed to be so special to late spring in England. A mother duck with six ducklings paddled out from the bank. A few punts, still out, came through the lock and were poled away down river, the girls in their summer frocks lying drowsily against the cushions. The moment seemed to Amy to distil everything that was beauty and peace, everything that was being so hideously destroyed.

'It's lovely, isn't it?' she said. 'You could only get this in England.'

'Nowhere like it,' Johnny said. 'Wherever I get to after the war I shall always want to come back.'

Amy hesitated. She found that she needed courage to ask. 'What will you do,' she said, 'after the war?'

His face was eager, his eyes bright. 'I don't know exactly, but I'd like to see a bit more of the world. There's so much out there. We've got an Australian pilot in the squadron and he has amazing stories. Do you know how big Australia is, Amy? How vast? They'll need aeroplanes. There's so much of the Empire, apart from anywhere else, Africa and India and Australia and New Zealand and Canada. Wild places, Amy. Just imagine it.'

Wild, she thought. That would attract him, of course. Wild and dangerous. She said nothing, and looked away across the river where shadows were gathering beneath the trees and low screening branches trailed in the water.

'I'm glad you met my mother,' he said. 'She's quite a character, isn't she?'

The change of subject took her by surprise. 'Yes,' she said. 'I was glad to meet her too. She is rather – formal, I suppose.'

He smiled. 'Old-fashioned, perhaps. Set in her ways.'

Amy paused, and then she said, 'Do you think she knows? Do you think she really realizes what is happening in France?'

'Not entirely,' he said. 'She thinks of war as battles, cavalry charges with sabres. Or brave regiments taking a stand at Rorke's Drift.' He took a swallow of his beer. 'She doesn't really understand what I'm doing in an aeroplane.'

'Can anyone know?' she said. 'Anyone who hasn't been there?'

'Perhaps my father knows,' he said. 'He's a thinking man, and he's doing something at the War Office. He doesn't say what.'

The mother duck sailed calmly back again, the little ones almost running after her across the water.

'Your mother seems to think that everything will go back to the way it was before,' Amy said. 'I don't think it will. People are changing.' She stopped, wondering whether to go on, but he was relaxed, watching the river. 'Women are changing. They are doing so many new things. Many of them are not going to be satisfied to go back into domestic service, or even just to stay at home and be wives and mothers.' She watched him, wondering how he would take that remark, wondering whether he would say how he felt about it.

He didn't seem to notice it. 'My mother won't change. She doesn't think women should have the vote.'

'What about you?' she said. 'What do you think?'

'I don't mind women having the vote. After all, they'll be bringing up the next generation.'

'What about women working, having careers? What do you think about that?'

He frowned. 'I don't know. I haven't really thought about it.' He looked at his watch. 'We'd better get on. I'll take you home and then I'll go to Town and stay at my club tonight.' He smiled at her. 'It'll be easier to get to you tomorrow.'

He led her to the car and helped her in. He hadn't answered her question. She could quite believe that he had never thought about it. Women of his class didn't work, didn't have careers; certainly not careers like medicine, a life that was so contained, so absorbing. Women like Florence Nightingale and Edith Cavell and Mrs Garrett

Anderson were few and far between.

He left her at the door of her house. He took her hand. 'Tomorrow,' he said. He put her hand to his lips and sighed. 'Tomorrow,' he said again. 'It's my last day. Ten o'clock?'

She nodded. 'Yes.' He got into the car, waved his hand, and drove away.

She took off her hat and coat in the hall. Her father was in the sitting-room, reading. He put his book down as she came in. 'Hello, my dear.'

She went over to him and kissed his cheek. 'Hello, Father.'

'Come and sit down,' he said. 'What have you been doing today?'

She sat opposite to him by the fireplace. The evening had cooled and a little fire was burning, her mother's screen moved to one side. 'Johnny took me to have tea with his mother. They have a house in Berkshire.'

'Meeting his mother? That sounds rather serious.' He paused expectantly. 'Is it serious, Amy?'

She bit her lips. 'I don't know.'

'Do you love him, Amy?'

She nodded, her eyes filling. 'Yes, I think I do, but his background is so different. If I try to ask him what he feels about women working he doesn't really answer. I don't think he's ever considered it except as a kind of philosophical question. It's not something that happens in that kind of family. Charity work, yes, but not a career. They would think that being a wife and mother was enough of a career.' She sighed. 'I know what his mother would think. She'd have a fit. She would want his wife to be there to support him, in every way, just as they always have been.'

He smiled, and then the smile faded. 'What are you going to do?'

She stared into the fire, her hands clasped and her shoulders drooping. 'Nothing. Wait.'

'Put it off, you mean?'

She sighed. 'I suppose so. I really don't want to bother him now. God knows, he has enough to think about – his flying, the war. I don't want him to be disturbed by anything. We just have to get through this war day by day. I don't want to distract him in the slightest way.'

'I understand,' he said. 'But you can't have a successful relationship unless it's based on honesty. Tell me, dear, has he mentioned marriage?'

'No,' she said. She thought suddenly of Dan, of his careful explanation of his attitudes. 'I don't think he would, under the circumstances.'

'But he must feel something for you, or he wouldn't want to see
you.'

'He does feel something for me, Father, I know that, but I don't
know whether his feeling for me is enough to overcome any prejudices
or objections he might have.' Her head drooped. 'And I don't know
whether I could give up medicine. It would be like giving up most of
my life.'

'Be careful, Amy,' he said. 'Wouldn't it be better to find out now,
before it goes any further? I just want you to be happy.'

She went to bed early, wanting to be alone, to think. She didn't really
know what Johnny's intentions were. Perhaps he didn't know himself.
How could anyone think clearly in this war? Could she give up medicine? The very thought made her feel strange, panicky and breathless.
It would be like losing a limb, losing her heart. Could she give up
Johnny? Could he give her up? Her thoughts went round and round
without any resolution. Johnny's mother was obviously concerned,
suspecting that they had more than a friendship. His father had told
her in a very diplomatic use of words that Johnny must make his own
decisions and live his own life. It was just possible, though unlikely,
that Johnny might be perfectly happy for his wife to have a job.

Wait, she thought. Wait. It was Johnny's last day tomorrow. She
wasn't going to spoil it by worrying. She probably wouldn't see him
again for months. There was no need to try to make decisions now.

Johnny collected her at ten the next morning and they drove to
London.

'What would you like to do?' he said. 'I think the Herbert Tree
production is still on at His Majesty's, if you'd like to go to a matinee.'

'No,' she said. 'It's a lovely day. Could we walk? Could we go to see
some of the Wren churches in the City? I've always wanted to do that.'

'Of course,' he said.

He parked the car near the Monument and they walked around the
City, to one or two of the lovely old churches, to St Mary Le Bow of the
Bow Bells, and then to St Paul's. Amy gazed up at the great cupola.
These churches held for her a deeply comforting atmosphere of hold-
ing fast, of endurance. 'It's so magnificent,' Amy said. 'You don't think
the Germans would ever—'

'No,' he said at once. 'I don't think even they would do that. Things like this belong to the world.' They came out into the sunshine. 'Let's have lunch and then I'll take you for a walk in the park.'

They had lunch at the Cheshire Cheese and then drove to Hyde Park Corner. Johnny parked in Park Lane. The park was busy with people enjoying the sunshine, women in bright summer clothes, young men in uniform, nannies in uniform pushing large baby carriages or sitting in chatting groups on the park benches. There were children everywhere, running about, throwing balls or bowling hoops.

Johnny took her hand. 'I want to be alone with you,' he said.

She laughed up at him. 'We are alone.'

He looked around him. 'Alone in Hyde Park? That isn't what I mean.' He stopped and turned her towards him. 'I want to be really alone with you.'

'I don't know, Johnny,' she began, but then stopped, silenced by his intensity, the physical tension in his body, his serious face.

'I want to kiss you,' he said. 'If you don't want to be kissed in front of all these people, I think you had better come with me.'

'Where?' she said.

He placed her hand under his arm and began to walk her away. 'We have an apartment here,' he said. 'Just off Park Lane.'

'We?' she said.

'The family. We used to have a house a generation ago, but I think it got a bit expensive, even for us. The apartment's shut up when no one's in London. There's no one there at the moment.'

She stopped and looked up at him, her heart beating so loudly that she thought he might hear it. 'Is that wise, Johnny?'

'No,' he said. 'Probably not. Is anything wise these days? We don't have time, do we, to be wise?'

She couldn't speak, her longing for him overwhelming her. She felt her body melt and dissolve until she seemed to be nothing but feeling. She knew that he sensed it. He looked at her intently; the muscles of his face suddenly relaxed. He took her hand.

He led her to a block of mansion flats and they walked up the stairs to the first floor. She noticed everything with a strange clarity, the spotless stairs, the brown carpet, the bowl of flowers on a side table. It was as if she were storing it all in her memory, like a series of photographs to be taken out later and looked at and cherished.

He took a key from his pocket and opened the door. He led her inside and closed the door behind her. 'Amy,' he said, his voice breathless, urgent.

He took off her hat and threw it behind him. He reached behind her and took the pins out of her hair so that it fell about her shoulders. He took her face in his hands and then he kissed her. It was so different from his last kiss. That had been gentle and tentative. This kiss was a new discovery, a new world. She felt her body leap towards him. He put his arms around her and his face against her hair. 'I want you, Amy,' he said, 'more than I have ever wanted anything.'

She felt helpless. She had lost all memory of reason or intelligence or control. She wanted him with a passion that she couldn't resist, that she didn't want to resist. 'Yes,' she murmured. 'Yes, Johnny. I've never. . . .'

'I know,' he said. 'Are you sure, Amy?'

'Yes,' she said again.

He picked her up in his arms and carried her to a bedroom. He undressed her slowly and kissed her breasts and she shuddered under his touch. He laid her, naked, on the bed and undressed himself. She knew his body. She had nursed and washed and fed it, but she was overcome again by his physical beauty.

He lay beside her and touched her hair as it spread out on the pillow. 'You're so beautiful, Amy,' he whispered. He ran his hands over her body and she melted into his touch. This is right, she thought. There is nothing wrong about it, nothing immoral or foolish. It is right. She cried out as he entered her, and then, at last, she cried out again.

They lay together, her head on his shoulder. He was so still. She moved away a little and looked at him. He seemed to be asleep, his face utterly relaxed, his fair eyelashes brushing his cheeks.

'I'm not asleep,' he said. He opened his eyes and smiled at her. 'Are you all right?'

She bent over him and kissed his lips. 'Yes,' she said. 'Of course.'

'Are you my girl now?'

'Yes,' she said.

He hung over her, touching her face and her hair, kissing her with small kisses as if he were gently devouring her. 'You're so beautiful.'

She lay down again on his shoulder and drifted into sleep. She woke again to find his lips on hers and his body pressed against her once more.

Afterwards she dressed and put up her hair and retrieved her hat. She looked at herself in the mirror. It's different now, she thought. She almost said the words aloud. Her father was right. She must tell him now. She must give them both the chance to decide on the future.

He drove her home in the late afternoon. All the way she was thinking, I must tell him; I must tell him now. He stopped the car outside her door.

'I won't come in,' he said. 'I've got to go early in the morning and I've got to pack. Give my regards to your father.'

She summoned up her courage. 'Johnny,' she began.

He put his finger over her mouth to silence her. 'You're frowning,' he said, 'so I don't want you to say anything. No frowns. Just kiss me.' He kissed her lightly on the lips. 'Don't forget you're my girl.' He got out of the car and opened the door for her. He got back into the car and drove away.

CHAPTER THIRTEEN

1916

HELEN had left for England when Amy got back to Paris; gone home to arrange her engagement. Amy felt, not envy exactly, but a longing to find things so easy – fall in love, get married, no problems. She felt different now; everything had changed. She had given herself to Johnny. At least, she had given her heart and her body, but what about her mind? She so wished that she could talk it over with someone, with Helen, perhaps, one day.

The war seemed to escalate in horror; her own problems seemed puny and unimportant. The talk around the hospital was dire. One of the men, shot in both legs, told her that two battalions of soldiers had been buried alive in their trenches by German artillery. When they got to them all they could see were rows of bayonets sticking up out of the ground. All the men were dead, suffocated as they stood. The picture was horrifying.

The wounded poured in. There were men with infections, not just surgical cases, men with typhoid, infective jaundice, pneumonia and dysentery. They had been put in the upstairs bedrooms to be nursed, isolated from the others.

Amy went back into theatre.

'I'm glad to see you back, Amy.' Dr Hanfield looked even more tired and drawn. 'I hope you had a good rest. I'm afraid you're going to be very busy. All the staff are tired out and are due for a rest but we're hoping for some new recruits.'

'I see we're taking medical cases now,' Amy said. 'They'll need a lot of nursing.'

Dr Hanfield nodded. 'We're getting a new doctor, thank goodness, a physician who can look after them, and some new nurses. The typhoid is getting worse, and now there's infective jaundice everywhere. Apparently the trenches are overrun with rats, spreading it about.'

Amy shuddered. The rats would have plenty to eat.

'There's no excuse for typhoid,' Sister said briskly. 'The British Army should have made inoculation compulsory, like the French did. I don't know why the men would refuse it. They go into all this but they're frightened of needles!'

On 1 July they knew that something dreadful had happened; the hospital was rife with rumour and filled with shocked, worried faces. A few days later M. Le Blanc came into the hospital, his face white and hands shaking and was closeted with Dr Hanfield for half an hour. After he'd gone, Theatre Sister asked Amy to go to the office to ask for more morphine. She knocked at the door. There was a long pause and then Dr Hanfield called, 'Come in.' She was standing by her desk and had a look on her face of utter despair. She'd obviously been crying. She looked at Amy with swollen eyes, for a moment unable to speak.

'What is it?' Amy said. 'What's happened?' For a dreadful moment she thought that the bad news was for her alone, that something had happened to Johnny. Then with a flood of relief she realized that was foolish. Whatever it was that was causing this despair, it could not be something so personal, so individual. The whole world seemed to be dying.

'They've started fighting on the Somme.' The doctor's voice was breaking. 'There were nearly sixty thousand British casualties on the first day. Sixty thousand, Amy, in one day. Nineteen thousand of those are dead.' She sat down at her desk and put her head in her hands. 'The aid posts and hospitals are overwhelmed. We'll be overwhelmed. I don't know how we can possibly cope.'

'What can I do?' Amy said. 'I'll do anything.'

Dr Hanfield wiped her hands over her face. 'We'll just have to do our best and carry on as normal. At least we've got some new staff coming. Ask Sister to come to me, please.'

Amy closed the door quietly. She gave the message to Sister and then went up to her room and sat down on her bed. Sixty thousand men. What on earth could it have been like, that hell? No horror that mankind had ever brought about could have been like that. Even the American Civil War couldn't have been like that. What was happening? Was it the end of the world? I have to do more, she thought. I have to do more.

After a week Helen came back, white-faced and appalled. She had brought with her some English newspapers. 'Do you know, Amy?' she said. 'Have you seen these?' The papers were filled with the horror and with endless lists of the wounded and dead. 'Look.' Helen was almost crying. 'They thought the British guns had wiped out the German trenches, but they hadn't. They still had their machine-gun posts. Our men were mown down like animals. And it was all for nothing.'

Amy put her arms around her. 'Oh, Helen.'

'Peter had to go back early,' Helen said. 'There are dead and dying everywhere, Amy. There are shell holes full of dead, trenches full of dead. Piles and piles of dead. And Peter's there now, in the middle of it all.'

'He's in a Clearing Station, Helen,' Amy said gently. 'He'll be all right. The Clearing Stations aren't that close to the trenches. It's not as if he's in an Aid Post at the front.'

'No, he's not in a Clearing Station any more.' Helen's face was grim. 'He and Dan have been posted to the hospitals at Étaples. That camp is right next to a railway line and there are hundreds of troops there. I'm frightened the Germans might bomb it.'

'They won't bomb hospitals, Helen.' Amy tried to sound positive and confident. 'They'll be all right.' She took Helen's hands in hers. 'Tell me about your engagement, Helen. Think about that instead. Did it all go well? What did your parents say?'

'It was wonderful.' Helen dried her eyes with the heel of her hand. 'His parents are dears and mine were so pleased. They loved Peter.'

'I knew they would.' Amy smiled, happy for Helen, but she wondered whether her father really approved of her relationship with Johnny. He had never really said anything against it, but she knew that he worried about it, about whether they were really suited to one another. She tried to concentrate on Helen. 'Aren't you going to show me the ring?'

'Oh yes!' Helen took her engagement ring out of her bodice, where it was hanging from a chain.

'It's lovely,' Amy said. 'Sapphire and diamonds.'

Helen held it in her hand. 'I want to be with him, Amy. I just want to be with him, all the time, wherever he is.'

'Oh, Helen,' Amy sighed. 'What can you do? We just have to keep going. What can anyone do?'

'I don't know yet.' Helen put her ring back in her bodice. 'Tell me about you. Did you see Johnny?'

'Yes, I did. He took me to see his mother.'

'What was she like?'

'Stiff,' Amy said. 'Very stiff. I don't think she really approved of me.'

'Oh dear. Why ever not?'

Amy shrugged. 'Not in the county set, I think. I saw his father too. He was very nice.' She took the little box out of a drawer and held out her brooch. 'Johnny gave me this.'

Helen took it in her hands. 'Oh, a sweetheart brooch.'

'What do you mean?'

'That's what they call them,' Helen said. 'Sweetheart wings. They are copies of the wings on the Flying Corps uniforms. The pilots give them to their sweethearts.'

Amy put the brooch carefully back in the box. 'I didn't know that,' she said.

Helen laughed. 'He's much more than a friend. Now do you believe me?'

Amy could almost feel his naked arms around her and his lips on hers. 'Yes,' she said, 'I believe you.'

The news from the Somme came every day and chilled the blood. Amy worked long hours in theatre, but she found it hard to sleep and her restlessness increased. She lay in bed at night, worrying. She was well aware that her restlessness and fearfulness were because she might possibly be pregnant. In retrospect she wondered how she could possibly have been so reckless. What would she do? Would Johnny do the honourable thing? Even if he did, what would her life be like then? She thought she knew. All decisions would be made for her. She was torn. One part of her longed to have Johnny's children, but not now and not until she had told him what she wanted to do. When she had a child, if she ever did, she wanted it to be longed and planned for, conceived in a love that was held in the permanence and commitment of marriage. She waited, counting off the days, terrified that they would go by and her fears would be confirmed. She woke on the expected day and found that she was bleeding. Her period had come on time. She was not pregnant.

But the restlessness stayed. She began to feel more and more that the relatively luxury of Paris was not what she wanted, when the world around her was a sink of suffering and death. She wanted to be with the men, to share their privations, to put herself to the test. She didn't want to come out of this war knowing that she had taken the easy way. New staff was coming to the hospital. They could manage very well without her.

Helen continued to look bereft. 'Amy,' she said one night when they were going to bed, 'I've been thinking.'

'What about?'

'About being with Peter. I can't think about anything else.' Helen stopped in the middle of brushing her hair. 'I've been thinking that perhaps I might apply to go to Étaples. They'd probably take me as a VAD.'

'How strange,' Amy said. 'I've been thinking more or less the same thing. Things are getting so much worse. They must be desperate for people with experience. I just have this feeling that I've done all I can here. Someone else can take my place. I want to do something more.'

Helen said, excitedly, 'Let's do it. Let's go together.'

They talked it over for several days. Amy could see nothing against it. Her father would not be happy about it, but he would have to accept, as they all did now, that the war was going on, there was no end in sight. He would know that she had to do everything she could, everything that she was allowed to do.

They went together to see Matron. She didn't try to dissuade them, but she tried to make sure that they knew what they were doing. 'Do you know what Étaples is like?' she said. 'It's a huge camp. Hundreds of troops are training there and coming and going all the time, and the hospitals there are overwhelmed. You won't have a nice room to stay in; a hut will be more likely. Are you quite sure you want to leave Paris?'

'Yes,' they said together.

'Very well then. I'm sorry to see you go, but best of luck.' She gave them both a reference to say that they were already experienced in hospital duties.

Dr Hanfield added a note for Amy to recommend that she should work in theatre. 'I'm sorry to lose you, Amy,' she said. 'But I understand how you feel. Best of luck.'

They sent in their applications, and they waited. Helen was impatient. 'Why don't we hear? I've told Peter that we're coming.' At last, at the end of August, the letters came. They had both been accepted. Amy wrote to her father and to Johnny.

They packed their meagre belongings. They spent an afternoon saying goodbye to Paris. They went to Nôtre Dame, the Place de la Concorde, the Place de l'Opera. The statues and monuments were surrounded by even more layers of sandbags.

'I'm going to come back after the war,' Helen said. 'I shall get Peter to bring me. We'll stay at our hotel and be proper tourists.'

Amy laughed. 'I'll come with you.'

They bought more toilet soap and some perfume. 'I think we might need this,' Helen said, 'if what we're told about Étaples is anything to go by.' They went to Printemps and bought sturdy boots and mackintoshes and several sets of warm underwear. Winter in a hut was a chilling prospect.

They said their goodbyes in Paris and took the train, crowded as usual, and arrived in Étaples in the late afternoon. The station was packed with wounded men waiting for trains to take them to Paris or to Boulogne and then a boat back to England and home.

They made their way out of the station. It was raining and the roads were thick with mud.

'God,' Helen said, 'if it's like this in August what is November going to be like?'

They left their bags at the station to be collected and walked to the camp. Long rows of huts came into view with sand hills and sparse grass here and there between them. The railway line ran alongside the huge camp between the huts and the sea and the road to Camiers ran close by.

As they drew nearer they heard a constant rumbling sound, the sound of traffic on the road. They watched in growing horror. The road was packed with troops and lorries and ambulances. Many of the wounded were on foot, men who looked half alive, eyes empty and faces drained of everything but the supreme effort of making it to the camp. Wounded men helped others more injured than themselves.

Many were on makeshift crutches. Many were without boots, their feet wrapped in ragged bits of cloth.

Helen clutched Amy's arm. 'Oh, Amy,' she said, her voice breaking. 'I knew it was bad, but I never imagined anything like this.'

They walked through the endless rows of huts, looking for the hospital they were to join. Here and there a few flowers bloomed, a few daisies or a brave rose. They found their hospital and reported to the matron, a small, round woman with a steely eye. 'Settle yourselves in,' she said, 'and report to me in the morning.'

They were led to the small hut that was to be their home. They looked around.

'Goodness,' Helen said. 'Matron in Paris didn't exaggerate, did she?'

The hut had two beds, a table and two hard chairs, a cupboard for each of them and a few nails hammered into the wall appeared to be all there was of a wardrobe.

'Real home from home,' Helen said.

Amy hung her dripping raincoat on one of the nails. 'A bit closer to reality,' she said grimly.

Helen grinned. 'A bit closer to Peter, anyway.'

They felt, rather than heard, a distant deep, vibrating rumbling, and the hut gave an almost imperceptible shake.

Helen paused from her unpacking, a pair of boots in her hand. 'What on earth's that?'

The rumbling came again. 'It's guns,' Amy said. 'Heavy guns, a long way away.'

Helen said nothing, just pressed her lips together and put her boots in the cupboard.

The next morning they reported to Matron. 'I see that you both have some experience,' she said. 'That's good. I've assigned you to the theatre, Miss Osborne. Report to Theatre Sister.'

Helen, to her shock and surprise, was assigned to the German ward. 'Germans?' she said, unable to hide her reluctance.

'They are patients,' Matron said sharply, 'just like everyone else, and most of them are very ill. You will treat them the same as our own men.'

'Of course,' Helen said quietly. 'Of course I will.' Later on, in their hut, she was still disappointed. 'The German Ward! Really!'

'We had Germans in Paris,' Amy said.

Helen sighed. 'Not a whole ward full.'

They are just men, Amy thought, caught up in this mess like everyone else. The propaganda about the Germans had been relentless. They were accused of doing appalling things, murdering prisoners, murdering woman and babies, looting and raping. Some of it might well be true. Hatred, she thought, is a powerful tool. Hatred of the enemy and patriotism and love of one's country were weapons more powerful than the guns. Why else would any man go through this? 'Even if what we're told is true,' she said, 'they won't be in any condition to do anything.'

'I suppose not,' Helen said, 'but I'll be on my guard.'

Amy reported to theatre and was given her duties. She was appalled by what she saw, injuries and wounds more dreadful than anyone could imagine, rows and rows of men in the huts and tents, waiting patiently for their turn, blood everywhere, pus-soaked bandages, a bin in theatre almost full of body parts.

She and Helen fell into bed that night, exhausted. 'How was it?' Amy asked.

Helen sighed, 'Just what Matron said. They're all too ill to speak. One of them died today. He was only nineteen.' She paused for a moment. 'How was theatre?'

'Dreadful. The men are so patient, waiting and waiting their turn. There just aren't enough surgeons.'

'There isn't enough anything.'

'There's a proper X-ray department,' Amy said. 'A permanent one. That's a real boon.' The X-ray department had been a very pleasant surprise. She was also delighted to see that blood transfusion was being used quite commonly. 'They're giving blood transfusions too,' she said. 'Using citrated blood.'

'What's that?' Helen said sleepily.

'The citrate stops the blood clotting,' Amy said. 'So they can store it for a little while and transport it. It means the donor doesn't actually have to be there.'

'I don't know how you know all these things,' Helen said. Then her voice brightened. 'I went to see Matron again. She says that I can meet Peter, seeing that we are engaged. She says we can meet at the mess hut for a cup of tea, but she wants you to be there as chaperon.'

'Chaperon?' Amy said. 'I thought those days had gone.'

'Not here,' Helen said. 'She's very strict. No hanky-panky.' She paused. 'I expect he'll bring Dan if he can.'

Amy laughed. 'Captain Fielding, you mean,' she said. 'We're strictly on official terms in theatre. Absolutely no first names. It's supposed to give a bad impression to the patients.'

'Captain Fielding, then.' Helen turned over and yawned. 'Got to sleep. Good night.'

Amy woke early the next day. She had been dreaming about Johnny, about flying with him over the peaceful fields of England. It seemed a million miles away.

She had known since they arrived that she would be seeing Dan. She realized that Helen was right and she would have to tell him about Johnny, but how? He had never actually made an approach to her. It would be presumptuous of her to assume that he ever would. It could be very embarrassing for them both. Helen seemed to be convinced that he cared for her, but she might well be wrong.

Over dinner with Helen she said, 'How am I going to tell Dan about Johnny? I can't just blurt it out, "Oh by the way, Dan, I'm involved with someone else". It might be dreadfully embarrassing. He might have someone else himself.'

'I know how to do it,' Helen said. 'Why don't you just wear your sweetheart brooch. He's bound to see it, and then he would know.'

'It's an idea,' Amy said. 'I'll think about it.'

Their tea took place a few days later. Helen put up her hair with great care and pinched her cheeks to give them some colour.

Amy laughed. 'You look as if you're getting ready for a deb's ball.'

'I do my best,' Helen said. 'I haven't seen him for weeks.'

Amy opened the little jeweller's box. She took out the brooch and looked at it for a few moments. Then she pinned it to her uniform. It seemed the best way.

They walked to the mess hut, skirting the puddles. There was no one else in the hut. Peter arrived first. Helen blushed pink and threw her arms around him. Amy smiled and sat down at the far end of the hut, giving them as much privacy as she could.

Dan arrived soon afterwards. He smiled broadly when he saw her and came to sit next to her. He took her hand. 'Hello, Amy,' he said. 'It's lovely to see you.'

'And you, Dan,' she said. He was looking at her with eyes full of unmistakable pleasure and affection. He pressed her hand gently.

A stray ray of sunshine came through the window and caught her brooch and the diamond must have gleamed. Dan looked down and stared at it for a moment, his face puzzled and shocked. 'Sweetheart wings?' he stammered. He let go of her hand.

Amy looked at him directly, desperately not wanting to hurt him, but knowing now that it couldn't be avoided.

'Yes,' she said. 'I have a friend in the Flying Corps.'

He was silent for a moment. 'I see,' he said at last. 'I didn't know. You didn't tell me.' He looked away, out of the window. 'Are you engaged to him, Amy?'

'No,' she said. 'Not exactly.'

He looked back at her. She could see in his face the conscious effort he was making to hide his feelings, to suppress his disappointment. 'I'm glad you have someone . . . to care for you,' he said.

She wanted to touch him, to tell him she was sorry, that she had never meant to hurt him, that he was a good man and a good friend.

His face closed down to a normal friendly expression. 'How are you getting on here?'

'I'm working in theatre again,' she said.

'I shall be seeing you now and again then.' He looked across the room to where Helen and Peter were murmuring together. 'Your friend. What is his name?'

'Johnny Maddox,' she said.

'How did you meet?'

'He was one of the wounded that I picked up in the ambulance, and then he was a patient at the hospital.'

'I see.' He got up. 'Must get back to work. I expect I'll see you about. I'm glad about Helen and Peter.' He walked away and left the hut.

She sat alone, looking out of the window. She knew now that she had underestimated his feelings and she was unhappy that she had hurt him. It was the last thing she wanted. But she was glad she had told him the truth. She was so tired of secrets. She would tell Johnny everything as soon as she possibly could. She wanted her life to be open and free again.

The Battle of the Somme ground on. The chaos was uncontained. The wounded poured in; through September and November there was no respite. Helen, to her relief, was transferred to one of the British surgical wards where they were desperate for staff. Sometimes they worked for several weeks without even a half-day's rest. The rain became almost constant and the mud almost ankle deep. 'God,' Helen said, 'it's like treacle.' The war seemed to have produced a special kind of mud, sucking and cloying. The wounded staggered in, coated from head to foot, feet rotting from standing in trenches half filled with water. Their stories were dreadful, of wounded men drowning in mud and filthy water in shell holes. Men lay in beds or on the floor in huts and tents waiting for surgery. Their patience broke Amy's heart. The surgeons, exhausted, moved from one operating table to another, often from one theatre to another. The patient would be anaesthetized and prepared so as not to waste time, and the surgeon would rush in, scrub up again, and perform the next surgery. Sometimes, by the time they got there, it was already too late.

Amy saw Dan frequently. They met in theatre with time only to nod to each other. He never sought her out at any other time. If ever they met by chance apart from work he was carefully polite and distant. He looked as all of them did, ready to drop, often unshaven and wearing crumpled clothes he might have slept in. The work was relentless. All of them worked doggedly on, snatching meals or a cup of tea or a few hours' sleep whenever they could. The surgeons often worked sixteen or seventeen hours a day, snatched a meal and slept. Sometimes it was even longer.

Amy was given more and more work in theatre; there could never be enough staff to deal with the endless tide of the wounded. Each time there was another push on the Somme the road was crammed and the noise of lorries and ambulances never ceased, night or day.

Even after the Somme offensive stopped in the middle of November, there was no respite. Christmas came, and poor and hopeless efforts to celebrate. The news came in. There had been more than 400,000 British casualties, and all for nothing. There was still stalemate.

Amy found herself becoming more and more tense. She felt like a volcano that was about to erupt. She would stand beside the operating table with Sister, waiting for the surgeon to arrive, knowing that men were often dying simply because they had to wait; that while they were waiting they bled to death. Every day she could feel more and more that a violent rage was rising within her, a rage that it was almost impossible to contain. The waste of her skills and training seemed like a crime against humanity, a crime against these dying men. She knew that one day it would overcome her. One day it would come to a head.

On Christmas Eve she stood beside Sister in theatre. The patient, anaesthetized, lay on the table between them. They were expecting Dan at any moment. On the table, the man's abdomen was split open. Covered with a loose, wet dressing, a piece of shattered small intestine protruded from the wound, leaking blood and body fluids. He was deathly pale with blood loss and shock. The seconds ticked by. In the theatre there was a tense, anxious silence. Somewhere outside they could hear a few voices singing 'Silent Night'.

'Where's Captain Fielding?' Sister said unhappily.

An orderly put his head around the door. 'The doctor's been delayed a bit,' he said. 'He'll be a minute or two.'

'He's going to die,' Sister said. 'It can't wait any longer.'

Quite suddenly Amy was filled with an extraordinary calm. It was as if a light had been turned on inside her. Her rage and frustration fled away. She knew now what she would do.

'Sister,' she said. She looked her in the eye. 'I haven't told you or anyone here the truth. I am a doctor, a surgeon. I can't explain it all to you now but I am going to do this surgery, at once. If I don't, he is going to die.' She reached over to the sister's tray and took the clamps. She placed them carefully over the intact ends of the shattered intestine.

For a moment Sister seemed too astonished to move, her eyes wide behind her mask. Then she gave a wail. 'No, Miss Osborne. Stop at once! Whatever are you doing? Don't touch him!'

Amy ignored her. She took a scalpel and cut out the shreds of intestine, clipping off the bleeding vessels, and dropped the bits of intestine into a dish. Amy didn't look at her, concentrating on what she was doing. 'I've told you, Sister. I am a surgeon. I know what I'm doing and I've done this before. If you try to stop me you'll be responsible for his death.' The anaesthetist was staring at her, his eyes also wide with astonishment.

Amy held out her hand. 'Hand me a suture,' she said firmly. 'Now. There is no time to lose.'

Sister hesitated for a moment, obviously not knowing what to do, but she picked up the suture. Amy took it from her. She began to stitch one side of the two ends of gut together. Sister watched her, hovering and undecided, but she seemed to realize that Amy really did know what she was doing. She seemed to make up her mind and held the retractors to expose the gut. Silently Amy stitched the ends of the gut together. The door opened suddenly and Dan came in.

'Captain Fielding. . . .' Sister began, her voice uncertain.

Dan came to the table and stood beside her. 'What on earth?' he said. 'Miss Osborne, what on earth do you think you are doing?'

'Repairing the gut,' Amy said quietly. 'As I have done before. Otherwise he would have died.' She could feel him beside her, tense and undecided, not knowing what to do. She went on with the surgery. He could hardly fight her over the patient. He couldn't snatch her hand away as she was stitching. She began to stitch the other side of the gut. She glanced at him and he was watching her intently. 'I am not Amy Osborne, Dan, I mean, Captain,' she said. 'I'm sorry I've had to deceive you. I am Amy Richmond. Perhaps you will understand now.'

CHAPTER FOURTEEN

1916

'A MY Richmond?' Dan sounded utterly puzzled. She glanced at him briefly. He was looking at her as if she were crazy.

She finished stitching the gut. She could feel Dan standing beside her tensely, hands hovering, ready to take over at any moment. The anastomosis looked neat and secure. 'I think that will do,' she said. She quickly examined the rest of the abdomen for any further injuries. All the other organs seemed to be intact. 'I think we can close up now.'

'Amy Richmond?' Dan said slowly, as if a light were slowly dawning.

'Doctor Amy Richmond,' Amy said.

'You mean you were the doctor who was—?'

'Yes,' She interrupted him hurriedly, concentrating on what she was doing. 'That's me. Perhaps I can just finish this before he suffers any more shock. I'll explain later.' Sister and the anaesthetist were silent, but the atmosphere crackled with their curiosity.

'Yes,' Dan said. 'It looks fine. Close him up.'

Carefully, and in silence, Amy closed up the peritoneum, leaving in a drain to remove any infected fluids that might gather inside. She closed the abdominal muscles and then the skin. She put on a dressing, then at last she turned and looked at Dan. He was still staring at her, still looking almost unbelieving.

He seemed to collect himself and turned to Sister. 'He can go back to the ward now, Sister. Fluids only by mouth.' He turned back to Amy. 'You did a good job, Miss Osborne,' he said. 'But I think I'd better take over now. We'll get on with the rest of the list, Sister. Let's have the next patient.'

Amy went back to her normal duties, her mind in a turmoil. She fetched and carried for him and for Sister, but now and again Dan asked for her assistance, holding a retractor to expose the operation site, or clipping off a bleeding vessel. The hours wore on and as she worked she had time to think about what she had done. She began to feel a kind of deflation, as if all her energy and determination had left her. She had revealed herself and performed active surgery. She had broken the rules. She had no doubt that it would be all over the hospitals the next day and no doubt would get back to the General Medical Council sooner or later. Sister, for one, looked as if she couldn't wait to pass on the news. What would happen then? She thought she knew.

They finished their shift. 'Would you wait for me, Miss Osborne?' Dan said. 'I would like to speak to you.'

She waited for him outside the theatre. The night was cold and clear and the stars were brilliant overhead. She leant against the wooden wall of the hut. I don't regret it, she thought. Not for a moment. I couldn't just watch him die. It would be inhuman.

Dan came out. 'Let's walk a bit, Amy,' he said. 'I think you'd better tell me what happened. I must say you put on a good act. You certainly had me fooled.' He sounded not annoyed exactly, more disappointed and hurt.

'I'm really sorry, Dan,' she said, 'but there didn't seem to be anything else that I could do.' She told him everything, about Bulford and his prejudices and his nauseating sexual advances, about her helplessness to defend herself, about her determination to get her licence back.

He listened in silence until she had finished. 'Why didn't you tell me all this before?' he said.

'I was afraid I'd be sent back. I didn't think the hospital would keep anyone with that kind of reputation. I couldn't bear the thought of doing nothing when there is so much death and suffering. I would have gone mad.'

She could see his face in the dim lights from the huts. She couldn't read his expression, except that he looked serious and thoughtful. They could hear more singing coming from the wards, more homesick Christmas carols.

183

'You could have trusted me,' he said at last.

'Dan.' She turned to face him and put her hand on his arm. 'I haven't told anyone. Not even Helen. I was so afraid of being sent away.' She very carefully didn't mention Johnny.

'I see,' he said quietly. 'Well, everyone will know now.'

Tears rose in Amy's eyes and she brushed them away. 'I know. What will happen to me? I suppose I'll have to go.'

'Amy,' he said, 'I've known you a long time now. I think I know you fairly well and I believe you, especially now I've seen you actually working. I believe what you said about Bulford. I've met men like him before, men who are fanatical about keeping women out of the profession. And I meant it, Amy, you probably saved that man's life. You did a good job.'

Her tears began to fall. 'I hope so. It might be the last one I ever do.'

'I'll speak to you in the morning,' he said gently. 'Now go to bed and try and get some sleep.' He smiled. 'Perhaps we shouldn't be seen lurking about together in the dark. Someone might get the wrong idea.'

He looked down at her in the dim light. He raised his hand and brushed away a tear from her cheek. Then he leant towards her slowly and kissed her gently on the mouth. 'It's Christmas Day tomorrow.' He walked away into the night.

He kissed me, she thought, surprised. The kiss had been light and gentle and without passion. Christmas Day tomorrow. What a farce. Everything was a disaster, her own life and the far greater horrors of the war. But amazingly, Dan had kissed her, and it had been surprisingly comforting.

When she got to the hut Helen was in bed but still awake. She sat up. 'Amy,' she said. 'You've been crying. What's happened?'

Amy sat down on her bed. 'Helen, I've got something to tell you. I should have told you ages ago.'

Helen listened, her eyes getting wider and wider. 'I always thought there was something,' she said. 'I always wondered why you knew all that medical stuff. Why didn't you tell me before?'

'I didn't want to tell anyone. I was frightened I might be kicked out. And if you knew about it you might have been kicked out too.'

'I think it's terrible.' Helen was highly indignant. 'It's just another example of women being suppressed and abused. That surgeon should be the one who's struck off.'

'Well, I've ruined it now. I'll almost certainly be sent away tomorrow.'

'Surely they can't do that.' Helen was even more indignant. 'You saved the man's life.'

'I broke the rules. I was told not to practise. That's all they'll care about.' She put her hands up to her face and rubbed her temples. 'It's all such a mess.'

Helen was silent for a moment and then she said, 'Have you told all this to Johnny?'

Amy shook her head. 'No. That's another thing. Absolutely no one knows about it except my father. Johnny doesn't know anything about it. There never seemed to be the right moment. I tried to tell him when I saw him in England but somehow it didn't happen.' She sighed. 'I don't think it would go down very well in that family.'

'You've got to tell him now,' Helen said. 'He'd find out anyway.'

'I know.'

'He'd be such a support to you, Amy. I know Peter would back me up with anything.'

'I don't know.'

Amy undressed and got into bed, lying on her back, staring at the roof. She felt utterly despondent and yet she knew that she could not have acted differently. After all, she thought, what did she matter? What mattered were all the men outside, patiently waiting, and patiently dying.

'It might be all right.' Helen said. 'They might overlook it.'

'Unlikely,' Amy said. Frustrated tears slipped down her cheeks. She wasn't crying for herself any more, but for the whole, horrified and horrifying world.

'It might be,' Helen said firmly. 'Don't give up, Amy.'

The next morning a runner came with a note. She was requested to meet Major Barnes, the acting DADMS at ten a.m. in his office.

'Who's that?' Helen said.

Amy gave a grim smile. 'The executioner. The acting Deputy Assistant Director of Medical Services. He's about to give me my marching orders.'

She arrived at the office and was shown in. Matron and Dan were already there, Matron looking as if she were about to burst with curiosity.

Major Barnes was intimidating, steel grey hair and sharp clear blue eyes. He was sitting behind his desk.

'Sit down, Miss Osborne,' he said. 'I think we should continue with that name for the time being.' Amy sat down on a hard chair in front of his desk. It was horribly reminiscent. It's happening again, she thought. All over again. He was the judge and jury. He looked at her sternly. 'Well, what have you got to say for yourself?'

She looked back at him defiantly. I've got nothing to lose now, she thought. I can say what I think. 'I've spent two years,' she said, 'watching wounded men coming and going and dying because the medical services are overwhelmed. I've spent two years knowing that if I tried to help them I would never be able to practise medicine again. Well, I just couldn't take it any more. I couldn't just watch that man die and do nothing. I took the Hippocratic oath and I don't care what Sir William Bulford says, or the GMC. They're not here, are they? They've no conception of what's really going on. I'm not sorry for what I did. I'm glad I did it.'

There was a long silence.

He looked at her, unsmiling. 'I suppose we all knew about you at the time,' he said. 'about you being struck off the Register. I'm sure you realize that given the evidence they had at the time, the GMC had no alternative.' He paused, looking stern. 'I can't say that I knew the details then. We were all too busy to concern ourselves with it. It would perhaps have caused more of a stir if there hadn't been other things to worry about.'

'You don't know the truth,' she said.

He rolled his pen between his fingers. 'I know Sir William Bulford,' he said.

She gave a short, cynical laugh. 'I'm sure you do.' She was quite reckless now. 'You all stick together, don't you?'

He raised his eyebrows. 'Captain Fielding has filled me in on the details, as you gave them.' She carefully didn't look at Dan. 'I did some training with Bulford,' Major Barnes went on. He stopped rolling his pen and smiled, a grim smile. 'I'm quite prepared to believe what you say. He is a most objectionable man, a total misogynist.' He paused again, and frowned. 'Except in certain areas. There was some trouble with a nurse, as I recall. All suppressed, of course.'

Amy stared at him, her mouth dropping open a little. She had certainly not expected this.

He got up and walked to the window and stood beside it, looking out. He was tall and held himself very straight, but she could sense the tension in his body, in his stiff shoulders and clenched fingers. 'How much are you prepared to risk, Miss Osborne?' he said.

She was puzzled. 'What do you mean?'

He continued to look out of the window. 'I mean that the General Medical Council might very well decide never to reinstate you.'

'It was only once,' she said defiantly. 'I only did the surgery once, and in extreme circumstances. Surely they could see that, if they have any idea of what's going on here.'

'Would you come here?' he said.

Puzzled, she got up and stood beside him by the window.

'Look out there,' he said. 'What do you see?'

She looked out at the appalling, unchanging scene, at men slipping and staggering and crawling, falling in the mud, blinded men being led by their mates, exhausted men carrying stretchers, streams of ambulances unloading.

'What do you see?' he said again.

Her voice caught in her throat. 'Hell,' she said. 'Armageddon.'

'Are you prepared to risk it?' He looked down at her and she met his eyes. 'Are you prepared to risk never being able to go back,' he went on, 'never being reinstated? They might forgive you one occasion, but they couldn't overlook it if you continued to do it.' She was even more puzzled.

'We need surgeons, Miss Osborne,' he said. 'We particularly need abdominal surgeons. I believe that is your field, and Captain Fielding tells me that he believes you to be very competent.'

Her heart leapt. 'Major Barnes,' she said, 'what are you saying? Are you asking me to do the surgery?'

He smiled and nodded. 'If you'll take the risk. I promise you that when the war is over and if you do the work well, I will do whatever I can to help you with the GMC. I would, of course, ask Captain Fielding to monitor you for a while, to make sure that your standards are consistently acceptable.'

She could hardly breathe. 'They will be. Of course I'll do it.'

He held out his hand and she shook it heartily. 'Welcome aboard,' he said. 'Happy Christmas.'

She shook hands with Matron and with Dan.

'I'll see you out,' Dan said.

They went out into the cold, damp air. 'Dan,' she said, 'How can I possibly thank you. You can't imagine what this means to me.'

'Don't thank me, we need you,' he said. 'You are quite sure? You know what a risk you are taking about your future.'

One of the stretcher-bearers slipped in the mud and nearly dropped his burden. The wounded man gave a muffled cry.

'I don't care about the future any more,' she said. 'I want to do what I can now. God knows, we might not be alive tomorrow.'

He looked down at her for a moment. 'I'm sorry about last night.'

'What do you mean?' she said.

'I'm sorry I kissed you. I shouldn't have done that.' He smiled. 'Or perhaps I should have done it a long time ago.'

She flushed a little. 'It's all right,' she said. 'I didn't mind.'

'Good,' he said. 'Report to theatre as soon as you can. They'll be expecting you.'

Amy walked back to the hut on air. She felt that she was redeemed, that her life now had a real purpose, whatever happened to her after the war – if the end ever came.

Helen was in the hut, preparing to go to an early lunch.

'What happened?' she said. 'Everybody's talking about it.' She grinned. 'Especially the soldier you operated on. He's something of a celebrity.'

'You won't believe it,' Amy said. 'I can hardly believe it myself. They've asked me to go on doing surgery. They are going to try and put it right with the GMC after the war.'

Helen threw her arms around her. 'Oh how wonderful. Tell me all about it. Let's have a cup of tea to celebrate.' She put the kettle on the primus stove and pumped up the stove to get the pressure up.

'There isn't much to tell.' Amy sat down at the table and Helen busied herself with the tea. 'They asked would I do it and I said yes.'

'I think it's wonderful, you being a surgeon.' Helen warmed up the teapot and made the tea. She sat down at the table. 'I think it's wonderful what all the women are doing. I wish I had the brains. I never really thought about having a job or a career. I just assumed that I'd get married and have a family one day.'

'You do more than enough,' Amy said. 'You work like a slave every day and you're cheerful and kind and you never give up. I don't know how I would have got through it all if it hadn't been for you. You're a good friend, Helen.'

'And so are you.' Helen put down her mug. 'What will your father say?'

'He'll be glad I'm doing what I want to do, and worried about me ever getting my licence back.'

'And what do you think Johnny will say?'

Amy sighed. 'I don't know, Helen. It's not the kind of family where women have careers outside marriage, certainly not careers like medicine where one is away from home so much. I know his mother would think it disgusting. I don't think it would go down very well at all.'

'What matters is what Johnny will think. Other women get married and still have careers.'

'Not many of them. I just don't know. He talks about things like travelling and seeing wild parts of the world. I can't see a career-minded wife fitting into all that.'

Helen frowned. Are you telling me that you'd have to choose? Marriage to Johnny or your career?'

Amy rested her head on her hands. 'That's what frightens me, Helen. I suppose I've just been a coward and put off telling him. Everything is so horrible in this war, so confused and chaotic. How can anyone make decisions about anything? I suppose I was hoping to leave it until the war was over. I never imagined it was going to last this long.'

'What a situation.' Helen said. 'I think I've been lucky. We just fell in love and that was that. No problems.'

'I envy you.'

'You'll have to tell him now,' Helen said. 'You won't be able to hide it any longer.'

'I know, but I want to do it when I'm with him.'

'Can't you just write to him?'

'I'll tell him next time I see him.' She took Helen's hand. 'I might need a friend then.'

'I'll be here,' Helen said.

Amy reported to theatre and began to work again, watched over carefully by Dan. She seemed to be readily accepted and she knew why. It wasn't the time for anyone to take attitudes about women doctors. But better than that, news of the success of the women's surgical groups had reached the camp – Dr Hanfield in Paris and Dr Elsie Inglis with her Scottish Women's Hospital at Royaumont. Dr Garrett Anderson had been given a hospital for the wounded in London. No one could say now that the women couldn't do it. They were doing it, very successfully.

New Year's Eve came round. Someone produced a few bottles of wine and the medical staff toasted the New Year in the mess hut. No one suggested singing 'Auld Lang Syne'. The losses were too great, the lost family and friends too many.

'1917,' Helen said. 'Do you think it will end this year? We just want to get married and settle down. It's been two and a half years. Surely it can't go on much longer.'

'I don't know Helen. We can only hope. Where's Peter?'

'In theatre – of course.'

Dan came in. Amy gave him a little wave and he came over to her. 'Happy New Year,' he said.

They met frequently now, in theatre or on the surgical wards. He certainly wasn't trying to avoid her any more, she thought. He couldn't if he tried. They stood beside each other every day at the operating table while he watched her and nodded his approval of her work. He treated her as a colleague and friend, nothing more. But occasionally, when she caught him unawares, he was looking at her with a thoughtful, speculative look that he quickly covered up.

Someone gave him a glass of wine and he looked about him, saying hello to the other staff. How much he has changed, Amy thought. That diffident rather shy young man she had first met was gone for ever. His shoulders were broader and she could almost imagine that he had grown even taller. He was leaner, harder, as much a soldier now as a doctor. Doctors were not supposed to engage in any kind of fighting, but if push ever came to shove she would be glad to have Dan beside her.

He looked down at her. 'The last week has gone very well,' he said. 'I think I can safely tell Major Barnes that you can go it alone. I don't think you need anyone to watch over you.'

'Thank you, Dan,' she said. 'I wouldn't be doing it at all if it wasn't for you.'

'Odd, isn't it,' he said, 'how one used to worry about opening an abdomen? Now we see them every day. If only we had something for infection, something to kill the little blighters.'

She nodded. 'One feels so helpless, sometimes.'

'We won't talk shop,' he said. 'How is your father?'

'He's well. Finding it a bit difficult to cope with the food shortages. Like everyone else, I suppose.'

He looked away from her across the room and took a sip of his wine. 'And how is your friend?'

'Johnny? He's well. He writes quite often. They're hoping to get new aircraft this year, faster and more manoeuvrable. They all want to have a chance at the Red Baron. He's shooting down too many British planes.'

He looked back at her. 'Baron von Richthofen. Flies a red triplane, I believe. Your friend must have an exciting life.'

'Yes,' she said.

He put down his wine, the glass still half full. 'There's someone I need to see on the ward. I'll see you tomorrow, I expect.'

She left shortly after he did. The party, such as it was, was quiet and subdued. No one knew what the New Year would bring. Or perhaps, she thought, they knew only too well. She walked back to the sparse hut she called home. I want to see Johnny; she almost said the words aloud. It was six months now. She wanted his arms around her and his kiss. She wanted all of him.

The year wore on, January and February and into March and bitter cold.

Amy and Helen came out of the mess hut after lunch and walked down the pathway between the huts. For once it was a dry day and apart from a few cotton-wool clouds the sky was clear and blue.

'I had a letter from my father,' Amy said. 'He says things are really tight at home – shortages of everything. He thinks there might be rationing soon.'

'I know,' Helen said. 'But it isn't any good worrying about it. There isn't anything we can do.'

'He also says there's something odd going on in Russia. It sounds as if there's some kind of revolution brewing. Against the Tsar.'

'Against the war more like,' Helen said. 'I wish everybody would revolt against that. Peter says it's weird. Our soldiers and theirs are just sitting opposite one another shooting at anything that moves but no one is doing any real attacking. It could go on for ever.'

'It's still spreading,' Amy sighed. 'My father says the German U-boats are sinking American ships now. Goodness knows what that will lead to.'

'Perhaps they'll come and help us.'

'Perhaps.'

They walked on in silence.

The noise started very faintly. 'What's that?' Helen said. Odd noises were always a worry. Amy was fine tuned now to the noises of the camp, but anything new always brought a new anxiety. The droning was very different from the usual sound of the endless traffic on the road.

They looked around them, and then Amy looked up. 'It's aircraft,' she said, and pointed. 'Look.' The planes were flying towards them from the east, the dots growing bigger until they could clearly see the wings. 'There are six of them.'

They stared into the sky. 'What are they? Helen said nervously. 'Are they theirs or ours?'

'I don't know yet,' Amy said.

A few seconds ticked by. Everyone in the camp knew how vulnerable they were to enemy attack from the air. So far they had been safe. So far the Germans seemed to respect the fact that there were hospitals on the site. The planes came closer, the droning louder.

Amy gasped. 'Oh my God, Helen, look! Black crosses! They're German.'

For a moment they seemed to be rooted to the spot. They could hear shouts now from the men here and there in the camp and sounds of running feet. A group of men rushed past them towards the anti-aircraft guns. 'Get under cover, ladies,' the sergeant shouted. 'They're German aircraft.'

'Come on, Helen.' Amy grabbed her arm and they began to run. 'We must get to the ward. We'll have to move the men.'

They burst into the ward. 'Enemy aircraft, Sister,' Amy said, breathless. The drone got louder. 'Quick, we must move the beds away from the windows.' They began to push and pull the beds into the middle of the hut, away from the windows and possible flying glass. They heard the crump of a falling bomb, but it sounded a good way away, on the edge of the camp. The windows rattled, but didn't break. They stood beside the beds in the middle of the ward.

'Anyone who can, get under the beds,' Amy ordered. They pulled the blankets over the heads of the men who couldn't get out of bed. Surely they will try to avoid the hospitals, Amy thought. Surely no one would bomb a hospital.

'Where next?' Sister whispered.

They waited fearfully for the next whistle of a falling bomb or the crump of another explosion, but nothing happened. Strained seconds went by. Then, amazingly, they heard the sound of cheering from outside.

'What on earth?' Amy ran to the door and looked out. One of the soldiers was waving his cap in the air. 'Here come the Flying Corps,' he shouted. 'Give 'em hell, boys.'

Amy stared up. British aircraft swooped down from above and the sky was suddenly filled with the chatter of machine-guns and the scream of the engines as they turned and climbed and dived. 'A dog fight!' the soldier shouted. 'A bloody dog fight!'

Helen and Sister came out and stood beside her. Overhead the planes looped and rolled and turned in a kind of dance. They appeared to move with a kind of lazy grace. They seemed to float, to glide, to appear and disappear as if by magic. It was mesmerizing. Amy had the strange thought that the dance would have been beautiful, if it hadn't been so deadly. It hardly seemed possible that up there, in the blue sky and among the shining clouds and glittering wings, men were fighting bitterly for their lives. Fighting for our lives too, she thought, everyone in this camp. The guns stuttered and sparked.

There was a sudden flash and one of the German planes burst into flames.

'Got his fuel tank,' the soldier said with relish.

They watched, horrified, as the German pilot climbed out of the cockpit and then threw himself out of the plane. They watched his body fall, slowly turning, to certain death. Helen clutched her mouth.

'Oh my God,' she said.

The soldier beside them drew in his breath. 'What a way to go,' he said. 'But I suppose it's better than burning.'

Amy closed her eyes, struggling not to think, trying with all her strength not to think of Johnny. She turned away and closed her eyes, sickened.

'Look,' the soldier said. 'They're going. Running away.'

The fight was quickly over. The German planes, harassed and separated, turned away for home. Two of them dropped their bombs on the open fields as they went. The British planes hovered above until the sky was clear and then they also turned for home.

'I suppose that man is dead,' Helen said. No one answered.

Amy fought down her horror. 'They won't give us those Guardian Angel parachutes,' Johnny had said, laughing. 'They think we might abandon the planes too soon.' Too soon? A young man was dead when he could have been saved.

They went back into the ward and began to put the beds back. All the men who could stand had been watching from the windows. A burly sergeant turned away. 'Only a matter of time, wasn't it?' he said. 'Bloody daft place to put hospitals, if you ask me, right next to a railway line and a training camp.'

'It's for the supplies,' Sister said sharply. 'It's the only way for us to get them. Otherwise they'd have to come by road or mule and take forever, and you wouldn't have your little comforts. Come on now, get back into bed.'

'I still think it's stupid,' he said. 'Like the rest of this bloody war.'

'Language,' Sister said.

CHAPTER FIFTEEN

1917

A MY stood outside the theatre, waiting for Dan. The sun was shining for once, the sky clear and blue. The atmosphere in the camp was different today. There was a feeling of hope. A group of smiling men passed her and called a cheery good morning. 'Dan,' she said, when he arrived, 'there's a rumour going about that the Americans have declared war on Germany.'

He smiled. 'It's true. It's official.'

She laughed with almost unbelieving relief. 'How wonderful! Surely that means the end of it? The Americans have so much – so much of everything and so many men. It will be like – like a whole new army.'

'I wouldn't get too excited just yet,' he said. 'Their standing army isn't even as big as ours. They'll have to train their men from scratch. It'll take months.'

Her face fell a little. 'But the Germans will know they're coming. It must dishearten them.'

'One hopes so,' he said. 'But I don't think we can expect any great change now, or for a long time yet I'm afraid.'

She sighed and closed her eyes briefly. 'I was just beginning to hope. . . .'

He touched her hand lightly. 'It will end, Amy, one day.'

She stared at him, her excitement and hope dying away, replaced with frustration and futile rage. 'It will have to end, won't it, when there are no more men left? No British, no French, no Germans. Nobody.' Her eyes filled with tears, tears of anger and disappointment.

He touched her hand again. 'We have to keep going, Amy. It's the only thing we can do.'

An orderly came out of the theatre. 'The patient is here,' she said.

They went in together. 'I want your help with this one,' Dan said. 'It might be a bit tricky. He has abdominal pain and shoulder-tip pain. There isn't an open abdominal wound, but I think he has a ruptured spleen. He must have had a nasty blow to the abdomen but he was knocked out and doesn't remember it. We'll probably have to remove it.'

'I haven't done that before,' she said.

'I've only done it twice.'

She met Helen later at lunch. 'What about the Americans,' Helen said, full of excitement. 'Isn't it wonderful?'

Amy smiled. 'Yes it is.' She didn't tell her about Dan's reservations.

'It'll be over soon.' Helen was beaming. 'Then we can all go home.'

That afternoon they had a few hours off to take a bath and have a walk for rest and exercise. They took their walk at the edge of the camp where the open countryside began.

'It looks so peaceful, doesn't it?' Helen said. 'Sometimes it looks so much like home that it nearly breaks my heart.'

Amy tried to lighten the moment. 'Where would you like to live after the war, Helen – you and Peter? Have you thought?'

'We talk about it all the time,' Helen said happily. 'Somewhere in the country where you can't hear anything but the birds and you can't smell anything but the flowers. I'm so utterly tired of these awful smells. When I get back to England I'm going to bathe in perfume and grow roses all over the house.'

'The birds are still singing,' Amy said. 'I can hear a blackbird.'

They walked on. Over the country sounds the drone of an aircraft came to them from the distance.

'Oh God,' Helen said. 'Not the Germans. Not again.'

Amy stared into the sky. 'We don't know what it is yet.'

'Come on!' Helen pulled at her arm. 'We can't take any chances. We'd best get under cover and we ought to get back to the ward.'

Amy gazed at the approaching plane. 'Just a minute, Helen.' She stared up, shading her eyes. 'Look,' she said. The aircraft did a slight turn and they could see the red white and blue roundel on the side. 'It's all right. It's one of ours. I think it's one of those new SE5s. Johnny's been telling me about them in his letters.'

'Thank goodness,' Helen breathed. 'I thought we were for it again.' They watched the plane approach. 'Look,' she said. 'I think it's coming down. I wonder if it's in trouble.'

'Oh no. Not that. I hope not. 'Amy could hardly look. She still had the horrified memory of the young German pilot falling to his death. She saw it in her dreams.

The aircraft disappeared behind a group of trees. They both waited, holding their breath, waiting for an explosion or a plume of smoke. The aircraft appeared again, bumping along a long field beside the camp. It turned and taxied back. The engine stopped, and then the pilot climbed out. He put chocks under the wheels and then began to walk towards them over the field. They watched him. As he got closer he took off his helmet and ran his hand through his hair, fair hair that shone in the sunshine.

Amy clutched Helen's arm. 'Helen, look.' She gave a jump of excitement. 'I think – it is! It's Johnny!' She climbed over the fence and ran towards him and met him as he walked towards the camp. 'Johnny!'

He put his arms around her and swung her round, laughing, and then he kissed her lightly on the mouth.

'Johnny,' she said again. 'How wonderful. What on earth are you doing here?'

'Come to see you, of course,' he said.

She clung to his arm. 'Are you allowed to just visit people? Won't you get into trouble?'

He laughed. 'Well, they won't know, will they?And if they find out I'll say I got lost and landed to ask the way.'

She laughed with him. 'They'd never believe that.'

'Oh they would,' he said. 'You'd be surprised. People do it all the time.'

They walked to the camp and he helped her over the fence. 'You remember Helen?' Amy asked. 'From Paris?'

'Of course.' He shook her hand.

'I'll finish my walk,' Helen said, carefully leaving them alone.

Amy led him into the camp. 'I'd better take you to the mess hut,' she said. 'Strictly no men in our own. Come and have a cup of tea.'

They walked into the camp. A corporal marched up to them and saluted smartly. 'I have been sent to ask if you need any assistance, sir,' he said.

'Thank you, Corporal,' Johnny said. 'Merely dropped in to ask the way. I shall need a couple of men to help me turn the aircraft shortly. Meanwhile I am being taken for a cup of tea.'

'Very good, sir. You are at Étaples, sir.'

'Thank you, Corporal.'

Amy led him to the mess. 'See?' he said. 'Nothing to it.'

She got him a cup of tea. 'I assume,' she said, laughing, 'that you'll be able to find your way back.'

'Of course.' He drank his tea. 'I've been here before. I thought you might have seen me.'

She shook her head, puzzled. 'No. When was that?'

'We had a little quarrel over here with some German planes a few weeks ago.'

She paled. 'That was you? One of those aircraft was you?'

He nodded. 'Good show, wasn't it?'

'Oh, Johnny.'

She couldn't hide her distress. He put his hand over hers. 'It's all right, my dear. I'm still here, hale and hearty.'

'It's so lovely to see you.'

'And you.' He paused, looking at her seriously. 'I assume there were no problems after – after London.'

'No,' she said. 'It was all right. Nothing happened.'

He looked relieved. 'That was lucky then.'

'Yes. Lucky.'

'It was wonderful, Amy. You don't regret it, do you?'

'No. I don't. Not ever. I miss you such a lot.'

'One day,' he said.

She saw Dan come into the mess. He had obviously seen them and seen Johnny's hand on hers. She slipped her hand away. Dan hesitated for a moment and then came over to them. Johnny got up as he approached.

'Dan,' she said. 'This is Johnny Maddox, my friend from the Flying Corps.' They shook hands. 'Dan is one of the surgeons here,' she said. 'A very good one.' She looked Dan in the eye, willing him to say nothing about her work.

'Have you any news?' Dan asked blandly. 'You fellows seem to know what's going on. We only know afterwards, when the results come pouring in here.'

Johnny shrugged. 'Something might be happening at Vimy, I think. Same old mess, I expect.'

Dan nodded. 'We'll have to be prepared then. I'd best get back to the ward. I'll get some tea there. Best of luck.'

'I'll see you later,' Amy said. 'I'm back on duty in an hour.' He left the hut. Johnny watched him go.

'Johnny,' she said, 'I've got something to tell you.'

He turned back to her and leant back in his chair. 'Has it by any chance got anything to do with your doctor friend?'

'No,' she said quickly. 'Not like that, anyway. He's just a friend and a colleague.'

'What then?'

'It's about me. I've been keeping something from you. I tried to tell you in England, but the moment never seemed to be right.'

'You look very serious, Amy.' He smiled. 'What have you done? Robbed a bank?'

She smiled briefly. 'No, it's not as bad as that.'

He listened to her without interruption, but he looked rather grim and puzzled.

'So,' he said, when she'd finished, 'you are telling me that you are a doctor, a surgeon.' She nodded. 'And you were removed from the medical register.' She nodded again. 'But nevertheless you are doing surgery here.'

'Yes,' she said emphatically. 'I've been asked to do it. The men are dying. You've seen it yourself. You know what it's like.'

'I do indeed. But you say you've put yourself in danger of never getting your licence back?'

She sat upright, stiffening her back and her resolve. 'I'll get it back. I will.'

Two of the sisters came in and sat at a far table with cups of tea, looking at them with interest.

Johnny smiled and leant towards her, lowering his voice. 'Does it really matter, Amy? If you marry me there won't be any necessity for you to do any kind of work.'

She gave a little gasp. 'Are you asking me to marry you, Johnny?'

He put his hand over hers again. 'Of course. I thought that was understood.'

Her eyes filled with tears. 'I do love you.'

He grinned. 'I sincerely hope so.' He glanced across at the sisters. 'I wish we could be alone. I can't even kiss you.'

'I know.'

He squeezed her hand. 'So you see, there's nothing to worry about. You won't have to work. You'll have plenty to do, believe me. My mother does a lot of charity work – she never stops.'

Her smile faded. 'But . . . what if I want to do it? I worked so hard to qualify, Johnny. It means a lot to me.'

His face changed a little. 'I don't quite see how it would be possible.'

She leant towards him, trying to show him how much it meant to her. 'Other women do it.'

'I don't want other women, Amy, I want you. Wouldn't you be satisfied and happy doing what other wives do, doing what my mother does?'

She began to have a strange feeling that something was shrivelling inside her, something that she couldn't grasp. 'I'm not the same as your mother, Johnny. Times are changing. Surely she would understand?'

He shook his head. 'No, she wouldn't. I don't think there is any reason for her to know anything about it.'

She lowered her head and bit her lip, confused and distressed.

He bent down and looked up into her eyes, smiling. 'I love you, Amy. Isn't that all that matters? We'll sort it out somehow. You might never get your licence back. There'd be no problem then.'

She smiled at him, a troubled smile.

'Let's leave it until the war is over,' he said. 'We can't do anything about it till then.'

She looked into his handsome face, wondering how she could ever be without him, wondering at the same time how she could live her life without her job.

'Yes,' she said. 'When the war's over.'

'I've got to go,' he said. 'Write to me, Amy. I'll see you when I can. Don't forget that you're my girl.'

They walked out together into the fitful sunshine and walked to the edge of the camp. Two soldiers were waiting by his aircraft to help him. He climbed over the fence then leant across and kissed her on the mouth. He strode away across the field, putting on his helmet. He climbed into the plane and the two Tommies turned the plane round, into the wind. The engine spluttered and roared and the plane rolled down the field and then up into the blue sky and away.

She walked back to the hut. Nothing had been resolved, but at least she had told him. Surely, she thought, they could work it out somehow. If they truly loved each other surely they could reach some compromise – square the circle. At the end of this endless war.

She went back to the theatre, to the ruptured intestines, damaged livers and spleens. She removed a shattered kidney, hoping that the boy was young and strong enough to lead a normal life with just one. Time after time the putrid smell of infection dashed any hope of recovery. One day it will end, she said to herself, over and over. One day it will end.

That night Helen was excited and curious. 'Fancy him flying in, just like that! Wasn't that wonderful? What did he say?'

Amy lay on her back, looking at the ceiling. 'He asked me to marry him.'

Helen gave a squeal and sat up in bed. 'There you are, I knew he would. You said yes, of course.'

'Yes.' Amy was still troubled. 'But I told him all about me and I don't think he was altogether pleased with the idea of a working wife. I know his mother wouldn't like it.'

'You're not marrying his mother.' Helen was indignant. 'Sooner or later everyone is going to have to accept that woman are different now.'

'He says we'll sort it out after the war.'

'After the war, after the war,' Helen said. 'All our lives are waiting until after the war.' She lay down again. 'I'm sick of it.'

'Your friend was right about something brewing,' Dan said, a few days later. 'There's been an attack by the Canadians at Vimy Ridge and another attack at Arras. Massive casualties, of course. We should be getting them any moment.'

The English newspapers arrived, several days late, and Amy began to read the accounts of the battle. The weather was appalling. Men had struggled through mud deep enough to drown a man. Then her heart leapt into her mouth. There had been a massive air battle over Vimy Ridge. In dreadful weather – rain and wind and a snowstorm – the planes had battled it out, and the Red Baron had added even more victims to his tally. She did her work in a constant fear for Johnny. She couldn't sleep. Any snatched moments led to nightmares of aeroplanes falling and crashing and the terrible repeated dream of the young German pilot.

She got a letter from Johnny and almost collapsed with relief. He had been there.

It was bad, Amy. It must have been hell for the men on the ground. The weather was appalling. They were slogging through mud and shell holes filled with water. The air was filled with shells and bullets; I don't know how we managed to fly through them unscathed. The ground was on fire with explosions and bursting shells. I was glad I was in the air.

He's alive, she thought. He came through it. He's alive. She slept that night like the dead.

The wounded arrived, endless, endless lines of men, soaked to the skin, covered in mud and lice, many with rat-bites. They toiled on.

A letter arrived from her father.

They've bombed London again. Fourteen Gotha bombers. Apparently you could see them from Kensington High Street; 162 people were killed and over four hundred wounded. They are killing women and children, Amy.

June was drier with occasional sunny days. 'Thank God it's stopped raining,' Dan said. 'Perhaps the men can get somewhere now. They can't fight in the mud.' He spoke too soon. The rain started again, torrential and continuous and the trenches and shell holes filled again. The army captured Messines Ridge and began the battle at Passchendaele.

'The Germans are using mustard gas again,' Dan said. 'God help the men.'

'The Americans won't be coming until next year,' Helen said, almost in tears. 'You know what that means.' There was nothing that Amy could say. 'It means it isn't going to end, not this year anyway.'

Amy felt overcome with weariness. Another year at least, and after that – who could know? They were all just waiting, endlessly waiting for any kind of normal life to come back again; Helen and Peter, she and Johnny, half the world.

That evening Helen bounced into the hut, her eyes shining. 'Amy!' she said. 'Guess what!'

Amy laughed. 'Whatever it is it's obviously something good.'

'We're not going to wait any longer.' Helen was excited and happy. 'We're going to get married now as soon as we can.'

Amy was thrilled. 'What? When? When did all this happen?'

'We decided today.' Helen stopped bouncing around the room and sat down at the table. 'We're not going home; it would take too long. We're going to get married in Paris. Peter wants Dan to be his best man, and I want you to be my maid of honour.'

For the next two weeks Helen was totally occupied with her wedding. She was given two days off to go to Paris to make arrangements. 'I'll have to let you go,' Matron said, smiling. 'You won't be any use until you've done it.'

When she came back she was beaming. 'I've organized the Embassy in Paris, and the English church, and I've booked hotels.'

'Can your parents come?' Amy asked, and for the first time Helen looked a little sad. 'I've sent cables,' she said. 'My father is coming if he can get a passage, but they don't think my mother or the girls should take the risk. Peter's father can't get away.' She brightened up again. 'That little dressmaker is making a dress for me.'

'I'll just wear my pink again,' Amy said. 'It's come in very handy.'

'After the war,' Helen said, 'we'll have another blessing and a real party in England. We'll really celebrate then.'

Somewhat to Amy's surprise they were all given two nights off to go to the wedding and Helen and Peter were to have two extra nights in Paris. 'I shall still have to share with you when we get back,' Helen said. 'Matron says we can't stay together.' She rolled her eyes. 'It would cause scandal and set a bad example.'

'At least you'll have a long weekend,' Amy said wistfully. It was more than she had ever had alone with Johnny.

They travelled to Paris on the train, the men decently housed in one hotel and the girls in another. Helen's father was there to give her away.

The simple ceremony touched Amy in the deepest way, far more than a lavish wedding in England would ever have done. The men standing proudly in their uniforms and Helen in her simple dress seemed to pare down the service to its real meaning – the simple joining of two fine people who loved each other.

She and Dan travelled back together on the train. She sat with her head against the seat back, staring drowsily out of the widow. She glanced at Dan and he was looking at her, his dark eyes brooding. Then he smiled at her, a cheerful, friendly smile.

'Post, Amy.' Helen put the letters on the table. Amy was dressing hurriedly; she was due in theatre. She glanced at the letters. One was from her father; she could see that. The other one she didn't recognize. She slipped them in her pocket to read later.

She spent the morning in theatre, and came back to the hut to tidy up her hair and get ready for the afternoon. She stood by the table and read her father's letter. He tried to keep cheerful, bless him, but he constantly worried about her.

She slit open the other letter. *Dear Amy*, it began. Puzzled, she read on. In a moment she felt suddenly as if she were not alive any more, as if her heart had stopped beating and she was not breathing. It isn't true, she thought, it can't be; it's some dreadful mistake, and for a few confused seconds she was comforted. Then she gave a cry, 'Helen!'

Helen was beside her at once. 'Amy, what is it? What's happened?'

Amy couldn't stand. She lowered herself slowly into a chair. Helen knelt beside her. She tried to take the letter but Amy wouldn't let it go. She clutched it to her in despair, as if it was the last contact she would ever have, as if his name, written on the paper, was his last touch.

'He's dead, Helen,' she whispered. 'Johnny is dead. The letter is from his father.'

'Oh no! Oh no!' Helen put her arms around her. She burst into tears.

'He can't be,' Amy said. 'He can't be dead.' But outside the door, in the road and the railway and the hospitals, death was a living, breathing, insatiable monster. She couldn't cry. She sat on the chair unmoving.

'Stay here,' Helen said. 'I'm going to get someone. I'm going to tell them you can't work today. Don't move, Amy.'

She didn't move. Slowly, very slowly, she had to realize, to accept the truth. Johnny was dead. Her bright, laughing Johnny was dead. She saw him standing before her, tall and upright in his uniform. She saw his smile, his shining hair as he walked to her across the field. She felt his arms around her and his kiss on her mouth. She saw his mother's roses that she had named for him, the bright, flaming flowers dancing free in the garden. Her face felt frozen; she couldn't cry.

The door opened quietly and Helen and Dan came in. Dan took her hands in his. 'I'm so sorry, Amy. I'm so sorry.'

She looked into his kind, concerned face and held on to his hands.

'I'll tell them you can't work for a while,' he said.

'I don't want to stop working,' she said dully. 'It'll be better if I go on. God knows I'm not the only one.'

'You must take your time, Amy.'

'I want to go to his funeral,' she said. 'The letter is from his father. He's being buried in a week, when – when he arrives home.'

'Of course,' Dan said. 'You shall go.'

'I'll stay with you today,' Helen said. 'You shouldn't be alone.'

'Call for me any time,' Dan said. He released her hands. 'I'll sort out compassionate leave for you. Just leave it to me. Look after her, Helen.'

'I'll go to see Matron,' Helen said. 'I'll get the day off to be with you. I'll be back very soon.'

They left the hut, leaving her alone. She walked about the hut, restless, in pain. It didn't seem possible that he had gone – a moment, a spark of time, and he was gone. She couldn't bear to think of how he died – surely not like the German pilot. She put the letter down carefully on the table. How they must be suffering, his mother and father and his brother. She remembered his mother's face, the fear in her eyes. This war – any war – takes the finest and the best.

Helen came back. 'Come out with me,' Amy said. 'I need to be outside in the open air.'

They walked down their usual walk at the edge of the camp. Helen took her hand. 'Do you want to talk about it, Amy?'

They walked a little further. 'His father got a letter from his commanding officer,' Amy said. 'He was shot down. He said that Johnny died instantly. He didn't suffer. I only hope that it was true.' They walked for most of the rest of the day. Amy was too restless to stay anywhere.

In the evening Dan came. 'I've arranged for you to go home,' he said. 'The day after tomorrow.' She nodded her thanks. 'Do you think you might come back, Amy? Or perhaps it's too soon for you to make such decisions.'

'Of course I'll come back,' she said. 'I need to work. It's the only thing I can do.'

205

After he had gone she got into bed, but she lay awake most of the night, only falling into a restless doze as dawn was breaking.

When she arrived in England it was raining. She sent a telegram to her father as soon as she left the boat: *Have arrived in England. Johnny is dead.* She took the train to London, to Victoria Station. The train was packed with soldiers. They sat in strained silence in the seats, or smoked, standing in the corridors, their eyes distant and guarded.

She arrived home exhausted. Her father met her at the door and put his arms around her and led her inside. The familiar atmosphere of home wrapped around her. She put her head on her father's shoulder and for the first time, she wept.

'What can I say, Amy?' Her father held her as her sobbing quietened. 'I'm so sorry.'

'There's nothing to say,' she said. 'He's gone; that's all.' Her head began to droop.

'You're exhausted,' he said. 'You must go to bed and rest.'

'Yes,' she said. 'Just for a little while.' She dragged herself upstairs and into her room and undressed and got into bed. She fell asleep instantly and slept until the next morning, without dreaming.

Her father was at the breakfast table when she came downstairs. He poured her a cup of tea. 'Did you sleep?'

She nodded. 'Yes.' She sipped her tea. 'The funeral is on Friday. At their home in Berkshire.'

'Do you want me to come with you?'

'No, dear,' she said. 'I'd rather go alone. I'm only going to the service. I'm not going to stay. I couldn't bear to stand around talking about him to people I don't know and who don't know me.'

'Come straight home afterwards,' he said. 'You can rest here with me.'

On Friday she took the train to London and then a train from Paddington. She took a taxi from the station to the church.

The little church was filled with people, all, to her distress, dressed in black. There was so much black everywhere. Johnny would not have wanted black.

She found a place at the back of the church. She could see Johnny's father in the front pew and beside him Johnny's mother. She looked smaller than ever, shrunken and bent, and heavily veiled.

The organ began to play quietly and the congregation stood up. The coffin was carried in, draped in the Union flag. It passed so close to her that she could have reached out and touched it – touched him. The tears began and ran silently down her cheeks. There were tears all around her.

She didn't hear the service. She stood up and sat down with everyone else. A few words came through from the prayers; courage, sacrifice, eternal life. I want him now, she thought. I want him now. The tears flowed. The service ended and the coffin was carried out into the little churchyard for the final goodbye.

Johnny's father saw her and made a little signal with his hand, reaching out to her. When the service was over he came to stand beside her.

'Amy,' he said. He took her hand. She could see the agony in his eyes. 'I want to talk to you,' he said. 'Will you come back to the house?'

'No,' she said. 'I couldn't bear it.'

He seemed to understand. 'Wait for me here,' he said. 'I'll take my wife home and I'll come back.'

'Yes,' she said. 'I'll wait.'

They climbed into their cars. Johnny's mother didn't speak to her, too devastated, Amy thought, to speak to anyone. She probably didn't know anything about her real relationship with Johnny. He probably hadn't told her yet. It was going to be after the war. Everything was after the war.

She stood beside the grave for a few moments with bowed head, saying her last goodbye. Then she went to sit in the little church. It was very quiet. The light slanted through the stained-glass windows, casting their colours on the stone floor. The ancient walls seemed to speak to her. She put out her hand and touched one of the stone pillars, solid, unchanging. Hundreds of years of English history folded around her. She could feel the presence of these ancient congregations. 'Life goes on,' they seemed to say. 'We accept; we go on.'

Sir Henry came into the church and sat beside her. 'My dear,' he said. There were tears in his eyes. 'I know that you loved him and I know that he loved you. I want you to know that I would have been proud to welcome you into the family.'

'Thank you,' she whispered.

'He told me,' he went on, 'about you being a doctor and about your troubles.'

'It hardly matters now,' she said.

'Yes, it does, Amy. You must go on with your life. I believe what you say. I'm not without contacts. I'll help you in any way I can.'

'I can't think about it now,' she said.

He took her hand. 'I know, but time heals, Amy. Don't let this war destroy you.'

'Thank you,' she whispered again.

He got up. 'I'll take you to the station. Go home to your father, Amy, and then go back to your work. Johnny admired you very much.'

He saw her on to the train. 'I'll be in touch,' he said.

She left Johnny in the churchyard. She went home to her father and then she went back to France, taking Johnny's free spirit with her.

CHAPTER SIXTEEN

1917-1918

A MY arrived back in France and took the train to Étaples. Once again it was raining. Rain, she thought, endless rain, as if the whole world were weeping. Rain and mud.

Helen was waiting for her in their hut. 'Take off your coat,' she said, 'you're soaking.' She made a cup of tea. 'Can I do anything, Amy?'

Amy shook her head. 'I'm glad I went. I don't think I quite believed it before.'

'I'm so sorry, Amy.'

Helen and Dan were concerned and kind, but there was no time for reflection or even for grieving. Only when she lay in bed could she think about Johnny and shed her private tears. The battle for Passchendaele went on in a nightmare of bullets, mud, and poison gas.

They were getting more and more shell-shocked men; so many that they opened a ward for them in one of the tents. There were men who couldn't stop screaming unless they were sedated into a restless sleep; men whose whole body shook and shuddered until they were skeletal and exhausted; men who couldn't walk – whose legs let them down as they tried to stand; men who couldn't see or hear, whose uninjured eyes and ears could no longer transmit their messages to a brain so stunned with horror that it would not receive them.

She was surprised to see that there were a few French women and children in the camp, women from the farms, by the look of them, weary and distraught.

'They're refugees from the villages,' Helen said. 'They've started to come into Étaples, into the town. Some of them have come here looking for a doctor.'

'Miss Osborne,' Sister said one morning. 'Captain Fielding wants you urgently in the female ward. There is an emergency there.' Amy hurried across, wondering what the problem was. The nurses and orderlies got colds and flu but they hadn't had a surgical emergency before.

She found, to her surprise, a woman in labour. 'She's from one of the villages,' Dan said. 'One of the refugees. We'll have to help her. She's been in labour too long already and she isn't getting anywhere.'

Amy felt her abdomen. The baby's head seemed to be lying freely to one side. She put on a glove and examined her. 'There's a limb down,' she said.

'Trouble,' Dan said. 'Is it an arm or a leg?'

Amy paused. If the baby's limb was a leg then it was a breech presentation and they could allow it to proceed normally. If it was an arm then the delivery was totally obstructed, the baby lying across the neck of the womb. In that case there was no way that the baby could be delivered normally. If they left her, the baby and probably the mother, would die. She felt again, her fingers touching the little limb. Was it a hand she was feeling, or a foot? She felt the tiny fingers move.

'It's a hand,' she said. 'We'll have to do a section. It's the only way.'

Dan looked at her across the patient who was moaning in pain, the sweat standing on her brow. 'Have you done one before?'

She nodded. 'Perhaps we could cross-match her and get a donor in case she needs blood. We'll use Group O if there's no match.'

He nodded briefly. 'Prepare her for theatre, Sister,' he said. 'I'll get it organized. I'll see you in theatre, Miss Osborne.'

The last thing Amy expected was that she would be doing a Caesarean section here in this army camp filled with the weapons of destruction. Between them she and Sister managed to explain to the mother what they were going to do. They took her to theatre where Dan and the anaesthetist were waiting.

Speed, Amy thought. Speed was essential. The baby's pulse rate was already too high. The anaesthetist put the mother to sleep.

She cut across the abdomen, through the muscles and the peritoneum. Then she cut through the uterus and the blood spurted, as she knew it would. She and Dan clamped off the bleeding vessels. She felt carefully for the baby's head and gently lifted him out – a little boy. She clipped off and cut the cord and laid him in the nurse's waiting arms. The afterbirth came away and she quickly began to repair the uterus and close the wound. Across the theatre she heard a little cough, and then the baby cried, a loud, healthy cry. She glanced up at Sister whose eyes were filled with tears.

The baby cried. Amy felt an unaccustomed surge of pleasure and joy. Among all the cries she heard in this camp day after day, this was a cry to warm the heart, a cry of new life, of hope and happiness.

'I hear you had a baby,' Helen said. 'How lovely,' and then she laughed and blushed. 'I'm so sorry. What a thing to say.'

Amy smiled. 'It's all right, I know what you mean. Just don't say it to anyone else.'

'I'm going to have lots of babies,' Helen said. 'Lots and lots.'

'Helen!' Amy said. 'You don't mean. . . .'

Helen blushed again. 'Oh no. I wouldn't be here if I was pregnant. Peter wouldn't let me stay. He's not too keen now, but I said we got married to be together, didn't we, so he'll have to put up with me.'

Amy laughed. 'I think he can manage that.'

In September the weather became fine and dry. 'Perhaps we'll get somewhere now,' Dan said, 'if the land dries out.' But once again he spoke too soon. By October it was raining again, daily, incessant rain. In November, after sixteen weeks of fighting, the Canadians took Passchendaele Ridge. Then the British attacked at Cambrai, but the British tanks bogged down in the mud. After 40,000 casualties, they were back where they started.

'Bad news,' Dan said one morning. 'The Russians are pulling out. The new government has obviously decided that they've had enough. Now the Huns can concentrate on us.'

Amy stared at him. 'Perhaps they're the only ones with any sense,' she said. 'I wish we could all do the same.'

'When will the Americans get here?' Helen said plaintively. 'I wish they would come.'

The men who poured into the hospital from Cambrai were exhausted beyond belief.

'They're beginning to fantasize again,' Helen said. 'They're talking about ghosts. One of them told me he saw his commanding officer helping the wounded off the battlefield, bullets flying all around, and when he got back he found out the officer had been dead for three days.' The rumours flew around, of dead soldiers coming back to help the living. More angels of Mons.

'They've had enough,' Amy said. 'They can't accept reality any more.'

Sometimes she almost believed them. She dreamt about Johnny almost every night. Then once, when she was walking at the edge of the camp, she thought she saw him walking towards her over the field, his fair hair shining. She had a crazed moment of unbelieving joy, she almost called out to him, almost climbed over the fence to run to him, and then in an instant he was gone. Slowly the acute and unbearable pain became a steady, nostalgic ache in her heart.

After Cambrai the flow of wounded began to ease a little, but they were replaced by an endless flow of sick men, men with pneumonia, typhus, influenza, hepatitis. Often they had raging fevers that were never diagnosed. Helen was transferred to a medical ward. 'There aren't nearly enough nurses or VADs,' she said. 'Sometimes I'm the only person on the ward. I give bedpans out in my dreams.'

'What's happening?' Amy said to Dan. 'Have you any news?'

'Not much,' he said. 'It seems to have gone back to the same old beginning, sitting in trenches staring at each other and shooting anything that moves.'

The winter came in and was bitter; deep, frozen cold and bitter winds. The water froze in the kettles and taps overnight. The nurses and VADs wore jerseys and sometimes overcoats on the wards. Keeping the men warm became a major battle.

The year crept towards its end. Just before Christmas Amy and Helen walked into Étaples town to buy some sweets and biscuits for the men. Even these simple pleasures were becoming scarce. The town was busy, a steady trickle of refugees along the road in from the east. In the camp the men got up a Christmas concert. The medical and nursing staff crowded into the back of the tent, ready to leave if they were needed. There were the old, well-worn acts, music and songs and recitations – 'The boy stood on the burning deck' and 'The Ancient Mariner.' Then a young man came on to the makeshift stage, a young pilot from the RFC, his arm in a sling. He sang a song that he said was popular among the pilots. Amy listened with growing horror.

Take the cylinder out of my kidneys
The connecting rod out of my brain
From the small of my back take the camshaft
And assemble the engine again.

She left the tent abruptly. Dan followed her out into the freezing night.

'I'm sorry, Amy,' he said. 'You shouldn't have had to listen to that.' She was trying, unsuccessfully, to hold back the tears. 'Amy,' he said softly. He took her in his arms and held her close, stroking her hair, as you would comfort a child.

'It's all right,' she said at last. 'I'm sorry.'

He let her go. 'I wish I could take the pain away.' She nodded, without looking at him, and without words, and made her way back to the hut.

Helen came back later. '1918 in a week,' she said. 'I'm not going to celebrate New Year. How could anyone? I'm just going to spend the evening with Peter if I can, though I don't suppose we'll manage to be alone.'

A strange marriage, Amy thought, but at least they're together. Most people were not.

January was bitter. The wounded still came in steady but manageable numbers, and the sick flowed in.

In February there was news that delighted the female staff. 'It's happened, Amy.' Helen was dancing about the hut. 'Votes for women! Our great and wonderful government' – she made a face – 'has at last decided that women can vote. We are no longer classed with criminals and lunatics.' She pulled another face. 'You've got to be thirty, though.'

'About time too. And I don't understand why they've made it only over thirty.' Amy thought of all the women here and at home, the nurses and VADs and the WAACs and WRENS and the Land Army and the ambulance drivers – most of them under thirty. 'I suppose it's a start.'

Helen pinned her suffragist badge to her apron. 'They can't stop me wearing this today.' She smiled broadly. 'We can be Members of Parliament too.'

Amy laughed. 'I can certainly think of someone who might do that.'

Helen was serious. 'I'll have to wait for a few years, but I shall certainly keep it in mind.'

'What are you all so happy about?' one of the patients asked, a grizzled sergeant, wounded in the leg.

'We've got the vote,' Amy said. 'Women have got the vote. What do you think of that?'

'Good for you,' he said. 'You can't do worse than the lot we've got now. Maybe you can stop this bleeding war.'

In March the weather eased a little, icy days and nights changing to cold, cold rain. Amy was in a strange, restless mood. She took to wandering about the edge of the camp in her time off, or occasionally walked into Étaples, looking at the shops, watching the steady trickle of refugees from the east, away from the enemy lines. Do they know something we don't, she thought? Or are they just getting as far away as they can? She felt as if this were the lull before a storm. Everywhere there was a dreadful sense of weariness, of want and despair. The only laughter came from the children, playing with their meagre toys in the streets.

She saw Dan almost daily. 'I'm stifled, Dan,' she said. 'I just have this awful feeling, and it's not only me. The men are restless and the shell-shock cases are worse. It's as if there's a black cloud hanging over us.'

'You're tired, Amy,' he said. 'We're all tired to death.'

'I just feel as if there's something coming,' she said.

Dan smiled wearily. 'There's always something coming.'

On 21 March, they knew what it was. The camp was struck with unbelieving shock. The Germans had launched a massive offensive, pouring shells and explosives and phosgene and mustard gas into the British lines. By nightfall they had broken through and the British were falling back.

Amy and Dan were in the surgical ward when the news came through. Dan visibly paled before her eyes.

'It'll take nearly two days before the wounded get here,' he said. 'God knows what it will be like. We must be prepared. Get what sleep you can, Amy.' He turned to Sister. 'Stock up the theatres and the wards, Sister. As many dressings and bandages as you can get. I'll try to get more blood. We must transfer more of the nurses and VADs to the surgical wards.'

Amy lay in bed at night, waiting. She felt as she had when she first qualified, afraid of what might be coming in, hoping that she would be able to cope.

They heard the rumbling of the ambulances and lorries on the road half an hour before they arrived. They waited in the theatres and wards, silent, apprehensive.

The ambulances began to unload. Amy was dazed by the scenes before her. There were hundreds of men, their wounds covered in filthy, stinking bandages and sodden dressings, shattered limbs bound to splints with filthy rags, spilling intestines under dirty wet towels; the gassed men coughing up their lives, their eyes swollen and purulent. The men were crying, dismayed. 'There's thousands of them,' one of the young soldiers sobbed. 'There's ten of them for every one of us.'

Amy and Helen looked at each other, horrified. Where had all these German soldiers come from? For the very first time it occurred to Amy that the Allies might lose the war. The thought was devastating, paralysing. Was it possible? All this, and then to lose? Was German cavalry going to ride down Whitehall?

The men came on, in trucks, farm carts, anything they could get. One of the officers was near to tears. 'It's chaos,' he said. 'We've lost dozens of the men; they're scattered everywhere.'

'Miss Osborne,' Sister whispered, 'they've shelled Paris! They've got guns that can shell from seventy-five miles away.'

One morning Amy and Helen were walking to the hospital when a column of soldiers marched down the road nearby. 'Who on earth are they?' Helen said. They were so tall, so upright, and seemed so cheerful. Helen clutched Amy's arm. 'Amy! It's the Americans!' Amy watched them go by, impressed by their height and strength. What a contrast, she thought, to our own men, beaten down by years of war, and beaten down by neglect and want before that. There were so many things that needed changing at home, after the war.

By May the Germans were only thirty-seven miles from Paris. Her father's letters spoke of more air raids on England, and there were air raids on Paris. No one was safe now. Amy woke every day, wondering how long it would be before German planes attacked the camp. How could they escape it? There was the railway and the railway bridge, hundreds of men in training. It must be a prime target. So far they seemed to have been protected by the presence of the hospitals, but how long would that last? German planes frequently flew over, on reconnaissance, she supposed. Then there was an unsettling rumour that they had dropped a message, saying, 'Move your hospitals or move your railway.'

'They wouldn't,' Helen said. 'Even they wouldn't bomb hospitals.'

They were woken one morning by an enormous explosion.

'My God!' Helen jumped out of bed. 'What's that?'

They dressed hurriedly, knowing already what it was. They peered out of the door. Several German Taube aircraft were overhead. There was another explosion.

'Oh God, Oh God,' Helen stepped outside. 'We'd better get to the hospital.'

They slipped between the buildings, hugging the walls. They could hear shouting from everywhere, and then a thin screaming from the shell-shock tent. One of the men, wild eyed, ran out across the camp towards the fields. Helen made to go after him but Amy stopped her. 'They're machine-gunning, Helen. Stay here.'

They reached the ward and stumbled inside. The staff were standing by the door, unable to do anything, just waiting until it was over.

'They're after the railway bridge,' Dan said, 'but their aim isn't good. God knows what's going on out there.'

The explosions stopped; the sound of the aircraft faded away. They went outside. One of the ward tents had collapsed, the men exposed to the open air, but apart from that the damage seemed to be confined to the railway area.

They struggled to get the men under cover. 'Thank goodness there was so little damage,' Amy said. 'It could have been so much worse.'

Dan looked shocked. 'We haven't seen the last of them, Amy, I'm afraid. They'll come back.'

They came back that night, and the next, and the next. In the wards and in their own huts they crouched in the dark, hoping and waiting until the attacks were over. During the day they continued, endlessly, in the theatres. One day several nurses and VADs straggled into the camp, with nothing but the clothes they stood up in. They had retreated, with the men, from Casualty Clearing Stations that were about to be overrun by the advancing Germans.

The bombs seemed to fall mainly on the town and on the railway. 'They seem to be trying to avoid the hospitals,' Dan said. 'At least they are doing that.'

Amy found it very difficult even to remember the last raid, this time in the daytime. Somehow her brain and her memory shied away from it. Some part of her brain was protecting her from memories too terrible to bear.

The Taubes came over again, in the middle of the morning. As they left, one of them dropped its bomb on the camp. She remembered a nurse, running screaming from outside the mess hut, men running towards it, shouting, tearing at the wreckage with their bare hands. All she remembered after that was several bodies being carried out, and one of them was Helen.

She sat alone in their hut. Helen's coat hung on the nail, her little possessions scattered about. Helen was gone, her cheerfulness and affection and sympathy were gone from a world that needed them so badly.

Dan broke the rules and sat with her often in the hut, just being there, or holding her while she cried. There was little that he could say. Peter, wild eyed and distraught, insisted on being transferred to a forward First Aid Post, as near to the fighting as he could get. Helen was gone.

Slowly, haltingly, the tide turned. American troops, fresh and eager, poured in. The Germans were driven back. They had played their last hand, and they had failed.

At long last Amy began to believe that the end might be near. 'It's over, surely,' she said to Dan. 'Why don't they just stop? Why don't they stop the killing?'

At last they knew that the end was coming. The armistice was signed on the morning of 11 November, and at eleven o'clock, the killing stopped. The war was over.

*

They stood outside among the men in fitful, drizzling rain. The minutes and the seconds ticked by. Then, on the moment of eleven o'clock, somewhere in the camp, a bugler played the slow, melancholy notes of the Last Post. The men listened in silence, their heads bowed, and then, when it was over, there were a few spasmodic cheers. It was as if no one could believe it, as if they thought it was some kind of evil German hoax. Then the normal sounds began again, the shouted orders, the rumbling of traffic on the road.

Amy watched the ambulances coming in. It seemed an extraordinary thought that these would be the last of the wounded, that slowly the numbers would diminish, and then stop. All the men would be going home. Now the ambulances were also bringing in more and more men who were sick with influenza, the dreadful strain of the disease that was beginning to kill people all over Europe, and even, she had heard, in America. She felt a dreadful sense of inevitability, as if death would not give up, as if it would not be satisfied with mere human folly, but would want to display its own overwhelming power, devouring more and more.

'It's over, Amy,' Dan said softly. 'We can go home.'

It will never be over, she thought. Johnny and Helen and all the dead men will never come back. It will never be over.

She turned to him and forced a smile. 'Yes,' she said. 'Home.'

'We still have work to do,' he said. 'I expect we will have for some time.' They began to walk back to the theatre.

'What now, I wonder?' Dan said.

'At least it will stop,' Amy said, 'the carnage. We should get all the remaining wounded in the next few weeks.'

'This influenza worries me.' Dan looked sombre. 'It's killing people just as effectively as the war and it's just as relentless, just as mindless.'

'What's happened to us, Dan?' The war's end hadn't brought what Amy had hoped – a true feeling of evil conquered, a new beginning. She had an unaccountable feeling of dread, as if something dark had merely been covered over, not rooted out for ever. She sighed. Perhaps these thoughts were just the result of years of a horror that could never have been predicted or imagined.

'I think the world has fallen into a kind of pit,' he said. 'We'll just have to pull ourselves out of it.'

'How?'

'I suppose,' he said, 'by leading good lives.' He paused. 'That sounds really pompous, doesn't it, but I don't mean it that way.' He frowned, searching for words. 'I don't mean simply not doing deliberate harm. I mean looking after other people; our countrymen for a start. Some of these boys got better food, even in the trenches, than they did at home.'

'I think you are absolutely right,' she said. His words gave her a kind of warmth, a sense of purpose for the future.

The wounded still came. The fighting had apparently gone on until the very last moment. One of the officers told her that the Germans had continued to fire on them till the very end – a German officer had seen to that. Then at eleven o'clock he had stood up, taken off his helmet, bowed, and led his men away. His own men had been reluctant, fearing that it was some kind of trick. Then, slowly, they began to stand up in the trenches, amazed that they could do so without getting shot.

Slowly, the stream of wounded slowed to a trickle. They were replaced by men sick with the influenza, and slowly they were repatriated home. The camp began to disband, the Americans and Canadians and Anzacs and all the other Empire troops going home.

Dan was sent back to England, to work in one of the military hospitals in London. They said goodbye in the lane at the edge of the camp.

'Let me know as soon as you are back home,' he said. 'I'll come to see you. I'll write to you till then.'

She nodded, her eyes filling. He took her hands and then bent his head and kissed her gently on the cheek. 'I won't say goodbye. Just *au revoir*.'

She found herself in a personal no-man's land. Officially she wasn't there at all, except perhaps as a VAD. Very soon she would have to go home and face the future. She wondered if Major Barnes would remember his promise, if Sir Henry could ever do anything, if her work at the camp would stand her in good stead, or if it would count against her.

She plucked up her courage and went to see Major Barnes. 'Of course I remember, Miss Osborne,' he said. 'Or perhaps I should call you Dr Richmond now. I shall approach the General Medical Council as soon as I can.'

That, at least, was comforting. Her work at the camp was finishing. Perhaps her whole career was finishing. She would just have to wait.

Eventually, together with most of the other female staff, she was sent home. She took the train and the boat, and then the train again. Once more they were packed with soldiers going home, this time for good. She had expected that the men would be different, laughing, joking, larking about. To her surprise they were not. They were as quiet and subdued as the last time she had travelled, smoking incessantly, eyes hooded, withdrawn. She saw the same in London, men standing on the streets alone or in small groups, smoking, looking into the distance with empty eyes.

Her father greeted her with his arms open wide. He looks older, she thought, much more than four years older.

'Here I am, Father,' she said. 'Home again, safe and sound.'

He led her into the sitting-room, weeping. 'Thank God,' he said, his voice breaking. They sat together beside the fire, the unaccustomed warmth glowing on her face. 'I don't know what to say to you, Amy,' he said. 'I can't imagine what you have been through. I only thank God that you are home.'

She found that it wasn't possible to talk to her father about the war. She could see his concern, his eagerness to help her put it behind her, but no words would come. There were no words to describe the wounds, the filth, the horror and the pain, the danger and the death. She knew that he was waiting for her to tell him, but she could not. No matter how often she tried, the words would not come. She thought of the soldiers on the train, their eyes far away. She recognized their new battle.

She felt totally lost, confused and empty. She woke in the night, every night, disturbed and startled by the unnatural quiet, and found it hard to go to sleep again. She woke every morning, facing another day with nothing to do, nothing to distract her from her memories.

She wrote to Dan to tell him that she was home and a few days later he came to the house. She was so glad to see him that she almost cried, clutching his hands. She introduced him to her father and then took him out to walk, to be alone with him.

'You're still in uniform,' she said.

'Yes,' he said. 'I should be demobbed soon.'

'What will you do then?'

'I've been offered a job at St Bartholomew's – on the surgical staff.' He said it almost apologetically.

'How wonderful,' she said. 'I'm so happy for you Dan.'

'What are you doing, Amy?'

'Waiting,' she said. 'Just waiting.'

'I've been to the GMC,' he said.

'Oh Dan!'

'And they told me unofficially that they'd heard from Major Barnes. They also told me that they'd had a letter from Sir Henry Maddox.'

She looked away for a moment, a lump in her throat.

He took her hand. 'Do you think you might ever get over it, Amy? I don't mean forget him, I know you can never do that.' He paused. 'I don't really know what I mean. Am I being insensitive?'

She looked up at him. His face was filled with caring and concern.

'He's dead, Dan, and Helen's dead. I'll never forget them but I've accepted it now. I've had to. I can't look around me without seeing what has happened here. God knows, I'm not the only one.' She squeezed his hand gently. 'It's so good to see you, Dan. I don't have to say anything to you or explain anything. You know.'

'I know,' he said. He walked home with her. 'I'll see you soon.'

Two weeks later a letter arrived, inviting her to call at the GMC offices in London.

'I'm frightened, Father,' she said.

'Do you want me to come with you, Amy?'

She shook her head. 'No, dear.' She gave a wry smile. 'If I'm going to have a nervous breakdown I'll be better alone.'

She was shown into a small office and shortly afterwards one man came in, the one she remembered, the only man on the committee who'd shown her some sympathy.

He smiled at her. 'Sit down, Dr Richmond.' He sat down beside her, not behind a desk, this time, she noted.

He looked, she thought, slightly embarrassed. 'We have had several letters,' he said, 'on your behalf, concerning your fitness to practise.' She waited. 'We have also received a letter from Sir Henry Maddox, a character reference it would be hard to ignore.' She waited again, her heart thumping. 'There is something more,' he said. He looked even more embarrassed. 'We have had another – shall we say – complaint,

221

from the theatre sister at the hospital where you used to work.' She stared at him, puzzled. 'I will merely say,' he went on, 'that William Bulford has taken early retirement.' He coloured. 'I am sure you will understand me.'

She could not stop a look of disgust. 'I do.'

'Therefore,' he said, 'the General Medical Council have withdrawn unreservedly their decision of four years ago and your name has been restored to the Medical Register without any mark against you.' He smiled. 'I am sure that your surgical experience in France has far exceeded anything that you could have gained here at home, and will stand you and your patients in very good stead.'

He stood up and held out his hand and she shook it until he laughed and stopped her. 'Goodbye, Dr Richmond. You will be getting a letter of confirmation very shortly.'

She left the office on air. She travelled home and flew into the house, calling for her father. He ran out of the sitting-room, his face strained with worry.

She threw her arms around him. 'It's all right,' she said. 'They've taken it all back. I'm a doctor again.'

She wrote to Dan, and to Major Barnes and Sir Henry. She thought it best not to contact the sister, even if she had known where to find her. Dan sent a telegram to say that he would be with her at the weekend when he was off duty.

'I think we must get a telephone put in,' her father said with a smile, 'now that you are home again and people want to see you.'

She waited for Dan with impatience. She wanted to celebrate with him. He was the only person now who had been with her through it all. He was the only one who had worked beside her, the only one with whom she could face the past in healing silence, who understood. She didn't know if he still felt the same way about her. Too much had happened. Perhaps he was content to be just a good friend. But she missed him when he wasn't there; she trusted and admired him, she felt safe and content with him.

I love him, she thought, almost surprised. I want him. But there was one more obstacle. She would have to tell him about Johnny. She walked about the garden and about the town, worried and undecided. Things had changed in the war; attitudes to morality had been stretched, but they were still there, and there was, as in most things, one law for men and another for women. She had slept with Johnny. She didn't have to tell Dan, and he need never know, but she knew that she couldn't do that. She couldn't start a marriage with secrets. She might never marry; she would have her career. But she knew now that she wanted Dan. She shrank away from telling him, but if he wanted her, she would have to do it.

He arrived on Saturday afternoon. She had no doubt now that he felt the same, his face glowing with pleasure and yes – with love. Her father took one look at him and disappeared into his study with his pipe.

She took him into the sitting-room.

'I'm so glad, Amy,' he said. 'It's wonderful news. Not that I ever doubted it.'

She looked at him, unable to conceal her feeling for him. He took her in his arms, his cheek against her hair. 'You know I'm in love with you, Amy, don't you? I've loved you since I first saw you. That's a terrible old cliché, but it's true.' He drew back and looked down at her. 'Could you love me, Amy?'

'I do love you,' she said. He went to take her in his arms again but she held him back. 'I've got something to tell you.'

She met his eyes. 'It's Johnny,' she said. He opened his mouth to speak but she stopped him. 'I slept with him,' she said. 'Once. I loved him and I slept with him.'

He was silent for a moment. It's over, she thought. He won't want me now.

'I assumed that you had,' he said. 'I'm not blind, Amy. Is that what you wanted to tell me?'

She nodded. He took her face in his hands. 'It doesn't matter. It's like the war, it's past and gone. Marry me, Amy.'

'Yes!' she almost shouted, and threw her arms around him. 'Yes, yes, yes!'

He swung her round, laughing. 'Tomorrow?'

'Yes. As long as you are happy for me to work.'

He smiled. 'I'd be cross with you if you didn't. It would be such a waste.'

They sat down on the sofa together. 'I should tell you,' he said, 'that I would like to have children. It would mean a lot to me.'

'Of course,' she said. 'I want them too. We've lost so much. There is so much to put back.'

She looked around the tranquil room, with all its memories of her childhood. 'At least we know,' she said, 'that our children will never have to go through that hell. That madness will never happen again, will it?'

He took her in his arms and held her close, saying nothing.